Down Pour

MAGGIE GATES

Copyright © 2024 Maggie C. Gates. All Rights Reserved

No part of this publication may be reproduced, transmitted, or distributed in any form or by any means including photocopying, recording, information storage and retrieval systems, without prior written permission from the publisher except in the case of brief quotation embodied in book reviews.

No part of this work may be used to create, feed, or refine artificial intelligence models, for any purpose, without written permission from the author.

This book is a work of fiction. The characters and events in this book are fictitious. Any similarity to real places or persons, living or dead, is purely coincidental and not intended by the author or are used fictitiously.

The author acknowledges the trademark status and trademark owners of various products, brands, and/or establishments referenced in this work of fiction. The publication/use of these trademarks is not associated with, or sponsored by the trademark owners.

This book is intended for mature audiences.

ISBN: 9798321829752

Edited By Jordan Loft

Cover Design by Melissa Doughty - Mel D. Designs

To my Father-in-Law. The real Iron Man.

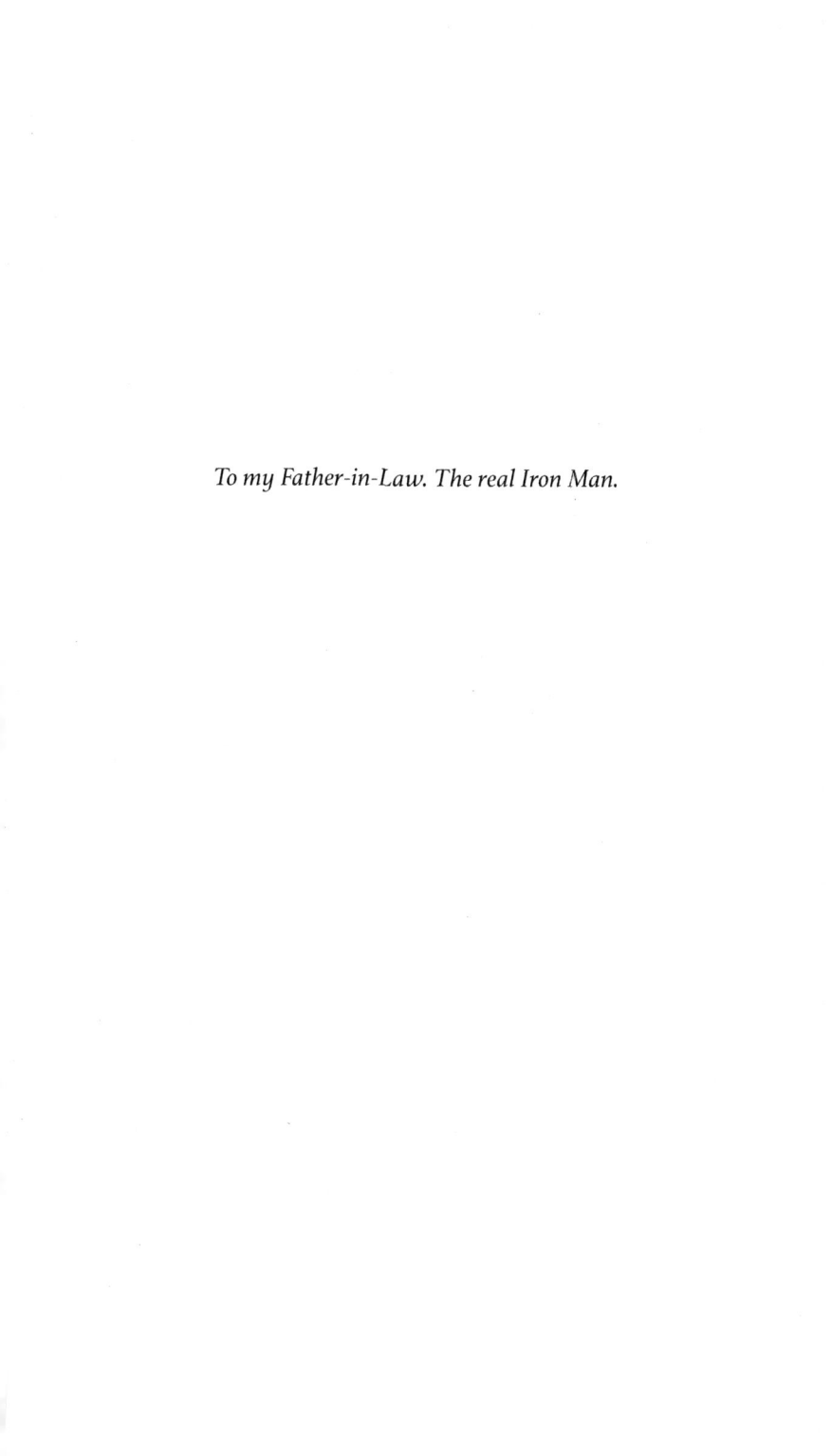

Down Pour

CONTENT WARNINGS

Downpour: A Grumpy Sunshine Romance contains strong themes of medical content, (spinal cord injury, quadriplegia, paraplegia) injuries associated with professional bull riding, suicidal thoughts and ideations, depression, theft/burglary, arson, the loss of parental figures, and drug and alcohol abuse.

The portrayal of Ray Griffith's spinal cord injury in *Downpour* is just one possible outcome of this type of injury. It does not reflect the full range of emotions, experiences, or recovery paths that individuals with spinal cord injuries may face. Each person's journey is unique and can differ significantly. This depiction is not intended to represent all possible experiences or outcomes.

This book features rope play and bondage. The acts performed in this book are fictional, and are not intended to be used as a guide or educational resource. Please research these practices thoroughly, and only engage in acts in safe, informed, sane, and consensual ways.

Treat yourself with care and happy reading!

With Love,
Maggie Gates

PROLOGUE
RAY

Do you know what it sounds like when seventy thousand people fall silent at the same time? I do.

"Tight legs, loose hips," Marty said. "You all taped up?"

I nodded and blocked everything out. The crowd, the announcer—even the two-thousand-pound beast under my ass. It all faded away.

I was in the zone, and I wasn't leaving until the title was mine.

"Rider ready."

Seventy thousand people holding their breath sounds like the hush before a thunderclap.

The chute boss placed a steady hand on my shoulder, ready to catch me in case Homewrecker decided to slam me into the gate before it opened.

"Go Uncle Ray!" my nieces cheered, bouncing up and down.

"You got this, brother!" Christian shouted, followed by a sharp whistle.

Eight seconds.

I never bothered counting in my head. Some riders did, but time had a way of freezing when a beast the size of a wrecking ball was trying to end me. The pain ripping through my shoulder made it hard to tell seven seconds from eight.

I shut my eyes, blocking out everything until all I heard was silence.

The gate swung wide, but Homewrecker paused.

Aw, shit.

Nothing worse than a boring bull.

I needed him to bring everything he had. Fifty points were on me, but the other fifty for bucking and intensity were all up to the animal.

With a grunt, Homewrecker threw me in the air, but I held on. The animal twisted like a tornado, slamming forward and back with each buck.

My hand ached and burned as every muscle and tendon stretched to its limit. I squeezed harder, fighting for every second.

The crowd's roar crushed my mental block.

Had it been eight seconds or was I just putting on a good show?

Homewrecker veered left then snapped right, catching me off guard. I shifted my hips to counter, but I could tell he was done with me.

He thrashed left and right until my grip failed and he threw me into the air. A hoof connected with my side, and pain exploded through my body.

The ground rushed up to meet me and I slammed into the dirt head-first. The pain stopped immediately.

That's weird.

I tried to roll onto my knees to get out of the ring, but nothing happened no matter how much I jerked.

Remember how I said the seventy-thousand-strong silence felt like waiting for thunder?

I couldn't feel a thing, but I sensed the weight of that gasp.

Then shouts erupted like a storm.

"MEDICAL! MEDICAL! GET THE SPINEBOARD!"

"RAY!"

"Stay still," someone commanded as figures swarmed around me.

No problem there. I wasn't sure why I couldn't move, but I just laid there as bodies flooded around me.

My older brother, Christian, had jumped the barrier and was in the ring, kneeling beside me.

That was nice of him.

I didn't feel anything when he picked up my hand.

Might be here for a while. I could use a nap.

That was the last thing I remembered thinking before it all went black.

Downpour.

~

ONE WEEK AFTER THE ACCIDENT

THAT BEEPING WAS FUCKING ANNOYING. *Someone needed to shut the damn machine off.*

Familiar voices echoed in the distance, like my brothers shouting through a dense haze.

Beep…

Jesus Christ—I wanted to pull the plug myself just so I could get some fucking sleep.

I struggled to wrench my eyes open, desperate to locate the source of that infuriating noise, but my lids felt glued shut. My body was numb. Like it didn't exist. My throat hurt like a bitch, though. Why couldn't the numbness fix that?

It was like being awake and asleep at the same time—teetering on the threshold of heaven and hell. Eternal limbo.

Beep... Beep... Beep...

Fuck me.

∼

THREE WEEKS AFTER THE ACCIDENT

Beep... Beep...

Was this what hell was like? Just one annoying beeping sound for all eternity?

Fuck me sideways. It was grating.

The voices had grown louder. Maybe I was going insane.

Orbs of gray and white floated across my field of vision, bending the darkness.

Goddamnit!

Fire lit up my throat in a blaze. It felt like a knife ripping through my windpipe. I wanted to scream, but couldn't.

Why couldn't I scream? Was I still in the ring? My head rocked, but I wasn't the one controlling it.

Something soft was behind my skull. It didn't feel like the dirt of the arena.

The burning eased to a simmer and the beeping slowed.

Thank fuck for that. It was still annoying, though.

The orbs of light widened, mellowing the blackness to a bleak storm.

Pain lanced down the back of my neck like a bolt of lightning. With each shot of agony, the grayness grew to familiar pink.

Huh. I could see the veins behind my eyelids. That was new.

Could I lift them?

I focused my effort and peered through protein-crusted lashes at the blurry lump to my left.

Was that Christian? Spectators weren't supposed to get in the ring. What was he doing here?

I tried calling out to tell him to get the fuck out of the arena, but I couldn't form the words.

Bright stabs of light split my head open like a watermelon falling off the back of a pickup truck.

Motherfucker! Nope. Not doing that.

I slammed my eyes shut again. I tried to breathe through the migraine, but that was a bad idea, too. My throat was coated in acid, and lifting my chest to fill my lungs was damn near impossible.

My cheek itched but I couldn't find my hand to scratch it.

I tried to call out to Christian again, but I couldn't get the words out.

My mouth was sandy and parched. I had eaten dirt more times than I could count in my bull riding career, but this felt different.

I debated taking another look. The pounding migraine was coming either way.

I forced my eyes open.

Christian was sitting beside me, reading a book. I had

thumbed through that one when I was at his house last week.

It was a Jordan Loft title that had a twist at the end. From the look on his face, he hadn't gotten to it yet.

"Chris," I croaked, and this time, he glanced up.

"Ray?" he rasped.

I blinked.

Damn, he looked like shit. That publicist he was seeing must've been keeping him busy at night.

My mouth felt like a cotton ball. I tried to lick my lips, but my tongue was dry too. I tried to ask him why I wasn't at the arena, but the darkness grew again, floating around the edges of my vision.

My head rocked as he slammed his hand into the panel beside me. Something hard and plastic pressed against my mouth.

Maybe that was why he couldn't hear me.

A wrecking ball rolled around in my head as I flicked my eyes down to get a look at it.

Christian reached over and lifted the thing off my mouth.

"My score?"

Goddamn, it hurt to talk. What the hell was wrong with my throat?

Christian reached into his pocket and pulled out the championship buckle. He placed it in my hand, but I couldn't feel it.

"Ninety-one point nine," he said.

I'd won.

So why wasn't the crowd cheering?

∼

TWO MONTHS AFTER THE ACCIDENT

I WAS FULLY CONVINCED that whoever stippled popcorn ceilings did it in patterns that mimicked those psychology tests. For sixty endless days, I'd been trapped in this childhood bedroom turned prison.

Sixty motherfucking days of pissing in a bedpan. Sixty excruciating days of Mom feeding me like an infant and wiping the drool and crumbs from my chin. Sixty insufferable days of my brothers carrying my body around the goddamn house just so I could see something beyond these four fucking walls.

Sixty days of wishing I had died in that arena.

∽

FOUR MONTHS AFTER THE ACCIDENT

MY HANDS ITCHED like a thousand fire ants were crawling under my skin. It was annoying as hell, and it had been happening more and more after each visit to my sadistic physical therapist. Probably because she took joy in electrocuting me.

According to her, functional electrical stimulation was supposed to help me regain use of my body. So far all it did was make me itch so bad I wanted to claw my own flesh off.

I stared at my useless hands, desperate to scratch but unable to do anything about it. No way in hell was I going to call someone in here just to scratch my goddamn hand.

Then again, I was tired of being awake. I wanted to close the curtains, lay down, and pretend I didn't exist.

Sleeping was the closest I could get to being dead. Maybe that's why I craved it so much.

Muscle atrophy be damned.

I'd waste away in this room, slowly going mad staring at the fucking popcorn ceiling, counting the bumps until my mind turned to mush.

SIX MONTHS AFTER THE ACCIDENT

"THE SURGERY WENT AS EXPECTED. Like we all discussed during the trial screening, it's extremely invasive. The recovery is going to be rough. We'll continue to monitor the electrodes that were implanted along his spine for the next few days to make sure the surgery site starts healing and there are no complications. If all goes well, we'll be able to work with his care team to set up the pulse generator and start the rehab program."

I stared blankly at the wall as the surgeon updated my mom.

The surgeon sighed. "This kind of stimulation therapy is brand new and *very* experimental. It's one of just a few clinical trials in the world. I can't promise anything. We simply don't have the data to know what will happen."

Did the risk really matter at this point? Might as well be a lab rat for this experimental science shit. Not like my body was good for anything else.

EIGHT MONTHS AFTER THE ACCIDENT

THE ITCH in my hand flared up again. I swore under my breath and wrenched my eyes from the TV screen. The channel had shifted from the morning news to some unbearable soap opera. I hadn't bothered changing it with the clicker my brother, Nate, bought online.

He'd been so goddamn excited to set up that curved metal arm for me. *As if I should be thrilled to change the channel by biting down on a button with my teeth.*

I'd rather endure the melodramatic garbage.

I groaned and let my head fall back against the pillow, drained from the physical therapy session. I hadn't done much beyond being twisted and prodded like a lifeless doll, but it had still worn me out.

Christian had dragged me to the PT appointment today, going on about the benefits of therapy for his own mental well-being and the wonders the family counselor he took my nieces to had done for all of them.

Apparently, his therapist had an available appointment if I felt like opening up.

I didn't.

What was the point in dissecting the fact that I was quadriplegic. That I was unable to move an inch beyond my neck because I had to ride one more bull, had to claim one more championship? Because I just couldn't quit while I was ahead.

I didn't need to dig into any of it. It was what it was.

After months, the soreness from the breathing tube had finally faded, and the uncontrollable coughing had subsided. Unfortunate, really, since it meant people expected me to carry on a conversation when they barged into my room unannounced.

There was nothing to say.

I despised the empty platitudes, the hollow niceties, the patronizing smiles, and the well-meaning sentiments.

But what I hated most was the goddamn itch in my hand.

I shut my eyes, grasping at the fading memory of what it felt like to flex my muscles and move.

But I did.

My hand tilted to the side and brushed against a throw pillow. The coarse textured fabric soothed my itch.

Did I actually... I concentrated on my wrist—on the muscles there—as if I could will them back to life.

Sweat beaded on my forehead and the itch intensified. And then...

I moved.

My hand shifted left and right as I scratched the itch against the pillow.

∼

NINE MONTHS AFTER THE ACCIDENT

"WHAT THE HELL?" Christian stood in the doorway with his jaw on top of his boots.

I raised the hospital-grade cup to my lips and sipped through the bent straw.

The plate slipped from my brother's hand and crashed to the floor. Mashed potatoes splattered as peas scattered across the hardwood. A pang of sadness gripped me as the meatloaf landed on his boot.

Damn it... I loved meatloaf.

The scent had been taunting me for an hour, and I was starving.

Christian gaped. "I must be hallucinating from when I hit my head on the tractor earlier."

"Sorry," I said, setting the cup on the tray beside the

raised bed. The mattress felt like it had been sewn from Satan's flesh. I had it to thank for the ache in my shoulders and neck.

He stared with disbelief etched on his face. "Do that again."

I glanced up. "I'd rather not. It hurts like hell."

"What the fuck, man?" He ran his hand down his beard, his jaw tightening and his lips trembling.

I gritted my teeth as I watched the tears stream down his face. I hadn't shed a tear since waking in that hospital bed. So why was he crying?

"Ray, what the fuck? You're moving!"

"I was thirsty."

He didn't move for the plate, the squished potatoes, or the meatloaf. "Y-you...picked it up."

"I just learned how to use my hand again," I said. "Don't make me use it to flip you off."

I didn't mention the month of therapy I'd spent working on it.

Apparently, that itch was a good thing.

ONE YEAR AFTER THE ACCIDENT

THE SMELL of lumber and sawdust lingered in the air as I wheeled myself up the ramp to my new house.

It was a work in progress, with missing closet doors, exposed electrical sockets, and half-installed appliances. None of that mattered to me. I could always pay someone to deal with the details later.

I shoved on the wheels to push myself up the last bit of the wheelchair ramp, ignoring the ache in my arms.

This land had been mine since birth. All three of my brothers had their own plots, too. Christian and Nate had built their homes years ago. They were older and ready to settle down with their families. I'd held onto my piece even while living in Colorado for most of my twenties.

Sure, I let them use it for the cattle, but I never developed it myself.

I made it onto the porch and spun myself around with a sigh. I never thought my piece of the Griffith Brothers Ranch would need to be wheelchair accessible.

But at least I was alone.

Christian and Nate's houses stood to the east, with the main house a little north of that. Cassandra, Christian's fiancé and the ranch's property manager, was busy overseeing the construction of the lodge and restaurant on the west side.

Nobody ventured out to the south end where my house was tucked away. It was intentionally obscured by a veil of trees and accessible only by a dirt path winding around the ranch, out to the service road.

I pushed the front door open and breathed in the crisp smell of fresh paint.

"Oh, hello!" an unexpected voice greeted me from inside, shattering my moment of peace. "You must be Ray."

I sat, motionless, and stared at the stern-looking, gray-haired woman who was looking back at me. She'd invited herself into my home and was putting sheets on...

My jaw clenched.

That fucking hospital bed had been moved from my parents' place to mine.

I wanted to spin my chair around, slam the door shut, and set this place on fire.

"I don't care who you are," I growled, rolling back from the doorway. "Just get out of my house."

The woman laughed as if I was kidding.

I wasn't.

"Your momma told me you were a little prickly." She offered a warm smile. "But it doesn't bother me. I'm just here to help."

Her scrubs told me as much, but I wasn't having it.

I stabbed a finger at the door. "Out."

ONE YEAR AND ONE MONTH AFTER THE ACCIDENT

CHRISTIAN SAT ON MY COUCH, pressing his fingers to his eyes. "You can't keep firing people."

"That's the fourth CNA you've scared off this week," CJ pointed out. "Do you think these people grow on trees?"

Becks took a nicer approach. "It's a small town. There aren't many options."

Nate nodded in agreement.

I didn't bother looking up from the length of rope I was tying in knots. My brothers and sisters-in-law were the ones who staged this intervention. They weren't owed my attention.

I loosened the overhand knot so I could tie it again. It was a mind-numbing activity that helped improve the dexterity in my hands.

"Then stop sending people where they're not wanted," I muttered.

Cassandra snorted and glanced at Christian. "Told you."

My future sister-in-law was the only person I could

stand at the moment, but only because she was the only one who left me alone.

Nate tried again, his voice a mix of patience and exasperation. "I know it's not ideal—"

Ideal? Did they really think I enjoyed being waited on hand and foot?

"—but either you let us help you, or you stop firing the people who are hired to help you," he finished, making their terms clear.

I pulled the lever on my chair and rolled into the bedroom. "Send someone else out here and see what happens."

∼

ONE DAY AFTER THAT

"I QUIT. Never in my life have I been subjected to someone as rude and mean and—"

I slammed the door before the guy could finish his sentence.

Good riddance.

∼

ONE YEAR AND FOUR MONTHS AFTER THE ACCIDENT

"RAYMOND TYLER GRIFFITH! You did *not* change the locks on your doors."

My mother's furious shouts carried through the windowpane. No doubt, she had stormed down from her place after another home health aide failed to get in with the spare key.

At least the blinds were closed.

I stared at the kitchen ceiling as the cool floor tiles bit into my back. Sharp pain lanced through my hips and neck.

My wheelchair was toppled over a few feet away, surrounded by a mess of shattered glass. The steady stream from the tap was now joined by trickles of water cascading off the counter and onto the slowly flooding floor.

Lucky for me, Momma couldn't see me like this.

Not so lucky for me, I was stranded on the floor until I figured out how to get up.

1

BROOKE

I stretched out in my crisp, cool sheets as sunlight leaked through the blinds. Was there anything better than waking up in freshly washed bedding? I could already tell it was going to be a great day.

The window air conditioner rattled like maracas. The pair of googly eyes I had attached to it jiggled with every heave. Poor thing was dying in this sweltering June heat.

"You're doing great, little guy." I patted its rusted metal case. "Just keep going."

I shimmied into a relatively clean pair of shorts I found dangling off the bed frame. One flip-flop peeked out from under the bed, and I found the other on top of my dresser.

Bounding down the stairs, I greeted the sprawled-out figures on the couches on my way across the room.

Nick, the roommate who had lived here the longest out of all of us, lifted his head from the faded recliner. "Rent's due, Stacey."

"Really?" I laughed nervously and pawed through my pantry shelf. "I could have sworn I gave you money already."

I grabbed a box of granola bars with my name on it and

opened it up. *Empty*. Maybe one of my roommates got hungry and didn't have anything else? That was alright. I'd just have oatmeal.

Nope, that box was empty too.

"Hey, do you know if someone ate my food?" I asked.

A familiar blue and white wrapper was on Nick's lap. "Dunno," he grunted as he chased his bite with a swig of beer.

Chandler was passed out on the sofa with a mixing bowl of oatmeal resting on his stomach.

"No worries," I chirped, slinging my bag over my shoulder. "I'll just go by the store on my way back."

Stepping over a bulging garbage bag, I tiptoed past the mess of last night's party. Crushed beer cans skittered underfoot as I headed to the door.

"Don't forget about the money," Nick hollered as he scrolled his phone. "Cash this time. No checks."

The sun baked my skin as I skipped to my car, curls bouncing with each step. Mondays were the best. They were a fresh start. A new chance. Full of exciting possibilities.

I slid into the driver's seat and tossed my bag on the floorboard. The plastic flower pot on my dashboard wiggled as I turned the ignition.

"Aw, crap," I muttered, noticing the low fuel light. "That's fine, Madame Universe. Thanks for the excuse to grab a gas station snack."

I swung into the nearest station, chatting up the friendly cashier about the soap opera playing on the TV behind the counter as I paid for a snack cake and a few gallons of gas.

Everyone was being so nice today. Even Nick had almost gotten my name right. Usually, it was "Brenda," "Bonnie," or some other "B" name. But today, he called me by my last name like I was one of the bros.

The house was really starting to feel like home.

It was fun to always be surrounded by people. I always had someone to talk to or hang out with. It was like living in a dorm.

My own little found family.

I parked in front of the Caring Hands office and skipped up the brick steps. The door's jingling bells announced my arrival as I stepped into the cool air conditioning.

"Good morning, Peggy!" I greeted the office manager cheerfully.

She looked up from her desk with a frown. "You're late."

"Am I?" I pulled out my phone to check the time. "Oh shoot, it's dead. Do you have a charger?"

Peggy's eyebrow twitched.

"Oh my god! Your eyeshadow looks amazing today! The blue totally makes your eyes pop."

She huffed. "Have a seat, Brooke."

I plopped into the chair across from her desk, noticing a new addition. "Did you get a new plant? It's so cute! Does it have a name?"

Peggy sighed. "A name?"

"Yes! Plants have personalities. Naming them is a huge responsibility. It's like naming a baby."

Her fingers rattled against the keyboard. "I'm glad you brought up responsibility. Let's talk about that."

I bounced my feet and admired the cheery blue and yellow nail polish on my toes. It was bright like a sunny day against the dreary gray office carpet.

"Brooke," Peggy snapped, jolting me from my wistful thoughts.

I looked up. "So, who am I going to see today?"

Her jaw was locked. "You're going to have a light day. The only client you have is Mr. Wilson."

"Light day? Awesome! There's this antique store I've been dying to go to." I propped my elbow on her desk and rested my chin in my hand. "What's your day like? Do you wanna come with me? We could totally grab lunch and make an afternoon of it."

She huffed. "Let me clarify. You only have one client left."

I gasped. "Everyone got better? Even Mrs. Jones? I thought it would take months for her to recover. I mean, yeesh—breaking both your legs like that... But look at her go. She's a rockstar!"

Peggy pinched the bridge of her nose. "No one got better, Brooke. You cost the agency nine accounts. Nine valuable, paying clients left because of you."

"Really? I don't understand..."

My heart sank as she began to list off my failings—always running late, misplacing things, mixing up meds and meals. I tried to explain about my noisy roommates and lack of sleep, but she cut me off.

"I don't want to hear excuses. I can't keep giving you assignments if you're going to cost us money. This is your last chance."

My bottom lip trembled. "I'll do better. I promise."

"Don't bother coming back here if Mr. Wilson sends you away," she said, turning back to her computer and waving me off.

I retreated out of the office and slunk back to my car. The check engine light greeted me when I started the engine, and a knot formed in my stomach.

I needed this paycheck.

Rent, groceries, car repairs—being alive was expensive.

Being a home aid wasn't my dream job, but it gave me plenty of time to dream about other things. Plus, I loved helping my clients. Keeping them company, driving them to their appointments, chatting about their day while I cleaned their houses... People were awesome, and getting paid to do life with them was the best.

I just had to do better.

Two more years... I had to survive for two more years, and then everything would be fine.

2

RAY

I threaded the end of the rope through the loop and tightened it. My hand trembled. I bit the knot to loosen it so I could tie it again, all while ignoring the body on the other side of the room.

Unfortunately, the body was alive.

"I don't know why everyone said you're crabby," she said as she cleaned up from lunch. "You're just quiet. Nothing wrong with that, sweetheart. I don't mind the quiet. There's too much noise these days."

A dull ache pulsed behind my eyes. "Stop talking."

She huffed. "That grouchy act won't work on me. I raised six boys—including my husband. I can handle your attitude."

The rope fell as I unlocked my chair and rolled to the door. "Out."

She propped her hands on her hips. "I just got here."

"And now you're leaving." I opened the front door and wheeled away. "Don't bother locking up."

It was already time to change the locks again. Seemed like I spent more money on doorknobs than anything else.

Fortunately, the drill was still on the side table in the living room.

Maybe a number lock would be easier than dealing with keys and all that bullshit. I could just reprogram the code.

"Mr. Griffith, there's no reason for you to speak to me that way."

"There's no reason for you to still be here."

"But I—"

"I believe he told you to leave." Cassandra, my brother's fiancé, appeared in the doorway. She hitched her thumb over her shoulder. "Beat it."

The old lady glowered. "Who do you think you are, telling me to leave my job?"

Cassandra's cold stare made it clear the old lady was fucked. "It doesn't matter who I am. Ray told you to get out of his house. Now leave. You're trespassing, and this is Texas."

"I have a job to do."

"I fired you," I clipped.

Cassandra looked like she was about to claw the woman's eyes out. "If you don't leave, you have two choices. Either I can find someone to shoot you and bury you in the south pasture, or I can beat you to death with that kitchen towel in your hand. Take your pick."

"This family is just as crazy as everyone said," she yammered as she grabbed her oversized quilted purse and stormed out.

I lifted my wrist and managed a half-decent middle finger. She should have listened the first time.

Why didn't people listen to me? They always thought I was joking or that I wasn't the final say on who got to set foot in my house.

Cassandra waited until the woman stomped to her car

before closing the door behind her. "I brought your mail down. Marty sent some documents for you to sign."

"Get Christian to do it," I grumbled. "He's my power of attorney."

"You really have to stop firing people," she said without the slightest bit of emotion. "We're getting a reputation."

"Isn't it your job to fix people's reputations? This should be child's play for you."

Cassandra dropped the mail on the table and pushed the chairs in. She picked up the tea towel the loud-mouthed grandma had dropped so it wouldn't get caught under my chair, and hung it over the dishwasher handle.

"I offered to bring you on as a client. You said no, remember? I don't offer twice. If you want my help, you know where to find me."

I rolled into the living room and parked myself in front of the sliding door. "I don't need a publicist."

"Marty says otherwise, and I agree with him."

The thought of Marty and his new rider made my blood boil. They could both go to hell as far as I was concerned.

Cassandra tapped a manicured nail on the envelopes. "Sign them and let me know when they're done. I'll put them with the outgoing mail."

"Chris can do it."

"Fine," she said, all too agreeably for my comfort. Cassandra was anything but agreeable.

Maybe that's why we got along so well.

"But that means he's going to come down here and lecture you. Do you really want him asking why you fired *another* CNA?"

I glared at her. "Leave a pen on the table."

She smirked, knowing she had won. "Call if you need something."

"I won't."

She shrugged like it was no big deal. "Suit yourself."

The door closed behind her and I waited until the click of her high heels faded into the distance before I breathed again.

Finally alone.

I eased up to the kitchen table and made a reach for the first envelope. My physical therapist had chewed my ass out this morning for not working on my left hand, but I didn't feel like failing today.

I knew what was stuffed in the envelopes. Contract terminations from two more sponsors.

Rule number one of almost dying: make sure someone knows your passwords. It's hard to cancel your phone plan if you're dead.

Rule number two of almost dying: make sure your house is clean before you walk up the steps to the pearly gates. It makes selling off your life easier.

I tried to rip the damn thing open, but I couldn't pinch the envelope.

The rope was fine. It was half an inch thick. Paper was thin, and I didn't have the dexterity to hold it and tear it open.

Unlike Christian, who would have opened the envelopes and laid out the pages, Cassandra left them sealed. Deliberately.

I managed to get my pocket knife open and sliced open the letter. The cool handle pressed against my palm as I slid the knife down and pressed my thumb behind the blade.

The sound of boots thudding against the wooden ramp outside startled me. The knife twisted in my hand and the sharp edge slid across the pad of my thumb.

"Shit," I hissed and yanked my hand away. Crimson

droplets spattered across the crisp white paper and onto my lap, staining my sweatpants.

Just fucking great. I quickly pressed my thumb to my shirt to stop the bleeding.

The doorknob clicked and the door creaked open.

Christian halted in his tracks at the sight of me before rushing over in a panic. "What the hell happened to you? Cass *just* left."

"Accident," I muttered. "Why're you here?"

"Just checkin' on you," he said. He grabbed the knife, wiped it off, closed it, and turned toward my bedroom. "Sit tight. I'll grab a change of clothes for you."

"Don't want 'em."

Christian paused with his hands braced on the bedroom door frame. "We've gotta talk about this."

"Don't you have a ranch to run?" I said as I gingerly slipped my hand between the folded piece of paper and opened it up to see what my former manager had sent over. Marty would just have to deal with the bloodstains. "What did you do all fucking day when I was in Colorado and riding the circuit?"

There were days where all I wanted was to saddle up and ride through the plains until I couldn't see anything or anyone. I was jealous of CJ, the youngest of the four of us. He got to ride away from it all.

I had tried to do that. I tried to leave it all behind.

"I worry about people all day," Christian said. "Bree, Gracie, Cass, and the ranch used to be at the top of that list. Now it's you."

I bristled at the mention of my nieces. At one point in time, they had been like my own daughters.

When Christian's wife died and Nate was deployed, I'd

stepped in to help Christian with his girls, Bree and Gracie. Those two girls were my world.

To them, I was Superman.

Invincible and indestructible.

I stared at the table so he couldn't see the hurt boiling in my eyes. My hair hung over my face. I was long overdue for a trim. The shaggy mane was making me resemble Christian more with each passing day.

He sighed. "I know this sucks for you."

It sucks? Was he fucking kidding me?

A caustic laugh escaped me. "Really? I wasn't aware. Thanks for letting me know."

"Ray—"

"Fuck off," I said as I reached for the pen. I fisted it and jammed the end against the table to open it up. Slowly, I managed to scribble something that vaguely resembled *Ray Griffith*.

The three letters of my first name were a sloppy, childlike scrawl—wonky, misshapen, and inconsistent in size and spacing, sprawling across the entire signature line.

Christian watched from the other side of the room. "Why'd you fire Maude?"

Maude? What kind of name was that?

"She talked too much."

"That's what you said about Brian. You know—the one you fired three days ago?"

"He talked too much, *and* he ate an egg salad sandwich in the car. It was ninety degrees out and he left the windows up."

Christian pinched the bridge of his nose. "And what about Mary-Beth last week?"

"She read to me. Out loud. Like it was elementary school story time or some shit."

He sighed. "We've gone through two agencies. You've cleared the roster for both."

"Good. Maybe now you'll stop sending people out here."

Christian didn't have a temper. Not like me, Nate, and CJ. Part of me wanted him to get pissed off just to see what would happen. If I could make him crack, it would be the most entertaining part of my day.

"I love you, man, but you've gotta stop firing people. Either you learn to get along with whoever we can find to come out here, or it's gonna be me and momma checking on you every hour."

"Or maybe you'll finally listen to me and just fucking leave me be." It was only ten in the morning, but I was done with this bullshit. I wanted to go back to bed.

Christian sighed. "We both know that's not an option right now."

As if I wasn't fucking aware of it.

The x-rays were seared in my mind. The medical team showed them when I woke up, unable to move. Those images were the only thing that forced me to accept the reality of the accident.

My spine snapped when I was flung off that bull and hit the ground.

For nine months, I was at the mercy of whoever was around to keep me alive. Apparently, Cassandra had been the one to pull strings and get me into an SCI clinical trial. The epidural electrical stimulation for my spinal cord injury would have cost millions if they hadn't been looking for human lab rats.

I had put away a decent amount of money from my winnings on the professional circuit, but millions every year over my lifetime—or what was left of it—wasn't in the cards.

But it worked. Well, it worked better on the actual rats. But apparently beggars couldn't be choosers.

But it did make me downgrade from quadriplegia to paraplegia.

Now, I had a rod in the back of my neck, electrodes in my spine, and storm clouds in my head.

Some days, the only reason I forced myself to go through physical therapy was to get my upper body mobility back enough to be left the hell alone.

Spite was a decent motivator.

I knew Christian meant well. All of them did. The doctors said I was lucky to have such a supportive family.

Maybe I was.

But that didn't make it better.

"I can hire help. I can have someone cart me around and do my bidding like I'm a fucking princess. But that doesn't give me my life back," I snapped. "So, stop being delusional and acting like if someone's here to put me on the goddamn toilet, that it's all sunshine and fucking roses."

Christian's face was passive behind his beard, but a quiet sigh slipped. "Grief is hard. When Gretchen died, I—"

"Just leave," I growled, wheeling past him. He could let himself out.

3

BROOKE

"Shit!" I squeaked as my foot caught on the uneven sidewalk outside Mr. Wilson's house, sending me sprawling. My palms slammed against the cement and my knee followed. The concrete's jagged edge bit into my skin and blood trickled down my shin.

I bit my lip, rolled onto my butt, and poked at the gash to examine the damage. That only made it bleed more.

On the bright side, at least I was done with my only client for the day and could enjoy the glorious weather with a good book and my feet propped up.

I brushed myself off and hobbled to my car, grimacing at the sharp ache in my knee. As I settled into the driver's seat, a truck whizzed by, making my car shake. I held my breath, hoping the mirrors would stay on.

Just as I pulled away from the curb, I spotted a blob of tapioca pudding on my shirt. Typical. But it wasn't enough to ruin my day.

I slowed to a stop at the next light and peeled off the Caring Hands uniform polo, swapping it for a workout tank top from the floorboard.

As I struggled out of one top and into the other, an impatient honk sounded from behind me. I waved apologetically and eased through the intersection.

My phone buzzed. With one hand on the wheel, I rummaged through my bag. "Hello?"

"Brooke, are you done at Mr. Wilson's house?" Peggy's voice echoed.

"Yes, ma'am. I just left."

"You have another client. I'm texting you the address. It's half an hour away, so don't dilly dally."

I eyed the fuel gauge. "I thought Mr. Wilson was my only client?"

"Do you want the job or not? There's a cash bonus today, and double pay if you last longer than a week."

Money today? Double in a week? Sold. I needed the cash more than a relaxing afternoon in the park. Hopefully, the family and the client wouldn't mind that I wasn't in the proper uniform. Mr. Wilson certainly didn't care, and Peggy didn't have eyes everywhere.

Or did she? Maybe that's why she was adding to my route.

"I'm on my way," I chirped.

Peggy chuckled ominously. "Good luck."

I punched the address into my GPS and swung a U-turn at the next light.

I drove with the windows down, singing my heart out to the radio. Five wrong turns and a pit-stop for gas later, I found myself speeding down a dirt road.

Dust whipped up from beneath my tires as I drove under a timber gate, that read *Griffith Brothers Ranch*.

Wide plains rolled across the horizon in an endless sea of green. Peggy hadn't been kidding—this place was in the middle of nowhere.

Gosh, it was gorgeous.

My tires skidded through each turn as I navigated the dirt path, following Peggy's brief directions on how to find the client's house. I passed a picturesque house with white siding and a blue star on the side, then took a left at the split in the path.

The next two houses were nearly identical, with covered porches and neat landscaping. The second of the pair had bicycles in the yard. Barns and warehouses were scattered across the grounds.

And standing right in the middle of the dirt road was a cow with pink and yellow pool noodles on its horns.

I stopped and poked my head out of the window. "Hi, friend! Could you move out of the way, please? I don't want to turn you into ground beef."

To my surprise, the cow obliged and sauntered toward one of the buildings that had corrugated metal siding.

I followed the long road a few more miles until I spotted the white-sided house peeking out from behind a thick grove of trees.

The car bumped as the tires went from dirt to a freshly paved driveway. The black asphalt glimmered in the waves of afternoon heat. A brand-new wheelchair ramp was accented with a patriotic garden flag at the very end.

I pulled up beside a truck covered in a tarp, grabbed my gas station haul, and hopped out.

"Hello?" I called out as I propped the bags on my hip and knocked on the door. When no one answered, I gave the handle a jiggle for good measure. It was locked.

Silence for miles. No engines. No voices. No car horns. Nothing.

The trees rustled as a gentle breeze danced across the yard. The house was picturesque. Neatly edged flower beds were covered in dark mulch. The house had a star on the side, matching the one on the house at the front of the property.

I really should have walked around to try to find the client Peggy had assigned me, but the sun felt too good. I plopped down on the front step and took it all in. Today was the perfect day to stop and smell the roses.

The scrape of hooves made me look up from the plant on my lap. The cow with pool noodles on his horns sauntered up the drive and gave me a curious look.

"Oh, hello again." I couldn't help but smile at the pool noodles. "Are you friendly? You look friendly. Can I pet you?"

As if he understood me, the cow eased up and settled down in front of the steps. His head was heavy against my leg.

"Well, aren't you just the sweetest thing?" I smoothed my hand down his nose. "What's your name, handsome boy?"

He let out a soft grunt and promptly fell asleep right then and there.

"That settles it," I said as I scratched beneath his copper-colored chin. "I'll just wait here until they get home."

It was common law that if an animal laid on you, you were to be their bed until they deemed it time to get up. I shuffled my things to the side so his head could take up full residency on my lap.

A rumble like thunder started low in the distance. The growl of the engine grew closer and closer until I spotted the nose of the truck poking through the opening in the trees.

The cow didn't stir. Poor guy must've been tuckered out.

A heavyset man with a thick beard leaned out of the driver's side window as he navigated the curving driveway.

Two other people were in the truck, but the glare from the sun obscured them from view.

I nudged the cow. "Hey, fella. I need to get up now."

It didn't even open an eye.

The truck came to a stop five feet from my knees, and the door opened.

"Hello!" I said, waving at the driver.

His hair was tied back in a neat bun, though most of it was hidden beneath his cowboy hat. Brown boots scraped against the paved driveway.

"Ma'am," he said with a nod.

The passenger's side door opened, and a woman stepped out. She took one look at me and raised an eyebrow. "Who are you?"

Oh my god, she was hot. And scary.

"Who? Me?" I clarified.

She rolled her eyes. "No, I meant Mickey. Of course, I mean you."

At the mention of his name, the cow—Mickey—lifted his head and looked at the woman.

"Get lost," she shooed.

"Cass," the cowboy said as a warning as he reached into the bed of the truck and lifted a wheelchair out.

I scrambled to grab the plastic gas station bag and my plant as the cow heaved himself back to his feet.

"Bye, Mickey." I patted his back as he wandered off. "Thanks for the snuggles."

The cowboy set the wheelchair on the ground. His body was hidden behind the back door as he reached in to help the third person from the truck.

"Who are you?" the woman asked sharply.

She ignored my outstretched hand and hit me with a bone-chilling stare. "We aren't hiring yet."

"O-oh..." I stammered before I finally got the words out. "No, I was sent here from Caring Hands Home Help."

"Then you can leave." The voice came from behind the truck door.

I watched curiously as the cowboy shut the door.

Oh my stars.

The guy in the wheelchair was hot. Like panty-dropping hot. Like, melt my clothes off with one glance h-o-t.

I looked down to make sure my tank top hadn't spontaneously combusted.

Tattoos covered every inch of his arms, and I caught a glimpse of ink peeking out from the collar of his shirt as the art extended up his neck. His jaw was sharp like an arrowhead and covered in dark scruff. He had cheekbones that models would kill for. Brown eyes pierced through me. His hair was disheveled in a way that screamed, "Hello, sir, she calls me daddy, too." His nose was adorably crooked as if it had been broken and reset. It gave him an edge that made my heart flutter.

Wait. *He* was the client?

Oh, no, no, no. I assisted elderly people. Really unattractive, one-foot-in-the-grave elderly people. I picked up their prescriptions, cooked their meals, and provided companionship so their loved ones could have a break. Most of them thought I was their granddaughter. I usually played along. It was easier than correcting them.

I didn't work for hot men who made my heart skip. I couldn't do this job with a cardiac condition. Heart skipping had to be a dealbreaker, right?

"Be nice," the cowboy scolded. "Both of you."

The man in the wheelchair and the woman growled at the same time.

"Well, Brooke from Caring Hands," the woman said.

"You were supposed to be here an hour and a half ago. Ray almost missed his PT appointment because you were late. Is this going to be a regular pattern of behavior for you?"

"I got lost, and then I had to stop for gas." I looked down at the plant in my hand. "And there was this lady at the gas station selling these plants on a table outside. They all seemed like they were dying because of the heat, so I bought one to save it. It's a rescue plant—you know, like a rescue puppy, but a—"

She lifted her hand. "That's quite enough."

The guy in the wheelchair seemed slightly amused, but the threat in his eyes quickly returned.

The cowboy sighed. "For god's sake. Use your manners, you feral heathens. My children and the animals behave better than you two."

When he looked at the woman, there was a warmth in his eyes. There was a softer side to their relationship.

"Nice to meet you, Brooke," the cowboy said. "I'm Christian Griffith. I run the ranch. If you need anything, just let me know."

"Pleasure to meet you, Mr. Griffith," I said. Some people only said to reach out as a polite gesture, but I believed him when he said it.

I shifted my weight uneasily in my flip-flops. *Should I ask to go inside?* The sun was scorching my shoulders.

Christian nudged the man in the wheelchair.

He grumbled something at Christian before huffing at me. "I'm Ray."

I gasped. "Oh my god! Your name is Ray? Like a ray of sunshine? I love it!"

I held up the plant for him to see. "I brought this for you! I can help you name her if you want. All plants need names, you know? I'm still trying to figure out her personality, but

'Betty' seems like a good fit. The lady at the gas station said it'll bloom when you meet the love of your life. Isn't that fun?"

Ray's gaze dropped to my knee. "You're bleeding." His stern timber made my head spin and my heart flutter.

Was it normal to feel like you were going to pass out when talking to a man?

"Oh, that?" I laughed neurotically. "I tripped." I tried to wave it off casually, but accidentally dropped the plant. The terracotta pot shattered on the asphalt. The already wilting leaves sizzled on the blacktop.

The woman cackled. "This'll be fun to watch. I sincerely hope you last longer than the last one. We could use some entertainment around here."

Ray remained silent. The disdain in his eyes said it all.

That was fine. I enjoyed a challenge.

4

RAY

Two days had passed since Brooke showed up at my doorstep with skinned knees and a smile plastered on her face. And for the past two days, she hadn't stopped talking.

No matter how many times I told her to shut up, she just...wouldn't.

Mickey, my niece's accidental pet cow, had taken up permanent residence on my back deck. Apparently, he was in love with the girl.

Thankfully, I'd gotten a few hours of peace today. It was one of those rare mornings when I didn't have to go into town for physical therapy. Babbling Brooke wasn't scheduled to return until the afternoon. Since I hadn't fired anyone in the past forty-eight hours, my brothers and parents had left me alone.

Wheeling myself back into the kitchen, I stowed the empty watering can under the sink. My back was giving me hell today—not an unusual occurrence, but certainly an irritating one.

My phone vibrated in my lap.

CJ

You good?

I didn't bother responding. CJ, my younger brother, knew I'd call if I needed something.

Not like he could help me anyway. He was probably as far away from people as humanly possible. It wasn't lost on me that he had been moving the herd of cattle farther and farther from the civilized part of the property, and it had nothing to do with the construction of the lodge and restaurant.

The sliding door was propped open today, letting a breeze sweep through the screen. If I was being honest, I wanted to go outside and drive through the property.

For the first time, the ranch was bustling from sunrise to sunset, and it wasn't because of the cattle.

I had been urging my dad for years to diversify the ranch's financial interests. Finally, he listened.

Cassandra was brought in. She fell in love with my brother, Christian, and the ranch revitalization project was born.

She was swamped, coordinating the budding equine program while the framing for the restaurant and lodge was going up. It would be worth it in the end.

Putting all your eggs in one basket was foolish. Everyone needed a backup plan. Turns out, I was the pot calling the kettle black.

I shifted to try and ease the ache that radiated down my sciatic nerve. It made my knee throb. That was new.

I had been feeling weird muscle sensations for a few weeks. My physical therapist knew, but we kept it between the two of us.

I eased away from the kitchen counter and locked my

wheelchair. Carefully, I cupped the back of my knee and lifted my foot off the footrest. I closed my eyes, braced against the arm-rests, then did what the physical therapist said and focused on the muscles that I remembered.

I felt the memory of tension pulling from my hip to my knee to my ankle as I slid my foot an inch. Moving my leg was an out-of-body experience.

My upper body gross motor skills had returned more easily than my fine motor skills. It was frustrating to have to spend my time in physical therapy learning how to use a pencil or use my phone.

Thank God for voice notes and voice-to-text. Not that I was ever the one to reach out to people. I used it for brief responses and middle finger emojis.

I glanced at the clock as I wedged my hands under my knee and slowly lifted my foot back onto the metal rest. It was almost two in the afternoon.

Brooke was supposed to have been here at one.

Today was her first day flying solo.

The day she showed up in my driveway with a fucking love plant, Chris and Cassandra had been there to act as a buffer. My mom was the one who showed up yesterday to make sure I didn't fire her.

The clock ticked on, but the driveway was empty.

I was generally irritated with someone being in my house, so why was I annoyed that she was late?

Ten minutes later, a rattling engine ker-plunked to a stop in the driveway. Mickey perked up from his nap on the back deck and wandered out front at the sound of Brooke's car.

The tension in my chest released, then immediately worked back up at the snap of her flip-flops.

Did she not have real shoes? The snap-snap sound as she stomped her way to the door was grating.

"Hello!" Brooke sang as she let herself in.

I hadn't bothered to change the locks or attempt to keep her out. Door knobs were getting expensive.

She kicked the door closed with a flip-flopped foot. Her toes were painted bright purple today. She had two cups in her hands, a bag on her shoulder, and three grocery bags hanging from the crook of her elbow.

"It's so pretty outside today," she said. "I just love the drive out here. How's your day going? Have you had lunch yet? There was a taco truck on my way in, so I hope you like barbacoa."

I did like barbacoa. But with coffee?

She took a slurp from a straw that was stuffed into a whipped cream and sprinkle-covered frozen concoction as she strolled into the kitchen. "I haven't figured out your coffee aura yet, so I got you an iced coffee, black. I figured we'll start there."

Why did she get me coffee?

Brooke blew out a breath. "Anyway. Enough about me. How's your day going?"

Curly brown hair was plastered to her forehead and neck. Her tanned skin was pink from the heat and covered in a sheen of sweat. She was in another pair of tiny denim shorts, and a tank top that was loose and low enough for me to see her ribs and bra.

"Fine," I muttered.

Brooke didn't pay me any mind. Because, of course, she didn't. Tornadoes don't care who they bother.

She dropped the drinks and her bags on the counter. "I picked up your prescriptions on the way in, and the groceries your mom texted me about. Give me just a sec to put them away, and then we can hang out."

I didn't want to hang out.

Brooke was odd. She wasn't a nurse. Wasn't a CNA. She was a glorified gopher who could talk the paint off the walls.

"Taco?" She handed me a lump wrapped in parchment.

I just glared.

"Do you want it on a plate? We could go outside and eat on the deck. I love the heat. Is Mickey out there?" She tugged a red box out of one of the grocery bags. "I found cow treats! I wanna see if he likes them."

This fucking woman and her excitement over cow treats...

When I didn't answer, she set my taco on the counter and grabbed hers. "Suit yourself. I'll be outside if you wanna join."

I stared at her ass as she strutted out of the kitchen, yanked the sliding screen open, and squealed when she spotted Mickey.

Great. Now I had a headache too.

I yanked open the junk drawer and found the bottle of ibuprofen. Medicine bottles were stupid. I couldn't get a good enough grip on the safety cap to open it.

I tried again, pressing the lid against the palm of my left hand. I had better grip strength in my right, but it still wasn't effective. I couldn't get the goddamn thing open.

Anger surged through me, and I threw the pill bottle across the room. Useless shit.

Brooke poked her head in. "Are you okay?" She spotted the pill bottle and came inside. "Ugh. I hate those. They should really make some with the safety caps and some without them."

I clenched my jaw as she knelt, grabbed the bottle, and popped it open.

"How many do you want?" Her eyes met mine. They reminded me of bluebonnets and an endless summer sky.

I blinked away the momentary stupor. "I'm fine. It just fell."

Brooke laughed. "I get that. I'm such a klutz. This morning, I forgot to grab my phone charger and I tripped up the stairs on the way to get it. I'll leave three pills here just in case."

I watched as she counted them out in her palm, then left them in a little pile on the edge of the countertop.

"Just holler if you need anything." She skipped back out to the deck and propped her feet up on a chair, talking to Mickey as she ate.

When I was sure that she was deep in conversation with the cow, I scooped the pills off the edge of the counter and into my palm, then tossed them back.

I wrapped both hands around the plastic iced coffee cup. The condensation beading on the side made it slippery, but I took it slow and washed the painkillers down with a sip from the straw.

Black coffee was terrible.

I grabbed the taco to chase away the taste of burnt coffee beans. Damn. It smelled good.

I was half-tempted to join her on the deck, just so I could stare at those bronze legs. *Damn.*

My dick twitched. That was inconvenient, especially because I was in gym shorts.

Those legs dropped from their perch, and Brooke strolled in. "Oh good! I was worried I caught you too late and you wouldn't be hungry! How do you like it?"

Fuck me. I needed my dick to calm down. I dropped my hand and the taco to my crotch to hide the growing tent in my pants.

Her ass peeked out the bottom of her shorts as she

tossed her balled up parchment into the garbage and bent over to tie the trash bag.

Most of the people who were sent out here wore scrubs. There was no way in hell she was supposed to wear barely-there denim cutoffs and a tank top that showed off her fine little body.

"You can go," I snapped. Honestly, I should have sat back and let myself look at something pretty, but all it did was remind me of everything I had lost.

Brooke paused. "What?"

"Leave."

She laughed. "I just got here."

I clenched my fist and pressed it against the armrest of my chair. "Go."

Her eyes dropped to my shorts, and she frowned. "Do you want me to get you a plate? I really don't mind helping. That's why I'm here. I just didn't want to bother you."

She was already on her tiptoes, reaching into my cabinet.

"I don't want a plate!" I roared. "I want you out of my house!"

Brooke froze in shock. Her eyes widened and welled up with tears, turning a glassy blue like the pond outside.

"I—I'm sorry," she whispered. "I'll do better. I'll—"

I stared at the floor so I didn't have to see the hurt on her face. "Get out."

Her feet scrambled as I added, "And don't come back."

∼

THE HOUSE WAS DARK. Moonlight filtered in through the windows. It was the middle of the night, but I couldn't sleep.

I had been lying in bed for hours, staring at the ceiling the way I used to.

Except this time, there were no popcorn ceilings to see patterns in. That was my fault. I had told the builders to make the ceilings smooth.

Now all I stared at was plain white paint.

I should have put some of those glow-in-the-dark stars up there. Or maybe a TV. That would have been smart.

But all I could do was stare into the blackness and wait for daybreak.

5

BROOKE

My stomach churned as I drove under the timber gate of the Griffith Brothers Cattle Ranch. Ray's mom, Claire, was on her porch as I passed. She beamed from ear to ear and waved.

I rounded the bend, passing the two other houses—Christian and Cassandra's, and Nate and Becks's—Ray's two brothers and their families.

I had yet to meet his youngest brother, and part of me wondered if I ever would. Maybe I'd meet him when they hauled me off the land for trespassing.

The squat metal building that housed the ranch office came into view, and I spotted Cassandra walking inside. She looked over her shoulder and watched with an unsettling gaze as I passed.

I continued driving, soaking up the last of the peace as Ray's grove of trees appeared in the distance. The truck was under its usual tarp, and the blinds were closed as always. Everything was familiar, except for the two teenagers knocking on the front door.

They turned and stared when I pulled into the driveway.

"Who are you?" the younger one asked when I got out and closed the door.

"Brooke. Who are you?"

"Gracie," she said.

The older one knocked again, but there was no answer.

"Is Ray not home?" I asked. He was supposed to be, according to his digital calendar.

The older one shrugged with teenage indifference. "I dunno. He won't let us see him." Her dejected sigh broke my heart.

"Which grown-up do you belong to?" I asked.

"Christian is our dad," the older one said.

"And Cassandra is our evil stepmother-to-be," the younger one added.

I laughed. "So Ray is your uncle?"

The younger one nodded. "I'm Gracie. And this is my sister, Bree."

I smiled weakly. "Well, it's nice to meet you."

"What are you doing here?" Bree asked. If I had to guess, she was around fourteen or fifteen.

I checked the time on my phone. "I'm here to hang out with your uncle."

Gracie's eyebrows lifted. "Will you ask him if we can hang out with him too? Maybe he'll say yes to you."

"I'll ask."

"Thank you!" Gracie flung her arms around me in a tight hug.

The girls raced down the ramp and cut through the trees. They had almost disappeared among the leaves when I saw the blinds crack.

I waited a moment, then knocked. When he didn't answer, I tried the handle. To my surprise, it was unlocked.

The lights were off, but sunshine streamed in from the

window by the door. Ray was in the recliner today, with the TV on but muted.

"What are you doing here?" he hissed.

I swallowed my pride and closed the door behind me. "I'm here to work."

"I told you not to come back."

"I know."

He cocked a brow. "And yet you're standing in my house."

"I really need this job," I croaked out.

Ray remained silent.

"Look, I think we got off on the wrong foot. Maybe we just need to sit down and talk and get to know each other so I know what you want from me."

Still nothing.

"I can't get fired," I admitted. "If I lose another client, they won't give me anymore. And I'm already behind on my bills as it is, and I just..." I squared my shoulders. "I swear I'll try harder."

He studied me from a distance, jaw flexing as he worked my plea over in his mind. "You can start by being on time for once."

I nodded as I hurried in and dropped my bags on the floor. "I'll try. I usually have a stop before you and sometimes it's hard to get away, and I—"

"Stop talking," he clipped.

I froze on the spot. "Yes, sir."

"Don't fucking call me that."

"Mr. Griffith?"

He closed his eyes and huffed. "Ray's fine."

"Your nieces were here."

"I know," he snapped.

"Do you... want me to go find them and let them in?"

"No."

"Okay…" I sighed. *Work with me here, man.*

Ray flicked his eyes to the deck. "Let's go sit out there."

I hurried to help him out of the recliner, but my foot caught the handle of my bag. I squealed as I tumbled forward and smacked the floor.

Ray huffed. "Jesus Christ."

I scrambled up, wiggled my foot free from the fabric strap, and hurried over.

Ray sat up and I pulled his wheelchair over.

"Don't fucking touch me," he snapped as I reached for him. The anger in his voice was palpable.

I jolted back.

"Go wait outside."

"But I'm supposed to—"

"Are you going to wait outside or are you going to get fired?"

I slipped outside with my tail between my legs and waited. The sun was high in the sky, and not a cloud was in sight. His deck had a breathtaking view, but curiosity got the better of me.

Through the open sliding door, I watched as Ray leaned forward in the recliner. He turned his chest to the side and slowly shuffled backward into his wheelchair. He lifted his legs onto the footrests before unlocking the brake and pushing himself out to meet me.

"Let's make one thing clear," Ray said as he rolled up to the edge of the deck, staring at the horizon. "I don't want you here."

"Okay." I swallowed my hurt and embarrassment. "I promise I'll stay out of your way. I can clean and do whatever you want. I just… I can't get fired again."

"You can drive me into town," he said.

"Yeah. Of course. I'd love to. I really do want to help any way I can."

He stared at me for a long moment. "Aren't you supposed to be wearing a uniform or something?"

I laughed and looked down at my shorts and tank top. "Yeah. But Mr. Wilson—the man I check on in the mornings—doesn't always know who I am, and he gets mad and throws things at me. This morning it was grits. I figured you wouldn't want me covered in it. It gets crusty after a while. So I changed in my car."

Something flashed across his face, but he didn't say a word.

"Do you... want me to—"

"It's fine," he groused.

I looked down at my hands, wishing I could melt into the ground.

Ray hadn't stopped staring at me. It was unnerving. There was so much I didn't know about him. But instead of sitting in the presence of a stranger, I was in the presence of a lion who hadn't eaten in days.

"Why can't you get fired?" he asked.

I lifted my chin. "Why don't you want me here?"

"You first."

"Living is expensive," I said.

That made him crack a smile, but it quickly disappeared. "Go find another job."

I huffed. "I've been fired from every job I've ever had. I don't have family, and I'm already behind on things as it is. I just need to hold on to this one a little longer until I can figure things out."

"Figure what out?"

I shrugged. "I dunno. What I'm doing with my life?"

"How much is a little longer?" Ray hedged. He was negotiating, and I was more than willing to play ball.

"Two years."

He scoffed.

"I'm serious. I just need to hold onto a steady job until I turn twenty-five, and then I get access to my trust fund."

He reached into his pocket and pulled out a length of rope. I watched as he started tying it in knots, over and over again. "So, you're going to wait two years to figure out what you're doing with your life?"

"What about you?"

He didn't look up from the rope as he tried to feed the tail through the loop with his left hand, but he couldn't quite get it. "What about me?"

"What do you do?"

Ray didn't answer.

"Will you tell me anything about you? It's fine if you don't want to. I'll just make up little stories in my head and speculate wildly while I clean your house and run your errands."

Ray's head snapped toward me. "Don't get it twisted. I just want my family to leave me alone. I don't want you here."

I couldn't help the way my lip quivered. "You've made that very clear."

His exacting gaze lifted from the rope. Ray stared at me for a beat before licking his lips. "I was a bull rider."

"Really? That's so cool!"

He let a caustic laugh slip. "Is everything cool to you?"

"Well, yeah. People are cool. I like getting to know whoever the universe sees fit to put me near."

"People suck."

"So..." I stared at the wooden planks of the deck. "You'll let me stay?"

He used his left hand to slide the tail of the rope through a loop and pulled it tight. "What's your backup plan if I fire you?"

I laughed. "I ran out of backup plans like ten backup plans ago."

It felt like the tension between us began to loosen. Maybe we wouldn't be friends, but we could coexist.

"What was your backup plan?" I asked. "You know, after bull riding. I can't imagine that being something you could do forever."

Ray continued to fiddle with the rope, not even bothering to glance up at me. "I never had one."

∼

"Jesus Christ," Ray shouted as he pushed his wheelchair through the kitchen and opened the front door. "What the hell are you doing?"

Three days into our truce, and he was still yelling at me.

Rule number one of trying to not get fired: don't piss off the grumpy bull rider.

Rule number two? When you do get fired, keep your chin up. The grumpy bull rider was hot.

"It's fine!" I said as I grabbed a dish towel and waved the smoke away from the pan.

Ray coughed in the haze. "You are a fucking disaster. You know that?"

I dropped the towel and shoved the window above the sink open to let the breeze in.

"There," I said as I stepped back and wiped my hands on

my shorts. "The smoke will be out in no time. No harm, no foul."

Something crackled behind me. I turned and shrieked. "Oh my god!"

Ray swore loudly. "You didn't turn the burner off, and you put a fucking towel on top of it?"

"I forgot!" I squealed as flames licked up the cotton cloth.

"It happened five seconds ago!"

"I was trying to get the smoke out!"

"Jesus! What the hell is going on in here?" Cassandra stood in the doorway with her hand clasped over her nose and mouth.

She stomped over in her high heels and pantsuit, turned the burner off, yanked the towel away, dropped it onto the floor, and stomped on it until the fire was out.

"I was just trying to fry an egg," I said as I scrambled to clean up the charred tea towel.

She pinched the bridge of her nose. "Whatever. You're Ray's problem."

"Gee, thanks," Ray grumbled.

Cassandra stabbed a finger at him. "You, however, are my problem."

"What crawled up your ass?" he sneered. "Trouble in paradise with your Griffith brother?"

"Nope," she snapped. "You were an ass to my girls the other day. That means I get to be an ass to you. Get the picture?"

Ray scoffed and pushed on the wheel to turn his chair away from her. "I didn't do jack shit."

"You locked them out."

"The door wasn't locked."

"Yeah? Well they were raised to be respectful, unlike

you. Now get your head out of your ass or you'll have hell to pay."

I stared, wide-eyed, as Cassandra stormed out in a tornado of blonde hair and expensive perfume.

"I think I'm in love with her," I whispered.

He didn't say a word.

"Why won't you see your nieces?" I asked, tossing the corpse of a towel into the trash and used a paper towel to wipe the black streaks off the floor.

Still no answer.

"Are you close to them?"

He flinched. It was barely noticeable, but it looked a lot like guilt. "Used to be."

"What happened?"

Ray arched an eyebrow. "Do you really think that's any of your business?"

I laughed. "Come on. We need to get to know each other."

"We don't." He grabbed the handle of the frying pan and dumped the charred remains of the egg into the garbage.

"I'm great at keeping secrets. This one time, my roommate told me that she worked her way up to being the general manager of the restaurant she's at and has never changed the paper towels because she doesn't know how to unlock the machine and put the new roll in. So, she just tells the new staff to do it and pretends to be busy. And I never told anyone."

Ray tipped his chin back and huffed. "Brooke."

"What?"

"You just told me."

"Come on," I begged. "You don't talk to me at all when I'm here. It's been days, and I'm going crazy."

"You talk enough for the both of us."

"If I promise to stop talking, will you tell me?"

Ray stared at me. I smiled at him. He didn't smile back.

"Please?" I begged.

Ray pushed his wheelchair over to the fridge and pawed around for a snack. "Their mother—my sister-in-law—died when the girls were little." He slammed the fridge door, making the condiment bottles rattle. "I was living in Colorado. Came back to the ranch for a few months. Christian was grieving and dealing with the ranch. Nate was deployed. CJ was a kid. So, I stayed at the house with the girls. Eventually, I went back to my life and they grew up. I used to surprise them when I'd come into town. I'd kidnap them from school, take them to lunch, and hang out like we used to. That's all."

Dear God. He couldn't be hot *and* good with kids. That combination was irresistible.

I grabbed an egg from the fridge to start the frying process again. Ray had mentioned a fried egg sandwich sounded good, and dammit—I was going to make him one.

"You should have them over. Order a pizza or something. Oh! We could have a game night! That'd be so much fun! They still want to hang out with you even though they've grown up."

"I don't want to hang out with them." And with that, he left the room.

6

BROOKE

Today wasn't going to be a good day. It was going to be a *great* day. Mr. Wilson didn't throw oatmeal at me today, so my company polo was still pristine. I left his house at noon on the dot and had time to spare for a coffee stop before I drove out to the ranch.

The sun was shining, the birds were singing, the barista gave me an extra drink that someone didn't like, and I had a day off tomorrow.

Life was an amazing thing.

The bells of the coffee shop door jingled as I stepped into the summer sun.

I took a slurp from the straw and headed down the sidewalk to my car. The aroma of nail polish and remover wafted out from the open salon door. It had been a while since I got my nails done. But with the extra pay from not getting fired in my first week with Ray, maybe I could splurge.

My pantry was stocked, my gas tank was full, my phone bill was paid, and I had already squirreled away my portion of the rent money for the month.

I had my shit together, and it felt so good.

"Yo, Stacey!"

I whirled around and spotted Nick heading down the sidewalk with his hands in his pockets. "Oh my god!" I mumbled through the mouthful of espresso and ice cream. "Hey!"

The chain hanging from his wallet jingled as he strolled up to me. "What are you doing out here? Shouldn't you be working?"

"Oh, I am!" I said as I wiggled the plastic cup that was quickly being covered in teardrops of condensation. "I just stopped for a little pick-me-up before I head out to the ranch."

He ran his thumb over his emaciated pencil mustache. "The ranch?"

"The Griffith Brothers Ranch."

"Right..." He studied the coffees in my hand. "Look, I think you shorted me on utilities last month."

My heart sank. I had been so careful... I paid in cash and counted every dollar. "Really?"

Nick crossed his arms and tipped his head back. "Look, if you can't pay your share, we'll give your room to someone else." He shrugged. "Your choice. Pay up or lose your spot."

"I swear, I gave you the right amount. I just—"

"Is there a problem here, sweetheart?" A giant shadow engulfed me.

I turned and found Christian Griffith standing behind me. "Hi, Mr. Griffith!"

He didn't look at me. Instead, his gaze was trained on Nick. "This fella' bothering you, Brooke?"

"Who?" I tipped my head toward Nick. "Him? Oh, no. This is my roommate. Well, one of them at least." I laughed. "Six of us share the house."

Mr. Griffith let out a low hum that sounded more like a growl. He crossed one thick arm over the other, resting them on top of his belly. "You headin' out our way?"

"Yes, sir," I said.

Nick started to back away. It was like Mr. Griffith had scared him away with one stern look from under that cowboy hat. "I'll see you back at the house, Stacey."

"It's Brooke," I called after him.

Christian circled around to stand in front of me. "That your boyfriend or something?"

I giggled. "That's funny."

But he didn't smile. "Does he speak to you like that all the time?"

I shrugged it off. "It's not a big deal. Nick is just... Nick."

Christian looked around. "Do you need a ride out to the ranch?"

"Oh, no. Thanks, though. I'm just getting a little pick-me-up before I go deal with the human storm cloud."

That made him laugh. "You're doing great, sweetheart." He squeezed my arm in a way that made me miss my dad. "I know Ray's being difficult about having help, but you've stuck around longer than any of the others."

I worked my lip between my teeth. "I think Ray's fine having help. I mean, who wouldn't want help? Most of my clients want help. It's the families who forget that they're capable of asking for it."

He stared at me for a moment, then nodded. "I'm glad I ran into you. I've gotta finish up in town, but I'll see you back at the ranch."

"See ya," I said as I waved and headed off to my car.

I ignored the rattling in my engine by blasting the radio as loud as it would go while I made the drive to the ranch.

The check engine light glowed like sunshine from behind the smiley face sticker.

The ranch was a welcomed sight. I passed two trucks emblazoned with construction company logos. I didn't know much about the building projects that were going on, but it was fascinating to watch.

I waved to Claire and Silas, Ray's parents, as I passed their house. Nate and Becks's house was dark, but it was because they were out of the country. I slowed and waved as I passed Bree and Gracie, Ray's nieces, as they ran down the dirt path.

I loved it here. Everyone was so friendly.

With the developed part of the ranch in the distance, Ray's grove of trees came into view. The leaves swallowed my car as I pulled down the drive. Suddenly, it was like I was in my own little world.

The ranch didn't exist outside of the tree line. Ray's house was completely closed off. Part of me wondered if that was on purpose.

I hopped out and carted my things inside, but Ray was nowhere to be found. Did I get the schedule wrong? Did I run into Mr. Griffith in town because he had to take Ray to an appointment? Where was he?

"Ray?"

His bedroom door was closed. I pressed my ear to it, listening for proof of life.

I knocked again. "Ray, it's me. Just letting you know I'm here."

Still nothing.

"Ray?"

My stomach churned. What if something was wrong? Where was he? Who did I call? Should I call someone, or should I just go hunt someone down on the ranch?

Wait.

The sliding door that led to the deck was open.

I poked my head outside and let out a sigh of relief. Ray was down by the pond, tying knots. I grabbed the coffees and the bag I brought in and headed down the deck ramp.

The grass was soft under my flip-flops as I strode across the yard to meet him. "Hey, you!"

Ray didn't look up from the knots he was tying. They were different today. He wasn't just keeping his hands busy with a mindless task; he was creating a pattern. His left hand looked a little stronger as he looped and tugged the smooth rope.

"How's your day?" I asked as I got closer. "Need anything from the house before I settle into leaving you alone?"

"Nah," he grunted.

"How'd you get your wheelchair down the grass?" I asked, setting the coffees on the ground and rummaging around in my bag.

He let out a weighted breath. "Pretty much the only workout I get."

"Is that why you don't use a power chair?"

"Yeah," he muttered.

"Someone's chatty today," I noted. "I like it."

He rolled his eyes as he went to work untying all the knots.

"I like the pond," I said, pulling the cup holder out and attaching it to the arm of his wheelchair. "Is it natural or did you have it put in?"

He eyed me warily. "Natural. What are you doing?"

I dropped the extra coffee into the cup holder. "I found this cup holder for suitcases and figured it might work for you. Now you can have coffee with me and not have to hold it. There's nothing worse than lukewarm iced coffee. It's worse than room-temperature hot coffee. It's like drinking a dry heave."

He arched an eyebrow. "What is it?"

"Iced latte with caramel. They gave it to me for free."

Ray took a sip, then grimaced.

"Not a fan?"

"Nope."

I switched our cups. "Try mine."

He glared at me.

"What? Do you think I'm trying to poison you or something? I'm trying to read your coffee aura."

A caustic laugh slipped. "My what?"

"Your coffee aura. You know, it's like your star sign, but way more important. The kind of coffee someone likes says a lot about them as a person."

Ray stared at my blended whipped cream concoction topped with chocolate drizzle, then at me, then back at the coffee.

"Please?" I begged. "Do it for your friendly neighborhood Sagittarius."

Ray took a sip. His face was completely void of any kind of reaction. "Try again."

"Okay, but are we getting warmer? Colder? Tell me where we're at. I need to know if I'm getting close."

Ray went back to tying knots. "Like drinking a dry heave."

I laughed as I wiggled my flip flops off and stretched out in the grass. "I think I'm getting close. You just don't want to admit it. Give me another week and I'll have you figured out."

"Awfully bold of you to assume I won't fire you before then."

"You like me," I said, closing my eyes and soaking in the sun.

Ray just grunted.

We spent an hour in companionable silence. Ray tied pattern after pattern, and I studied the cloud shapes high in the sky.

"So has it worked?" I asked when the sun came out from behind the clouds and blinded me.

"Has what worked?"

I pawed around in my bag for my sunglasses, but ended up pulling out my bag of Sweet Tarts. "Me being here. Has your family left you alone?"

"Mostly," he said with a hint of frustration. His hands must have been getting tired because he was having trouble tying the knot.

"Why do you tie knots all the time?"

"Why do you ask so many questions?"

"Because I like you."

His dark brows knitted together. "You shouldn't."

"I do. And there's nothing you can do about it."

He eyed my candies.

"Want one?" I wiggled the bag around. "It's mostly green and yellow ones now."

"Why?"

"Why what? Why am I offering you one?"

"No. Why are the green and yellow ones left?"

"Oh. Because I don't like those," I said as I spotted a coveted blue candy. The blue ones were the best.

Ray reached out and slowly uncurled his fingers. "Green."

I dropped three in his palm. He tossed them back like pills and crunched on the candies.

"So, what's with the rope?"

"I didn't say we were talking."

"I'm just curious," I said as I found a pink one.

"Do you want me to fire you?"

"I thought asking questions in the workplace was encouraged."

"It's not."

"Come on. Tell me something," I begged. "I've been so good."

Ray lifted an eyebrow.

I pressed my palms together. "Please."

He huffed. "My fine motor skills are shit."

"They look pretty good to me."

"Don't patronize me, Sunnyside. I thought you were better than that."

"Aww! You think about me?" I giggled. "I'm touched."

"Don't let your head get big. I think about firing you at least three times a day."

"See? I knew you were funny behind all that growling. So. Rope tying. Was that something you did with bull riding?"

Ray stared at me, then laughed. "No. Some rodeos have roping competitions. I didn't do that."

"Oh. That's cool. I just figured it was something you liked doing. You know, since it's all you do."

"It's supposed to help my dexterity. I still have trouble with my hands."

"Can I ask what happened?"

"You already know."

"I can make some assumptions considering you said you were a bull rider, and now you're just a grumpy hermit. But I'd like to hear it from you."

"Google it."

My heart sank. I thought we were making progress. I

really thought I could wear him down into trusting me, even just a little bit.

He huffed and put his hand out. "Give me the bag."

I relented and offered the bag of candy. Ray put the bag in his lap and fished around. Slowly, he pinched a yellow one. One by one, he pulled out only yellow and green candies and dropped them in his palm.

He handed the bag back and tossed a yellow one into his mouth.

"Accident during the championship eighteen months ago. I got thrown off the bull. Landed on my head. Broke my spine. Had a punctured lung. Bunch of broken ribs. Internal bleeding. The works."

"Oh my god," I whispered. "That's so scary."

He shrugged. "I was knocked out. Didn't know how bad it was until I woke up three weeks later."

"So, you've been working on getting your mobility back?"

He let out a wry laugh. "I allowed myself to be used as a lab rat for a human trial. It worked out well for the rats, and I had nothing left to lose. It helped me regain some mobility. That, and physical therapy. I hate that shit."

I rested my arm on top of my knees and propped my chin in my palm. "That's incredible. You've come so far in a year and a half."

He finished the last of the candies and picked up the rope. "Alright. That's enough talking for today."

7

RAY

I couldn't stop thinking about Brooke, and I hated myself for it. The last time she had been in here, she was in a god-awful embroidered polo, but she still wore those Daisy Dukes that were painted across her ass.

Water from the shower streamed down my face as I rested on the seat fitted against the tile wall. I pushed my hair out of my eyes and tipped my head back, breathing in the steam.

For once, I didn't hate talking about the accident. I just had to cut myself off before I kept rambling on about it. She was curious, but not placating or patronizing.

And fuck me, she was fine as hell.

Big blue eyes. Thick curls of brown hair I wanted to dig my hands into. Cherry lips with a line down the middle that made them look like pillows. Legs like a gazelle and a laugh that broke the haze in my mind every time I heard it.

She was, arguably, terrible at her job. And yet, she was the only person in a year and a half who had done a somewhat acceptable job of tolerating me.

She still talked too much, but at least she didn't expect a response.

I wrapped my hand around my dick and let out a slow exhale. Thoughts of her filled my mind as I worked my shaft up and down.

My motions were inconsistent, but that didn't keep the pressure from simmering in my groin.

Goddamn, she was beautiful.

The other day, she had rolled over in the grass and laid on her stomach. I got to stare at that ass for an hour. I groaned as fantasies of her tangled in bedsheets filtered through my mind as my dick grew harder and harder.

My shoddy attempt at jerking off didn't matter. Within seconds, I was coming to the thought of Brooke. Her hair tossed. Her skin flushed. Her lips parted and panting.

It had been a long time since I'd wanted a woman.

It had been even longer since a woman had wanted me.

I finished washing off and cut the water. Usually, I would have used the bars and pulleys to get out of the shower, but the steam—and the orgasm—had loosened me up a bit.

I closed my eyes and ran through the gamut of mental exercises my physical therapist made me do before we worked on my legs.

Focus on the muscles. Remember what it felt like. Isolate those feelings and focus on each part of the movement.

I focused on my left knee like it was a diagram in a science class. I envisioned bending it to plant my foot on the shower floor. I thought about bending forward and pushing up to stand.

I had spent most of my therapy hours that week in a standing body brace, with my legs being worked like a baby who had gas. I had random bouts of muscle spasticity that made my therapist hopeful. I chalked it up to optimistic delusion.

But part of me held onto those threads of delusion too.

I gripped the wall bars and slowly, slowly focused on lifting my hamstrings and quads. My left thigh raised off the plastic shower seat. I squeezed my eyes shut even harder as I planted my foot flat on the textured shower floor. An odd sensation pooled in my ankle—or at least what I thought was my ankle.

I pushed up on the bars, lifting my body with just my arms, keeping the bulk of my weight off my legs.

Slowly, I kept a hold on the shower support bars but released some of the strain on my arms.

Goddamn it. My knees hurt like a bitch.

I gritted my teeth and didn't dare open my eyes as I slowly opened my left hand and let go of one bar.

Rivulets of water streamed down my body. The non-slip coating on the bottom of the shower didn't matter. It was still slick as shit, and I wasn't going to take a chance and fall.

But maybe…

I peered through lowered lids as I lifted my foot and took a step.

Holy shit.

I took another breath. My knuckles on the support bar turned white as I shifted my weight and focused on my right knee and hip. I planted my right foot on the floor and, with less hesitancy, put my weight on it.

My arm was stretched behind me. I couldn't take another step without letting go.

But I was standing.

I grabbed the next set of support bars and pulled myself out of the shower the way I had managed to do every other time.

I hadn't told my family about any of the progress I had made, and swore my therapy team to secrecy.

What happened if the electrodes in my back stopped working? What happened when I got old and my body gave out faster than the average person? What would happen if my muscles went back into paralysis?

I left the ranch at eighteen so I wouldn't be a burden. I was acutely aware of the risks of bull riding, but it had been my ticket out.

I dried off and dressed using my wheelchair since I didn't want to press my luck.

I had just gotten my gym shorts on when someone knocked on the door.

Brooke was supposed to be here later, but that didn't sound like her knock. Which meant it was—

"Ray?" my brother Nate called out as he let himself in.

Yeah. I really needed to get that passcode lock for my door.

No one locked their shit up around here except for me. And the Griffith walking through my kitchen was Exhibit A as to why.

"You're back," I said as I pushed my chair into the living room and did a neat pivot around the corner of the couch.

Nate had been traveling with his wife, Becks, for her job as a foreign affairs correspondent. He used to double as her security detail thanks to his time in the military, but now he was the designated parent when they were overseas.

"Got in last night," he said as he helped himself to my fridge. "Jet lag is a bitch."

"Where were you this time?"

"Becks was covering a conflict on the border of Afghanistan and Pakistan. The network had her staging out of Islamabad, so I hung out at the hotel with Charlie while she was in the field."

Charlie was my two-year-old niece who had a head of ginger hair that matched her mom's.

"Everything go alright for Becks?" I asked.

"Yeah. Nothing too crazy." Nate pulled a plastic-wrapped bowl out of the fridge and poked at the top. "What the hell is this?"

I laughed under my breath. "Something Brooke tried to cook. It tastes like a shoe."

"Right. The home aide that you haven't fired yet." He peeled the plastic back and sniffed the contents of the bowl. "Dear god, that smells worse than a week-old MRE."

"I warned you."

Before he could say anything else, the door opened again. Christian and CJ walked in.

"Don't you people have jobs or something?" I said with a huff as I scrolled through my phone. My social media pages were more or less defunct.

Marty used to post on them for me—mostly content for ad campaigns I was obligated to boost. But nothing had been posted since the night of my accident.

But I wasn't scrolling for me. I was scrolling to try to find *her*.

"I'm retired," Nate said.

"What's your excuse?" I asked CJ. He was the ranch's cow boss, taking over for Christian after he took over as the foreman for our father.

CJ shrugged. "I took Indy out this morning. Just turned her out and got Anny. Saw Chris heading over here and came along."

Indy was my horse, Independence. She was a pretty girl,

but a sharp contrast to Anarchy, the sinister-looking horse that tolerated CJ.

"Thanks," I muttered. It wasn't like I could take Indy out or care for her. It sucked. "What are you doing here?" I asked Christian.

He peered around the corner. "Looking for Brooke."

I rolled my eyes. "I haven't fired her yet, if that's what you're asking."

Christian lifted his cowboy hat and ran his hand back through his long hair.

Maybe I'd grow my hair out and stop shaving, too. Go full outlaw.

"No. I had a run-in with her in town the other day. She was with some guy."

The hairs on the back of my neck bristled.

"She said he was her roommate, but it looked like he was trying to shake her down for cash. She wouldn't say anything in front of him. I wanted to make sure she was alright."

My blood ran hot with rage. Why hadn't she said anything about it when she showed up for her shift? Brooke just skipped through the house like her normal, babbling self and hung out.

"She should be here in an hour," I said as I glanced at the clock. "Which means she'll be here in two hours."

Christian ran his hand down his beard. "Be nice to her. I don't know what's going on, but if it was one of my girls, I'd be worried."

I really didn't want him to bring up his daughters. I felt like shit every time I turned them away, but I couldn't let them see me like this.

I wasn't the uncle they remembered, or the one they deserved.

Downpour 73

"Give me a call when she gets here," Christian said. "I'll come back and check on her."

I didn't need him to fucking check on her.

I would fucking check on her.

After my brothers left, I spent the next hour and a half watching the clock and combing through Brooke's social media profiles to find out who this roommate was.

She mostly posted pictures of flowers and clouds with little captions about them being the prettiest she had ever seen. A few photos were of her. Those were the prettiest I had ever seen.

When she didn't show at the scheduled time, or the tardy time I had come to expect, I started to worry.

Nearly four hours later, I heard the ker-thunk of her car engine sputter down my driveway.

My stomach was in knots. I stuffed my phone into the cupholder she had gotten for my wheelchair and grabbed one of the ropes I kept around. Acting like everything was normal was better than admitting I had been thinking about her every waking second.

The door creaked open, and Brooke shuffled in. I waited for her usual sunny greeting, but it never came.

Her head was down as she closed the door behind her. A waterfall of brown ringlets shrouded her face.

I waited, mindlessly tying the rope into knots as she shuffled around in the kitchen. Brooke unloaded my prescription refills, organizing them on the kitchen counter with the rest of the pill bottles.

Still, I waited. I had sent her a list of groceries to get in town, and watched as she unloaded them into the fridge and lower cabinets. Minutes passed, and she said nothing.

"Hey," I said.

Brooke squeaked and smacked her head on the open

cabinet door. She clasped one hand to the back of her skull and pressed the other to her chest. "You scared me."

Still, she didn't look up.

Something was wrong. Brooke was a disaster, but she was a predictable disaster. Whatever this was, wasn't normal.

Her hair shifted, and I spotted the rim of her sunglasses.

"You can see better inside if you take those off."

She laughed, but it wasn't her normal, bubbly laugh. Something was definitely wrong.

Fuck it.

I pushed into the kitchen and trapped her against the cabinets with my wheelchair.

"What's the matter?"

She fidgeted with a box of pasta. "Nothing. Sorry I'm running late. I swear one of these days I'll—"

"Brooke."

Her sunglasses slipped down her button nose, and that's when I saw it.

A dark bruise marred her cheek. It bloomed up her eye lid and across her temple. A blood vessel had broken in her eye, and a deep cut was still open and damp, just above her cheekbone.

I grabbed her glasses and threw them onto the counter. Brooke winced, and a tear slid down from the corner of her eye.

"I—I'm sorry," she whispered. "Running errands took longer than I thought, and there was traffic, and I—"

I reached up, cupped her chin, and wiped away the tear with my thumb as a low growl slipped from my chest. "Who the fuck did this to you?"

Her cherry lips trembled, and she shook her head. "I'm fine. I'm sorry I'm late again."

"I don't give a shit that you're late. I wanna know what the hell happened."

Brooke swallowed and nearly strangled the box of pasta in her hands. "Please. Can we... Can we just ignore each other today?" She sniffed as her eyes welled up with tears. "I've been really looking forward to that."

She looked like she hadn't slept. There were bags under her eyes and more pain than the injuries warranted, though they were gruesome.

"Not until you tell me what the hell happened."

She hurried to finish putting away the rest of the groceries, but I grabbed her wrist.

"Brooke."

"Please," she whispered, sliding the sunglasses on top of her head. "Between the pharmacy and the grocery store, I've gotten enough weird looks today."

"Tell me what happened," I gritted out.

Brooke slumped against the counters. "It's been a long day."

"Then sit on the couch and tell me. I don't give a shit. But you're not getting out of this."

A roll of toilet paper from the pack in the closet was the best I could do since I didn't have tissues on hand.

I rolled up to the couch, set the toilet paper on the end table, and locked the brakes on my chair. "Give me your hand."

The couch was harder to get onto than the recliner. I used the padded arm to hold most of my weight as I braced against it with my hand and held onto Brooke with my other. I ungracefully flopped onto the cushion and turned until I was sitting beside her.

I grabbed the roll of toilet paper and handed it to her. "Talk."

"It's not what you think," she said with tear-filled eyes as she ripped a sheet of toilet paper from the roll.

"It looks like you haven't slept in a week, and that someone used your face as a punching bag. But please—correct me where I'm wrong."

She hunched forward and rested her elbows on her knees as she tried to steady her breathing. "My roommates have been partying a lot, and it's been so loud in the house. There's always tons of people coming in and out. It's hard to fall asleep."

My blood turned molten. If some fucker had touched her, I was going to find some way to rip his body limb from limb. We had a backhoe and plenty of space out here to hide a corpse where no one would ever find it.

Christian's comment about some guy trying to get money from her lodged in my brain.

"Did they do that to you?" I let out a long breath to try and keep from flying off the handle. It barely worked. "I swear to god, if one of them put a fucking hand on you—"

"No," she cried. Brooke carefully dabbed her eye and sniffed. "Mr. Wilson, the client I see before I come out here... He's a really sweet old man, but—"

"Don't fucking defend someone if they assaulted you."

"He has dementia and he was having a bad day and didn't know who I was. He hit me and threw a plate at my head." Her words spilled out, one on top of the other.

"Fuck that shit. You're not going back there. Call your boss and tell them to make that man someone else's problem."

Brooke shook her head. Tears streamed down her cheeks as a warbled plea slipped from her lips. "No one else will take him. If I lose another client, I'll get fired. And if I get fired, I'll lose my job. And if I lose my job, I'll lose my room in the house. I can't lose my job, Ray. I can't."

I wanted heads to roll for this. Unfortunately, I wasn't the one who could crack skulls anymore. But I knew someone who could.

I fired off a text to Cassandra while Brooke rummaged around in my kitchen, making some halfway edible pancakes and bacon for dinner.

She handed me a plate and settled on the couch beside me. Neither of us had much of an appetite.

"You pick," I said as I handed her the TV remote and managed to grab a piece of bacon with my left hand.

Brooke turned on some obnoxious Real Housewives spinoff, but it didn't look like she was paying much attention. Her eyes were glassy and heavy as the people argued on screen.

Fifteen minutes in, I found myself unfortunately interested in the dramatics on the TV, and Brooke's head was on my shoulder.

Carefully, I wrapped my arm around her and tilted my body so she was resting on my chest.

Her lips were parted as soft snores escaped. I had never seen Brooke this exhausted. Hell—she was usually the Energizer Bunny.

I grabbed a throw pillow and put it on my lap before gently guiding her down to rest. She curled up like a cat, tucking her hands under her cheek and drawing her knees to her chest. I tugged down the blanket from the back of the couch and draped it over her body.

I brushed her hair away from her face and closed my eyes as I tangled warm curls around my fingers. Her body relaxed as I stroked her head.

Brooke never woke, and I didn't sleep. Because for once, I wanted to be awake.

8

BROOKE

Soft light floated through the living room. Everything was quiet. The couch creaked as I eased up onto my elbow and blinked.

Oh no.

Oh no, no, no.

My stomach sank like an anvil as I blinked the sleep from my eyes and came to.

Oh my god. I fell asleep at Ray's house.

On Ray's couch.

On top of Ray.

The set of abs under my head was a startling wake-up call, but oh my god—he smelled so good.

I panicked, pawing around until I found my phone stuffed between the couch cushions.

It was only a few minutes after nine in the morning, but it was an hour past when I was supposed to be at Mr. Wilson's house.

Missed calls from Peggy at the main office filled my phone screen.

I was *so* getting fired.

Dread and anxiety roiled in my gut as I scrambled off the couch.

"Brooke?" Ray was still stretched out on the couch. He was awake, but drowsy. His hair was messy, hanging in his eyes. "What time is it?"

"Late. I've gotta go." I jumped into my flip-flops and grabbed my keys, but paused and braced my hands on the edge of the coffee table as my head spun.

I hissed and cradled my temple. It felt like I had been hit by a sledgehammer. How could one frail, old man do that much damage?

"You shouldn't be driving," he said as he held onto the arm of the couch and pushed up until he was sitting. "You could have a concussion."

As much as I wanted to stay and have a lazy morning with him, I didn't have the time. "I drove yesterday. I'll be fine. I have to go."

Ray's eyebrows knitted together in concern. "Brooke—"

The rough tone of his voice made my heart ache. Was he worried or angry?

Probably angry. I had fallen asleep on his couch—on him.

I wanted to stay, but I couldn't. In fact, I didn't know if I'd even be coming back.

I needed to call Peggy back, then use the rest of my drive back to town to figure out where I was going to start applying for jobs.

"I'm sorry," I whispered as I darted out of the house.

I waited to call Peggy until I had made it back onto the paved service road. The bumps and potholes along the ranch's dirt paths had the tendency to make my car scream like a banshee.

I felt like I was going to throw up as I waited for her to pick up.

"Caring Hands Home Help. This is Peggy. How may I help—"

"Peggy, it's Brooke. I'm so sorry. I—I overslept and I didn't hear my phone going off and I—"

She huffed. "I've been trying to get in touch with you all morning."

"I know. I'm so sorry. I'm heading to Mr. Wilson's house right now."

"Don't bother," she clipped.

My heart dropped.

I had been trying so hard. I didn't mean to be this much of a wreck, but sometimes I just was. I couldn't help that my roommates liked to operate on nocturnal schedules and throw parties. I couldn't help that my car wouldn't let me go over forty miles an hour. I couldn't help that I was always late to the ranch because Mr. Wilson made it hard to get away. I couldn't help that the agency only gave me one uniform shirt, so it was always dirty.

But I was trying. I really, really was.

I just wanted to be good at something.

"Am I getting fired?" I whispered.

Peggy huffed. "We'll talk when you get here."

I made the drive back to the office in silence. I couldn't even muster the desire to turn on the radio to something cheery. It was the perfect day to scream "Great Balls of Fire" at the top of my lungs and bop around in the driver's seat, but I couldn't be bothered. It felt like I was driving to my own execution.

I pulled up to the curb and didn't even bother waiting out the perfunctory three minutes before heading inside. I just unbuckled my seatbelt, got out, and loped up the steps to the office.

Peggy wasn't at her desk, so I sat in the chair across from hers and waited.

"Oh," she said when she bustled into the front, carrying a thick stack of papers that smelled like they were fresh from the copier. "You're here."

"Yes ma'am."

She dropped down into the rolling desk chair and practically threw the stack of papers at me. "Sign these."

"Am I getting fired?"

Peggy glared at me. "Much to my dismay, no. You're not. Now sign those if you still want to be employed. And what happened to your face?"

I started to thumb through them. "Is this like a workers' comp thing? I meant to call you when I left Mr. Wilson's house yesterday to tell you about what happened, but—"

"Let me guess. You forgot. You got busy. It slipped your mind." Her tone made me feel small. I wanted to melt into the floor.

"I was just trying to make it out to Mr. Griffith's house in time, and I had some errands to run for him in between."

"Well, it looks like you made a good impression. The Griffith family wants you full-time."

I froze. "What?"

She threw a pen at me. "Do you want the job or not?"

I started scribbling my name on the dotted line before she finished her sentence. "Yes. Um, of course. Yes. Please. Yes."

Full time? My bank account would be so freaking happy. And with Ray? I would be with him full time? My ovaries did a little dance.

"You'll live at Mr. Griffith's house. Saturday and Sunday

are your days off, so feel free to leave if you want. Otherwise, you'll be expected to be there to assist at all times. Read over the liabilities clause, the code of conduct, and review the compensation breakdown."

Peggy was quiet as I worked through each page, signing and dating as needed. I paused when I got to the compensation breakdown, and my eyes bugged out.

That was more money than I had ever made in my entire life. I'd be paid every week, and my living expenses would be covered since I would be at his house.

I'd still need to keep my room at my house, just in case, but this was...

This was a game changer.

I couldn't let myself think the job would last me the entire two years I needed to make it through. But maybe I could save up enough and coast into my trust fund when I turned twenty-five.

I left the office feeling like an unbearable weight had been lifted from my shoulders.

Peggy's last marching orders had been to go to my place and pack up all the things I wanted to have when I moved into Ray's house. I usually would have been expected at Ray's house this afternoon, but I had been given the day off to get my affairs in order.

Not that I had many affairs to get in order.

I had a backpack that doubled as a suitcase and a reusable grocery bag that held my toiletries. It wouldn't take me long to pack. I could get back to the ranch before dark.

Cars were lined up in the driveway and on the street in front of the house. I had to park a block away and hoof it up the cracked sidewalk filled with overgrown weeds. Beer cans and liquor bottles littered the lawn.

I didn't bother pulling my key out. The door was cracked

open. Bodies were strewn about the living room. The whole place reeked of old takeout that was fermenting on the counter, weed, and alcohol. A trash bag had been tied to the door handle because the garbage can was overflowing. It looked like they had tried to use it as a basketball goal, but none of the trash actually made it into the bag.

"Staceeeee." Nick lifted his head off the stained rug in the middle of the living room floor. He was barely coherent. "What's up? You missed a hell of a party last night." His eyes couldn't focus on one spot in particular.

I stepped around the assortment of bodies in various states of undress and made a beeline for the stairs. "Looks like it."

"Where ya going?" he called.

"To pack!" I hollered down.

"Pack?" he mumbled as he lumbered up the stairs. "Pack for what?"

I paid him no mind as he slumped in my doorway while I shoved clothes into my backpack. "A client wants me full time. I'll be there during the week and back here on the weekends."

"You're not living here anymore?"

"I'll still live here. I just won't sleep here every night."

"Right. You'll be...."

"At the Griffith Brothers Ranch." I let out a proud sigh. "This is just what I've been waiting for."

Nick pointed to the calendar I had tacked to the wall. I hadn't slashed out today since I had been at Ray's this morning.

"What's that?"

"What? My calendar? Oh, I'm just counting down the days until I turn twenty-five."

"Why?"

"Because then I'll have access to my trust fund, and my life will begin. I think I might go back to college. Maybe I'll get a dog. I'm definitely getting a new car. Maybe a convertible, so I can drive with the top down. I mark off every day and smile because I'm one day closer to getting out of here."

"Right," he said listlessly as his eyes glazed over again. "Don't forget that you owe us for the trash service. It's fifty bucks."

From the looks of the interior of the house, no one had bothered to take the trash bags to the bins outside.

Or put the trash from the floor into the trash bags.

I winced. "I don't have it on me right now. Can I pay you this weekend? I didn't know it was my month to cover it. I thought it was Chandler's."

Nick stroked his chin. "It's $115 with the late fee."

I sighed. "I get paid every Friday now. I'll have it to you then."

He shrugged and lumbered back down the stairs. "Your choice."

I crammed the rest of my things into my bags and waddled out to my car with my hands full and my pillows stuffed under my arms. I could sleep almost anywhere, but I had to have my own pillows.

Well, except last night when I fell asleep on Ray.

Between the panic of rushing out of Ray's house this morning, to showing up at the office thinking I was getting fired, to getting a better gig and packing my things, I hadn't given myself time to reconcile what had happened.

I fell asleep on Ray Griffith yesterday. And he didn't push me away.

Apart from the fact that he was arguably the hottest man I had ever seen and my boss, I felt safe with him.

Maybe I shouldn't have. He clearly had some anger he needed to work through.

But I did. I felt safe with him.

The ranch was peaceful and quiet. At his house, surrounded by the trees, it felt like we were the only two people on earth.

His arms had felt so safe.

I never slept well with my roommates up at all hours of the night. It had been so long since I'd had a full night of uninterrupted sleep.

I still had a wicked headache. My face looked like I had lost a fight with a mountain lion. But I didn't think Ray minded.

I felt so stupid for crying in front of him yesterday, but the feel of his hand on my cheek as he wiped away my tears was branded into my memory.

The gates of the ranch were a welcome sight. As I drove along the path to Ray's house, it was like watching a migration. Horses, trucks, ATVs, and people on foot headed to Claire and Silas's house.

I waved to everyone I passed as I made my way to Ray's grove of trees.

The house was quiet and dark, but I could see the glow from the TV as I let myself in.

"Hey," I said as I pack-muled my things inside.

Ray looked up from the recliner. "Hey."

"So...." I looked around. "I'm here full time now..."

He tipped his chin.

"Can I ask—"

Ray chuckled. "Has asking if you can ask ever stopped you from asking before?"

I felt a little sheepish at being called out like that, but he wasn't wrong. "Was this your doing or your family's doing? I just want to know how much I'm expected to ignore you."

Ray didn't let a hint of emotion slip, but I swear he was about to smile. "Cassandra made the call."

My heart dropped.

"Oh."

Before I could say anything else, he added, "But I told her to." Ray tipped his head to the door beside his bedroom. "Guest room's yours."

I nodded and squeezed through the door with all my things.

It was neat, but clearly unused. There was a closet, a dresser, a nightstand, and a queen-sized bed.

The bed I had been sleeping on back at the house was a twin. A queen mattress was going to feel amazing. It had been made up with pretty linens in a soft sky blue. White pillows with tufted cases were stacked against the headboard.

On top of the nightstand was a plastic bag of blue and pink Sweet Tarts.

9

RAY

This was a disaster. I don't know what I had been thinking when I requested that Brooke live here full time.

Actually, I know exactly what I was thinking. *And what I was thinking with.*

It had been three days and not a single one had gone smoothly. The upside was that my family had more or less left me alone. The downside was that this was the first time I had to ride in a vehicle with Brooke.

"Why is there a sticker on your dashboard?" I asked as I buckled my seatbelt.

Brooke plopped into the driver's seat. Her denim shorts rode up even higher.

Fuck me. I looked away quickly.

Since she was living with me and only reporting to her boss through phone calls, she had ditched the ugly polo.

I didn't mind at all, but it was an inconvenience.

"The check engine light has been on for a while. It's annoying. So I put a sticker over it."

I pressed my head against the back of the seat and

closed my eyes. "You've gotta be kidding me. How long has it been on?"

"Like a year or so. It's fine."

"And you haven't taken it in to get checked out?"

"Why would I do that?" she asked as she buckled her seatbelt. "It still runs."

I glanced at her odometer, then at the oil change reminder sticker in the corner of the windshield. "You're—" I groaned "—fifteen thousand miles past due for an oil change."

"Oil changes are expensive!"

"So is buying a new car!" I shouted. I pinched the bridge of my nose. "That fucking bull didn't kill me, but you and this car will."

Brooke laughed. "Look at you making jokes this morning. Someone's in a good mood." She twisted the key in the ignition, but nothing happened. She tried again. The engine sputtered, then went silent. "Sometimes this happens when I haven't driven her for a few days."

"I'm sorry. Her?"

"Yeah. Her name is Winnie. You're supposed to name cars."

"You're supposed to name *nice* cars."

"Winnie's a nice car!"

I shot her a sharp look.

"You and your grumpy, judgmental ass can keep your thoughts to yourself." The mirrors groaned as she adjusted them. "And if you behave at physical therapy, I'll bring you a coffee."

"If we even make it out of the driveway."

"Ye of little faith," she said as she twisted the key again and the engine heaved to life. "There we go!"

The car died before she could put it into drive.

As much as I didn't want to go to physical therapy this morning, I needed to. I huffed and unbuckled. "Get my chair out of the back and bring it around."

Brooke raised an eyebrow. "What?"

"Hop to it, Sunnyside. We're burning daylight and I want to get an early start on my afternoon of doing nothing."

Reluctantly, she got out and pulled my wheelchair out of the backseat, setting it up beside my open door.

"Pull the tarp off," I said, pointing to the other vehicle in the driveway. "The keys are tucked up in the visor."

Brooke's curiosity got the best of her. She pulled the tarp off my truck and balled it up. "Um. What the hell?"

"I didn't ask for commentary," I grunted as I shifted into the wheelchair, got settled, and slammed the door to her pile of scrap metal.

I knew what surprised her. The truck I hadn't driven since my accident was wrapped in brand logos from companies that used to sponsor me.

"Holy crap!" She propped her hands on her hips and walked slowly around the truck. "This was all you?"

I shoved on my wheelchair, glided over to the passenger's side of the truck, and reached up to yank open the door. "Just get over here."

Brooke's flip-flops snapped against the pavement as she scurried over.

"Hold the door steady. Don't let it push open," I said as I put one hand on the seat and one hand on the interior door handle.

Brooke braced her body against the door. "Are you sure you don't want me to help?"

"I'm fine," I grunted as I heaved myself up with my arms and paused with my ass on the floorboard. I could barely reach the "oh shit" handle at the top of the interior, but I managed to get my fingers around it. I took a breath and muscled myself up to the seat. "Just put the chair in the bed," I said as I slammed the door.

Brooke hopped behind the wheel and found the keys right where my brother, CJ, left them almost two years ago.

Honestly, I didn't know if the truck would crank up. It was basically new, but it hadn't been driven since it was brought back to the ranch after my accident.

Brooke didn't hesitate. She stuck the keys in, and the engine purred.

"It's so high up," she said as she adjusted the mirrors.

I was aware. My shoulders ached from getting up into the seat. Truthfully, I felt good this morning. Had Brooke not been around, I would have tried to stand up. But we didn't have time.

"Let's go," I said.

Brooke babbled the entire way into town. She drove the truck like she was driving a bulldozer. We hopped up on nearly every curb and straddled the painted lines.

I didn't let the air release from my lungs until I spotted the medical complex.

Brooke parked the truck at the back of the lot since she was too scared to try to pull it between other vehicles. Getting down into the wheelchair was easier than getting up into the truck. But because I was a stubborn asshole, I refused to let Brooke push my chair.

That old Sunday school saying about "pride comes before a fall" was fucking true. I was exhausted by the time I made it into the building.

"I'll be done in an hour," I said as I pressed the button for the elevator.

Brooke's eyebrows lifted. "Okay."

"I'll meet you in the lobby."

She chewed on her lip. "Are you sure you don't want me to come up with you?"

The elevator doors opened. "I'm not a child, Brooke. I don't need a chaperone."

She nodded. "See you in an hour."

I rolled into the elevator and watched her dejected face through the slit between the closing doors.

Great. Now I felt like shit.

It wasn't just her; I didn't let anyone come to therapy with me. I didn't have much privacy or agency, but that was one boundary I had put up early.

I had to give it to my therapy team. Maybe they were just used to dealing with jaded assholes, but they were never put off by my rancor.

But they did get their revenge for my attitude by putting me through a gauntlet of exercises.

By the time the hour was up, I was exhausted. Making the trip to the back of the parking lot was a dreadful thought.

Maybe Brooke would be late, and I could catch a cat nap in the lobby.

Nope. She was right on time, sitting in the lobby and chatting up a stranger.

"Hey! All done?" Brooke chirped as she jumped up from the bench. She waved to the old man. "It was so nice talking to you, Robert!"

The old guy beamed like he had just had a conversation with an angel.

"I pulled up to the curb and sweet-talked the tow truck guy out of hauling the truck off," Brooke said as she handed me a whipped cream covered coffee drink. "And that's for you."

I swore under my breath. "Just park next time."

"I figured you would be tired, and I didn't think to get the parking tag from your house before we left. I'll definitely grab it next time so we can park close."

I didn't even bother arguing. I just took a sip and didn't completely hate it.

Actually, it was pretty good.

Brooke looked hopeful. "Well?"

I took another sip. "Well, what?"

"How'd I do with the coffee?"

"Right. My aura." I stabbed the straw into the cloud of whipped cream. It was delicious. "It's fine," I grumbled.

"You like it!" she sang. "Our auras match! This is great. I knew we'd get along."

The truck idled on the curb. I managed to get up into the seat again, and buckled in as Brooke put my wheelchair in the back.

I missed driving.

I did a lot of it when I was traveling the rodeo circuit. I'd go from state to state, fueled by gas station coffee and radio shows. I liked the solace. Rodeo culture erred on the side of 'work hard, play harder.'

When I was winning, the money flowed like the booze did. Women were attracted to that.

The fact that I had a few men's underwear campaigns under my belt didn't hurt.

But my truck had always been my place to be alone with my thoughts.

It was my place to get away from the chaos and get my head right. This truck cab was my church.

"Do you want to get lunch or something before we go home?" Brooke asked.

Hearing Brooke call it home, like it was hers, did something funny to my chest.

Honestly, there was a little Mexican place around the corner that I had been craving.

I didn't go out in public unless I had to. I hated navigating places that were accessible to get into, but a crowded maze once I got through the doors. It was more hassle than it was worth.

"Nah."

"You sure? I mean, you just had a workout. I'm always starving after I exercise. Do you want take out? Or I can make us lunch when we get back to the ranch."

The thought of her cooking was enough to convince me to go the takeout route.

A few minutes later, we had food wrapped up in plastic bags and were headed back to the ranch.

I wanted to eat, shower, and take a nap. In that order.

Brooke brought my chair around while I eased down and sat on the edge of the floorboard.

It had been a good session, but I was fucking tired. I got up on my feet and worked on my joint stability using the parallel bars, but it had drained me.

We sat out on the deck and ate while Mickey hung out at our feet and caught the crumbs.

Brooke was unusually quiet.

"What's the matter?" I muttered as I shoved my used napkins back into the paper bag.

Brooke's eyes lifted from her aluminum container of chicken, rice, and cheese. "What?"

"You're quiet. What's wrong?"

She tilted her head curiously. "Did I do something wrong?"

"What do you mean?"

"You didn't want me to come up with you."

"It's not you. I don't let anyone go up with me."

Her brows furrowed. "Why not?"

"Because I don't need anyone to."

She swallowed. "Right."

"Thanks for suggesting lunch," I muttered.

Her lips turned up slightly, but it wasn't much. "Is this the part of the day where I'm supposed to start ignoring you?"

The twitch in my dick told me that it was for the best.

Because as much as I wanted her, I shouldn't.

10

BROOKE

The distant spray of the shower was the only thing that kept the house from being completely silent. I knew it was a job, but being with Ray didn't really feel like work.

He was completely capable and took care of himself. I was sure a lot of it came from the sheer stubbornness of not wanting to ask for help, but he had figured it all out on his own.

I plucked another piece of candy from the bag he had left on my nightstand—a blue one this time—and let it melt on my tongue.

I hadn't allowed myself to dwell on why there had been a bag of my favorite candies—in only the colors I liked—waiting for me when I moved in.

It was so simple, but it was the sweetest thing anyone had done for me in a long time.

It had to have been Ray. He let Cassandra help him sometimes, but she didn't seem like the type to sit and sort candy colors.

He was cranky and grouchy. But honestly, I would be too if people refused to listen to me all day.

There was an acute sadness in his eyes. A light that had been dimmed. But there was something behind it, too. Like lava simmering beneath black rock. Heat flashed in his irises every time he looked at me.

But maybe I was just imagining things.

The water shut off and I heard him rummaging around. It sounded like his shower had a sliding door.

My heart skipped, and I sat up. Did he need help getting out? Even accessible showers were slick. I had helped plenty of clients in and out of the shower. It wouldn't have even fazed me.

But would it bother him? Ray had given me strict orders to ignore him.

I waited and listened. It was silent.

Okay, that was probably good. He was being careful.

My heart thudded in my chest, and I held my breath.

A loud slam that sounded like a body falling echoed through the walls.

I bolted off the bed and ran into his room. "Ray!"

"Go away!" he roared.

I froze in my tracks. His wheelchair was in the bedroom, but he wasn't. The bathroom door was open and steam floated out.

"Oh my god," I whispered. I had to be hallucinating.

Ray was—he was standing.

Black boxers painted his ass, but that was the extent of his clothing. Tattoos covered his arms and chest. The inked designs flexed like waves as he held onto the bathroom vanity to support his weight.

"Go," he gritted out.

"You're standing," I whispered. "Am I dreaming?"

"Get the hell out of my room," he barked.

I snapped out of my haze and reached for his hand. "Can I help you?"

"Don't fucking touch me, Brooke."

I took a step back. That must've been good enough for Ray. I watched in amazement as he took small step after small step, crossing the three-foot space between the bathroom door and his bed. He used the vanity, the wall, and the nightstand for support, but he was doing it.

I cupped my hands over my mouth. "Ray, that's incredible."

Hair, dripping with water, hung in his eyes as he kept his head down, watching each small lift and slide of his feet. When he reached the edge of the nightstand and reached for the bed, his knees gave out. Ray fell toward the bed but caught the edge and managed to pull himself up on top of the mattress.

His sculpted chest heaved as he sucked in deep breaths. It must have been exhausting.

"You keep your mouth shut," he growled, then pointed a finger at me. "You hear me? If you say a fucking word about this, I'll fire you. Have I made myself clear?"

I couldn't even speak. He was furious at me, but I didn't care. "Ray, this is amazing. We should celebrate! What do you need? Do you need anything? What can I do to help?"

The heat I usually saw in his eyes had been replaced by something far more sinister. His head hung low. "Get the fuck out."

My heart dropped. "Ray—"

"I don't care what you do," he shouted. "Just get out."

Tears flooded my eyes at the hatred in his voice. I thought we had been making progress. I really thought we had started connecting.

I choked on the lump in my throat. "Are you okay?"

His laugh was maleficent. "Do I look okay? Don't be so fucking naïve."

"I won't say a word," I whispered. "Just let me be here for you."

And, like a switch had been flipped, all that heat, hatred, and fire in his eyes turned to ash.

"No. Leave."

I stumbled to the guest room and found my sneakers. I needed to move. I was going to go stir-crazy if I kept sitting here, knowing he was behind that door and wouldn't even let me near him.

I left a note on the kitchen counter so he wouldn't worry —not that I expected him to— and made sure the front door was unlocked before jogging down the ramp.

I found myself walking the dirt path that led back to the developed part of the ranch. Even though it was the middle of the day, it seemed deserted. I didn't know much about the cattle ranching operation—Ray never talked about it—but I guessed that everyone was out with the cows. Wherever that was.

I passed a cluster of sheds, but they seemed lifeless. I passed the office. Through the postcard window, I could see Cassandra typing away on a computer.

She scared me, so I kept walking.

A barn with neat landscaping and a fresh coat of paint called to me. I loved animals. Maybe a walkthrough wouldn't hurt. I wouldn't be bothering anyone. I just needed to get out of the house for a little bit.

The shade of the stables was a welcome reprieve from the midday Texas sun. The concrete floors looked freshly swept, and the rubber mats had been hosed off. It smelled like animals, but I didn't mind. The warmth of hay and feed was comforting.

"Oh, hello," I said to a beautiful chestnut horse when it stuck its head over the lip of the stall. I smoothed my hand up and down his nose. "You're a handsome fella."

"Beautiful," a man said.

I whipped around and clasped my hands behind my back like a kid who got caught making a move for the cookie jar.

The silhouette moved closer from the other end of the barn. "*She* is a pretty girl."

"I—I'm sorry. I was just—"

"What are you doing in my barn?" Cowboy boots thudded against the concrete as the man stepped into a beam of sunlight. "This is private property, sweetheart."

He shared similar features to Ray and Christian, but his hair and eyes were much lighter.

"I'm sorry. I was just taking a walk and I got curious."

He looked me up and down and made a snap judgment. "You're the girl Ray hasn't fired yet."

I laughed. "Well, that's one way to put it." I stuck my hand out. "Brooke Stacey."

He held up his dirt-covered palms. "Trust me, you don't want to shake my hand."

I laughed. "That's fair. Thank you. Are you one of Ray's brothers? You look like one of them."

He tipped his chin. "Yes, ma'am. Carson Griffith. Most folks around here just call me CJ."

"Nice to meet you, CJ." I looked around, still feeling like I was going to get scolded. "Sorry for crashing your barn. I just needed to get some fresh air."

He laughed. "It's no bother. You must be something special if Ray hasn't made you run for the hills yet."

The horse I had been petting nibbled at my hair. I giggled and tossed my ponytail out of the way.

"You like animals?"

"Love them," I said as I offered my open palm to let the horse get a sense of me. "I didn't have any growing up, so having a cow hanging out on Ray's deck is a little like living in a zoo."

CJ chuckled. "I bet." He stepped closer, reached in his pocket, and pulled out a peppermint. "This is Independence, but we call her Indy. She's Ray's horse."

I took the peppermint he offered and gave it to Indy. She gently nibbled at it. "Does everyone have their own horse?"

CJ nodded. "Most of them are out right now." He pointed to another horse a few stalls down. "That's Dottie. She's Bree's horse, but Cassandra rides her too. Christian rides Liberty, but they're in the fields today." He pointed to a black horse in the fenced area outside the barn. "That one's mine. The rest of them are fine with people approaching, but don't go near Anny."

"Anny... Short for—"

"Anarchy," he said.

And for some reason, that fit him.

"Is it okay if I hang out here for a little bit? I promise I won't mess with anything."

Concern marred his face. It wasn't fatherly like Christian's, but it lacked the heat of Ray's gaze. "Everything going alright at the house?"

"With Ray? Of course! Everything's great! Why wouldn't it be?"

Ugh. I was a terrible liar. Ray knew exactly where to shoot to kill, and I felt like I was bleeding out after he yelled at me.

CJ laughed. "I don't believe you, but okay."

I grimaced. "I'm trying really hard to not get fired, and I think we both need a little space."

Indy nuzzled my shoulder, and I returned her love with gentle strokes.

"I know you've got a job to do, but if you ever need a hand, there's always someone around. Okay?" He turned and motioned for me to follow. "See that house in the distance?"

I followed his finger as we stood at the threshold of the stables. "Yeah."

"That's the bunkhouse. The ranch hands and I live there. You probably pass the main house and Christian's house on the way in. Momma's always at her place, unless she's getting my nieces from school. Cass is usually in the office, but she and I go riding most afternoons. Nate and Becks travel a lot for her job, so it's a fifty-fifty shot whether someone's there or not."

"I never realized how many people live here."

"It's getting bigger by the day. Construction's going on for the restaurant and lodge." He looked around, surveying the property. "The peace and quiet won't last for long."

"Ray hasn't said much about that, but I've seen the construction crews coming and going."

"It's what Cassandra was brought in for. We had a rough few years, and the ranch almost went under. When we got back on our feet, my dad decided we needed to diversify. Cass secured some investors to put a significant amount of money into building a hotel and a restaurant."

CJ was trying his best to sound neutral about it all, but I could sense the disdain.

"Well..." I hesitated. "I'll try my best not to get in anyone's way."

His eyes softened. "We're just glad someone's sticking around for Ray. Holler if you need anything, alright?"

I nodded. "Thanks."

CJ walked toward the paddock where Anarchy was, then paused. "Brooke?"

"Yeah?"

"If you can get Ray to come to the family dinner tonight, I'll take you on a trail ride."

"Family dinner?"

CJ tipped his head toward the front of the property. "Momma cooks for everyone twice a week. Ray hasn't sat at the table since his accident. He always refuses."

I let out a caustic laugh by accident. "And you think *I* can convince him to go?"

He shrugged. "You've made it this long without getting fired. He must think you're something special."

11

RAY

I tried to take a nap, but sleep never came. I tried to watch TV, but the only shows on were crap. I watered and pruned that stupid plant in my room, but it didn't calm the war in my head. I sat outside on the deck and tied knots, but I never entered that mindlessly distracted state.

I felt sick every time I thought about the look on Brooke's face when I yelled at her. She was just trying to help, and I had lashed out at her because—well—that's what I did.

I hurt people.

I was an inconvenience.

I was a burden.

Today had been a good day. Therapy—as much as it sucked—went well. I had showered and managed to get out by myself. Any other day, I would have been borderline happy. I would have been proud of my progress.

Then I had to fuck it all up by yelling at her instead of handling my emotions like a grown man. Why couldn't I be more like Christian? Nothing bothered him. The man was a walking bottle of Xanax.

Nate had a short fuse, but he knew how to control it. The military made sure of that.

CJ just hung out with animals all day. They didn't care if he was in a sour mood.

I was the wild child whose path ended the way everyone always said it would. And now I was making it everyone else's problem.

That thought brought me back to Brooke. Where was she?

She had been gone for the better part of three hours, and I was starting to get worried. The ranch was big. Hell, I'd get lost if I went too far out.

The front door opened and I heard the soft rhythm of her footsteps. I dropped the rope in my hands and wheeled out to the living room.

Brooke froze at the kitchen sink like she had been caught red-handed. Her cheeks were flushed a sunset pink, and sweat coated her sun-kissed skin in a sheen.

"Hey," I grunted.

She looked down at the glass in her hand. "I just came in to get a drink. It's hot out. I'll be gone in a minute."

Shit.

"Brooke—"

"I won't tell anyone," she whispered. "I swear." Her fingers trembled against the edge of the sink. She looked like she was about to pass out.

"Brooke, sit down."

"I'm fine. I'm going back out—"

"Sit. Down."

She bobbled the glass in her hand and fell silent.

"On the couch," I said as I wheeled over and locked my chair. Brooke watched me as I lifted one knee, then the other and slowly put pressure on my feet.

Nope. It wasn't happening again today. Apparently, I had exhausted my lower extremities for the day. I couldn't lock my knees and my thighs were Jell-O. I sighed and used my arms to get on the couch.

At least physical therapy had ended with a massage. My shoulders were killing me, but the pain was a little more manageable.

It wasn't until I was fully on the couch that Brooke dared to come near.

"I'm not gonna bite," I grumbled as I moved the throw pillows out of the way.

"Yeah, I don't believe you," she said as she took the far end of the couch.

I leaned over and grabbed the rope I had been working on out of my wheelchair so I would have something to do with my hands. "Where did you go?"

She sat tall and proper as if she were at a job interview. "Outside."

"I figured as much. You got sunburned."

Brooke just dropped her shoulders. "I didn't have time to put on sunscreen. I went for a walk."

"Is that why you smell like the barn?"

"Am I in trouble? CJ said it was fine. I just hung out there for a little bit and then watched Anny."

Anarchy was an asshole. But for some reason, she and CJ got along just fine. That horse didn't like anyone but him.

I raised an eyebrow. "Anny let you watch her?"

Brooke nodded. "I didn't touch her or anything."

"Probably a good thing. She bites." But the fact that Anarchy had let Brooke near the paddock fence was surprising. If that horse was within lunging distance, she would snap.

Brooke picked at her fingers. "If that's all, I'll go back to making myself scarce."

I sighed as a headache brewed in my temples. "No."

She stiffened.

"I... I need to apologize."

That piqued her curiosity.

"I'm sorry."

Brooke waited. "For?"

"I'm just... Sorry. Okay?"

She shook her head. "It's not an apology if you don't say what you're sorry for."

I held back a growl and rubbed the throbbing in my temple. "I'm sorry for being a jackass. Not just today. I'm sorry for most days."

She relaxed a little bit. "Can I ask you a question?"

I knew what was coming. It was the inevitable question I didn't want to answer. But she deserved to know.

"How long have you been able to..."

"Use my legs?" It wasn't walking. It felt more like trying to use stilts blindfolded.

She nodded.

"A few weeks. It's hit or miss. I've been working on it in physical therapy. Sometimes my body decides it's going to cooperate and other times I can't get out of my wheelchair."

Warmth and pressure wrapped around my hand. I looked down to see that Brooke was squeezing it. "You can trust me. I won't tell."

Because she needed the money. Not because she wanted me. I couldn't let myself forget that.

"My therapy team thinks this is as far as I'm going to go. Everything after this is just maintenance. I don't want to get everyone's hopes up."

Brooke tilted her head to the side like a curious puppy. "Why not? Hope is a great thing."

"Because I could hear Christian praying when I was in a coma," I blurted out. "I can't explain it, but I remember hearing him. My brother's not a praying man, but he kept praying for miracles. Not telling them is more merciful than getting their hopes up and letting them down when I don't recover."

"But that's such a burden," she said softly. Her hand still hadn't left mine and it felt so fucking good.

"I should have died, Brooke. I should have died instantly, but I didn't. And then I wasn't supposed to wake up in the hospital, but I did. And then I wished I had died in that arena. I was supposed to be quadriplegic for the rest of my life, but I'm not. My hands weren't supposed to work, but they do. I was supposed to be paraplegic, and I am. It's not an all-or-nothing diagnosis. Some mobility doesn't change that. Everything I've gained could disappear tomorrow. I can't keep expecting miracles. I've already gotten my share and then some."

Her blue eyes were soft like a twilight sky. "Can I give you a hug?"

That... wasn't at all what I expected her to say. "Why?"

"Because I have a feeling that you haven't had one in a while. And if we're keeping secrets, what's one more? Besides, I like hugging it out after an apology. It seals the forgiveness."

I stared at her optimistic face for a moment before turning to face her on the couch and opening my arm. "Come here, Sunnyside."

Brooke laughed and scooted over.

She didn't go for a quick side-hug. Nope. She wrapped

her arms around me and rested her head on my chest. "See? Don't you feel so much better?"

I wrapped both arms around her and held her tight. "Yeah." I let out a heavy breath. "It feels good." And I didn't want to let go.

∽

Smoke filled the kitchen, and the fire alarm let out a piercing shriek. "What the hell are you murdering in here?"

Whatever it was, the smell was atrocious.

Brooke waved the oven mitts at the oven door to try and clear the smoke. "I thought I'd smoke a brisket. But brisket is super expensive. So, I bought a pound of ground beef and shaped it into a brisket. I mean, they both come from cows. It'll be great! I think the smoke is a good sign."

I paused. "Wait. What? Smoking a brisket takes at least twelve hours. And you don't do it in an oven."

"I know," she said, coughing. "That's why I turned the oven all the way up so it would cook faster."

"How high—" I froze when I looked at the oven. "Five hundred degrees?! Jesus, you're going to burn my house down. Turn the damn oven off. I didn't even know it went that high." I rolled across the kitchen and grabbed the oven mitt from her. "Open the front door and get the box fan out of the hall closet."

I yanked open the oven door and winced as smoke billowed out. I reached in blindly and found the baking sheet. I pulled it out, rolled over to the sink, and tossed it in. The little lump of charcoal in the middle looked like a petrified hamster.

Brooke hurried back, set the box fan on the kitchen counter, and plugged it in.

I glanced at the clock. It was already a quarter till seven. The thing that sucked about living on the ranch was the inability to order a fucking pizza. We were outside of the delivery radius for the handful of restaurants in town.

"Do we have sandwich stuff?" I asked.

"Tomorrow's grocery day. We used the last of the bread for lunch."

I had some frozen microwave dinners, but I would have preferred eating the charcoal in the sink.

Tonight was family dinner at my parents' house. I could text my mom and see if she'd set two plates aside, then send Brooke up there to get it.

But I'd feel like shit over it.

"Do you want to go into town?" Brooke asked. "It would be pretty late and I don't know what places would still be open. We could go to Buc-ees, but you probably hate crowds and it's always packed."

I didn't feel like going through the hassle of driving into town. Deep down, I knew I could show up for family dinner without giving mom a heads up. Even when I was living in Colorado, my mom always set a plate for me. Hell, she had probably been setting one for Brooke since she hadn't gone running for the hills yet.

But Christian's girls would be there.

Brooke's hand on the back of my shoulder snapped me back to the present. "You okay? Maybe I should open the sliding door and get the rest of the smoke out."

I coughed. "Yeah. I'll cut the ceiling fan on."

"What do you want to do for dinner? I can see if there's some pasta or something in the pantry I can throw together."

"No," I said before she could attempt culinary arson again.

Honestly, I would have been fine with a protein shake and a power bar, but Brooke needed dinner too. It had been a while since I had someone else to think about.

"Go get in the truck."

Brooke cocked her head. "I thought you said you didn't want to go into town? I can cook. I just have to figure out what we—"

I huffed. "Get in the truck, Brooke."

A few minutes later, we were bumping and bobbing down the dirt lane.

"Go up to the main house," I said, pointing to the left as we neared the split in the path.

A coy smile painted her lips. "Wanna tell me what we're doing?"

"Getting dinner."

She peered at me from behind the wheel. "At your parents' house? Shouldn't we tell them we're coming?"

"Momma will have a place set."

"Are you sure?"

"I'm sure."

"When do you want me to pick you up?"

I paused. "What?"

"I'll just hang out at your house until you're done. You can just text me when you're ready. I'll keep my phone on me."

I shook my head. "You're eating too."

12

RAY

The ramp leading up to my parents' porch rattled as I pushed myself up to the door. I could smell the pot roast from the door, and my stomach rumbled.

"Whatever that is, I want your mom to teach me how to make it," Brooke whispered.

I wasn't going to argue with that. Even though I was starving, my appetite vanished as soon as we got to the door.

"You okay?" Brooke said quietly.

I sighed and stared at the door. "I haven't been at a family dinner since before the accident."

"Not even when you were recovering?"

I shook my head. "I'd stay in my room. I couldn't use my hands. Someone always had to help me eat. And I..." Bile bubbled up my throat. "I hated it."

"I can't even imagine." Brooke squeezed my hand. "We can always turn around."

The fact that she offered to leave and meant it was everything to me.

"Nah. Letting you have my mom's pot roast is the least I can do for you."

Brooke laughed and opened the door.

The flurry of conversation inside died at the creak of the hinges.

Cassandra's jaw dropped, along with her fork. "Oh my god. Pollyanna got him to leave the house."

I flipped her the bird.

Brooke giggled.

My nieces were seated by Cassandra. I could feel their eyes on me as I wheeled inside.

God, they looked so grown. Bree was fifteen. She'd be driving soon. I remembered holding her when she was just a baby. Entertaining her as a toddler when Christian was dealing with funeral arrangements for his first wife.

Gracie was a fucking teenager now. Thirteen. Twelve years ago, she would fall asleep on my chest. For a while, I was the only one she would stop crying for.

I had watched them grow up like they were mine. I used to be Superman to them. Invincible. They used to look at me like I hung the moon.

Those two used to be my world.

My mom jumped up from the table, dabbing her eyes with her sleeve. "Come in. Come in. I've got places already set for you both. You're over by Nate, Becks, and Charlie."

Charlotte, or Charlie as everyone called her, looked absolutely giddy at the prospect of new people to give her attention. My newest niece's high chair was pulled up to the table, and she seemed to be having a gourmet dinner of Cheerios after an attempt at pot roast went awry.

I kept my head down as we went to the other side of the long farmhouse table. Nate pulled my chair out of the way and made space for me to park my wheelchair at the table. Brooke took a seat beside Becks and immediately started talking.

Becks was a journalist. If there was anyone who could keep up with Brooke's chatter, it was her.

Mom brought over two plates piled high with pot roast, potatoes, and carrots, and set them in front of Brooke and me.

"Thank you, Mrs. Griffith," Brooke said with the prettiest smile I'd ever seen.

Mom beamed. "Oh honey, just call me Claire or Momma Griffith."

Brooke's smile widened. "Momma it is."

Cassandra gagged. "Oh god. She's one of those."

Christian elbowed her, and my nieces laughed, but I kept my head down.

"Thanks," I muttered.

Conversation around the table died when I reached for the fork.

I hated people watching me. It was like waiting for rain. The downpour would let loose sooner or later. Whatever was anticipated was always a disappointment.

I could feel everyone's eyes on me. But unlike getting on the back of a bull in a packed arena, I couldn't block it out.

I heard the little gasp from my mom when I touched the smooth silver fork. I heard Christian stroke his beard. I heard Gracie and Bree whispering to each other, and Cassandra scolding them. I could hear CJ picking at the label on his beer.

It made my skin crawl. My neck tensed. I wanted to get out of there.

Then I felt her.

Brooke squeezed my left hand under the table. Her

slender fingers were so soft as they wrapped around mine. She picked up her fork and speared a carrot but never looked at me. "This smells so good. Thanks for saving us some."

I chanced a look at my mom. She was crying. *Just great.*

Mom dabbed her eyes with her napkin. "I always set a place for all my kids and make enough just in case. That includes you for as long as you're with us."

Behind the privacy of the tablecloth, Brooke's fingers slipped between mine. "The ranch is so cool. I love seeing all the animals. Mickey's the sweetest. Why does he have pool noodles on his horns? Do all the cows wear them?"

Christian chuckled, and the feeling of everyone's attention being on me shifted to Brooke.

I ate quietly while Christian and Gracie told the story of how Mickey became her accidental pet. Gracie told her how Mickey would always escape the herd and wander up to someone's porch. Brooke's responding laugh sounded like wind chimes dancing in the breeze as a storm passed.

Her thumb stroking across the top of mine was the break in the clouds. It was the promise of sunshine on the other side.

So I kept my head down and finished my plate. But Brooke never let go.

Mom set a pecan pie on the table and started slicing it up. Bree and Gracie joined in to distribute the plates around the long table.

"Hi, Brooke!" Gracie chirped as she set a piece in front of her.

"Hey, Gracie," Brooke said, copying her tone.

Bree put a piece of pie in front of me but kept her eyes down and didn't say a word.

"Thanks," I mumbled. The fork slipped out of my fingers when I stabbed the pie.

"Bree, I love your hair," Brooke said as she took a bite.

I watched out of the corner of my eye as Bree smiled softly. "Thanks. Cassandra did it."

"Well, you look amazing."

Why was the fork so goddamn flat? Why wouldn't my fingers just fucking work? I felt Christian staring at me as I struggled to pick up the fork.

"I'm full," I said, giving up. "Thanks, momma."

Brooke set her fork down. "Do you think I could take mine to-go? The pot roast was so good, and I don't want to waste the pie on a full stomach."

Momma smiled. "Of course. Let me get some plastic wrap, and I'll send two pieces with you."

From across the table, CJ tipped his chin at Brooke. She smiled.

I didn't like that. Didn't like it one bit.

"Here you go," Mom said, giving Brooke two slices of pie wrapped up on a plate. Everyone began to clear the table, except for Cassandra, who made a beeline for me.

"We need to talk."

I lifted an eyebrow. "About what? Why does Bree look like she hates me?"

Cassandra rolled her eyes. "She doesn't hate you, jackass."

"Takes one to know one."

"Exactly," Cassandra hissed. "So if I'm the one calling you a jackass, that should be a fucking wakeup call. Bree is upset. She's hurt. You were her favorite person, and then you blocked her out for a year and a half."

"I almost died."

"Almost," Cassandra hissed. "And if you keep acting like

a jackass to those two girls who still think you're the guy they tell me stories about, I will finish what the bull started."

Brooke watched Cassandra storm off. "I think I'm in love with her."

Cassandra was the only one I currently tolerated, and she was skating on thin ice.

"You ready to call it a night, or do you want to hang out a little bit?" Brooke asked.

I took it back.

Cassandra was the only one I feared, though I would never admit it to her.

Brooke was the only one I currently tolerated.

"I'm ready to go."

She nodded. "Do you want me here, or do you want me to go start the truck?"

I didn't want her more than a foot away from me. Actually, I wanted her hand in mine again. But I needed a minute with my mom. "Give me a sec, and I'll be out."

Brooke grabbed the leftovers, said her goodbyes, gave hugs to everyone, and headed out. I waited until the front door closed before carefully navigating the dining room and finding my mom.

"Thanks for dinner," I said as I stopped in front of the sink where she was drying the plates.

Her smile was weathered and worn. "You know me. I always have a place for you." She tipped her head toward the door. "And one for that sweet girl too. She was a lucky find, wasn't she?"

"Lightning in a bottle," I said under my breath.

Mom chuckled. "That's the truth."

I waited a moment, not saying anything at all as she drained the sink. "I should head back. I'm pretty tired."

"I'm cooking again on Saturday if you want some. It

won't be anything fancy. We might do burgers. I'll be keeping all the grandbabies so Nate, Christian, and their ladies can go have a date night. You and Brooke should come. There's food, so you know CJ will be here."

"Brooke will go home on the weekends."

Her smile was sad. "You should still come if you want. Or we can come to you."

"I'll think about it." But she knew that was a 'no.'

Before I could turn my wheelchair, she laid a hand on my shoulder. "The rain will stop, you know."

I glanced out the window. "It's not raining."

"I don't mean outside, sweetheart." She leaned down and dropped a kiss on my head, just like she used to when I was a boy. "If the clouds don't part where you are, keep going until you find your sunshine."

I slipped outside while everyone was distracted by Becks and Nate's little one. Brooke was waiting by the truck. While I pulled myself up into the cab, she put my wheelchair into the bed. We made the drive back to the house in silence. I was tired, but not ready for sleep.

"Just give me a sec. I want to change my clothes. I think I still smell like horses and smoke," Brooke said, disappearing into her room and closing the door.

When she returned, she was wearing a pair of cotton sleep shorts and a tank top that exposed her entire back, along with most of her ribs and waist. She grabbed the slices of pilfered pie and two forks from the utensil drawer.

"The deck or the couch?" Brooke asked.

We settled on the deck, each with our own slice of pie. A gentle breeze rustled through the trees as the crickets and frogs sang a quiet tune.

I took my time with my fork, not feeling as much pressure now that there weren't a dozen eyes watching.

Brooke devoured her pie in two bites.

I paused and observed as she wiped the crumbs off her lap. "You weren't full, were you?"

A mischievous glint appeared in her eyes. "I'll never tell."

13

BROOKE

"Are you sure I can't do anything for you?" I said, looking up from my phone.

Ray and I had fallen into some sort of routine. We went to therapy three days a week. I usually ran his errands in town while he was at his appointments. And then we just hung out at the house and did... nothing.

And I was starting to go crazy.

Ray looked up from the rope he was tying. It was a pattern he seemed to be following from his phone. It was plaited in an intricate design of knots and loops.

He cracked a smile. "Do I look like I need help right now?"

I huffed. "I know. I'm just bored. Don't get me wrong, I'm super grateful for the job. But I feel bad. I feel like I'm taking advantage of you. I'm not actually doing anything."

"You're keeping my family from dropping in unannounced four times a day."

"I know. But should I be cleaning or something?"

"The house is clean."

"Do you want me to cook something? A snack or a treat?"

"No," Ray said quickly. "I need to make sure my homeowners insurance is paid up before you go back in the kitchen."

I flopped on the couch. "Can I ask a kind of intrusive question?"

He lifted an eyebrow. "Has a 'no' ever stopped you before?"

"I'm just curious."

Ray sighed and dropped the rope. "Go on."

"How do you pay for all this? I mean—your house, all the physical therapy. I'm sure you have crazy medical bills."

Ray shrugged. "We didn't grow up having a lot. Cattle and four boys are expensive. My folks taught me how to stretch a dollar. When I wasn't traveling the rodeo circuit, I worked for a ranch in Colorado. I lived on my paycheck from the ranch and invested all my winnings, sponsor checks, and endorsements."

"So, you *did* have a backup plan."

"No," Ray said as he went back to following the pattern on his phone. His left hand looked more steady today, and he wasn't having trouble pinching the rope with his thumb and index finger like he had been. "A backup plan is what you'll do when you fail. Not when you live a different life. I have a nest egg. Not a backup plan."

"Sorry for asking," I said quietly.

"Go on a walk or something if you're going stir-crazy."

That did sound tempting... "Are you sure?"

"Don't wear flip-flops."

"I won't be gone long. Maybe half an hour?"

Ray tipped his head toward the door. "If I promise not to get out of my recliner until you get back, will you just go?"

I hopped off the couch. "Pinky swear?"

Ray huffed. "Are you twelve?"

I stuck my pinky out at him until he relented and offered his. Sparks danced up my arm when our hands touched. Our fingers curled together. We paused for a moment, frozen in time.

His thumb brushed my wrist, and his grip on my finger tightened.

"I won't be long," I rasped.

Ray let go, and dammit—I didn't want him to.

He said nothing as I rummaged around in my room to get socks and sneakers, then slipped out the door.

The sun was scorching. Waves of heat radiated off the horizon. Maybe this was a bad idea. Air conditioning was great. Why would anyone want to be out here?

But Ray was right. I was going stir crazy.

I started toward the front of the property, where all the barns were. I'd say hello to the ladies in the stables, dole out a few treats, and walk to the front gate and back.

But that was the only part of the property I had seen...

I turned on my heels and went the opposite direction. I vaguely remembered someone saying something about the lodge and restaurant being built out this way. It would be cool to see the progress.

Dry grass crunched under my sneakers as I traipsed through the pasture. The sheds and warehouses grew to specks in the distance.

The fresh air—hot as it was—felt good on my shoulders. I picked up my pace to a jog and let the burn in my lungs fight out the intrusive thoughts about Ray.

I had dreams of him. Dreams of those tattooed arms and his chest. Every night, I fell asleep to the delusion that I was back on the couch with my head in his lap. I fantasized about his fingers combing through my hair and gliding over my shoulder.

The cuts and bruises from Mr. Wilson's outburst had healed, but the memory of Ray cradling my chin in his hand hadn't gone anywhere.

He was so gentle when he wanted to be, but there were moments where he scared me. He was like the Beast, angry and hurt. I knew it was in his nature to be soft, but the circumstances had made it hard for him.

I stumbled over a rock, but caught myself. Where was the construction site? Surely I was getting close.

I looked at my phone. No service, but I had only been walking for about fifteen minutes. I'd go a little further and then turn around.

Thoughts of Ray's hand tangled with mine when we ate dinner at his parents' house floated through my mind. His hands were calloused from using his wheelchair, but they felt so strong. So safe. I didn't want to let go.

I stumbled over another rock, and my vision swam. Seriously? Where was that construction site? I turned around and tried to catch my bearings, but it was nothing but dirt, grass, and low shrubbery as far as the eye could see.

Had I been jogging in a straight line or did I make a turn somewhere? The sun hung straight above my head, so there was no way of knowing which way it had risen or would set.

My heart raced, and I looked at my phone. Of course, the battery had died.

Okay. Don't panic. Just turn around and go back.

I pivoted and kept walking. My mouth felt as dry as the dust that clouded up from the ground with each step.

I passed a grove of bushes that I didn't recognize, but maybe I just hadn't been paying attention the first time. I tended to zone out.

My head felt light as I tried to make my way back. I needed to stop and breathe for a minute. I had been going for a while, and it was awfully hot.

I braced my hands on my knees and tried to suck in a breath, but it was threadbare and short.

Oh my God, I was going to die out here.

They were going to find nothing but a dusty skeleton covered in sun-baked clothes. My body would be picked apart by buzzards.

I didn't want to become bird food!

Okay, now I was panicking.

The waves of heat lifted from the ground, blurring my vision. I stumbled as I started back in the direction I thought I came. I waited for buildings and barns to pop up out of the earth, but there was nothing. Just grass for miles and miles.

My blood pounded in my ears, and the earth swirled. Was I hallucinating, or was there a horse in front of me?

"What the hell are you doing out here?"

I blinked at the man's voice. "W-Where am I?"

He swore and jumped down from the horse. "Sit."

That wasn't hard to do. I dropped to the ground like a sack of potatoes.

He reached into a saddlebag and pulled out a metal water bottle. "Drink this."

"Are you a serial killer? Are you going to poison me?"

"No, but I might kill my brother after he tells me why he let you out this way."

The water was ice-cold. I could feel it running down my throat. I blinked and peered under the man's cowboy hat. "CJ?"

"Who else did you think it was?"

I looked up at the midnight black mare who was glaring at me. "I dunno."

His hand pressed against my cheek. "Jesus—you're three seconds from heatstroke."

"Where am I?" I said between sips. "I was just going on a walk to see the construction site."

"Wrong direction and you went way too far. You're lucky as hell I was coming up this way. It's a hundred degrees."

"Yeah," I groaned as I drained the rest of his water. "I'm starting to feel it."

"You gonna pass out if you stand up?" CJ asked.

"Only one way to find out." I closed up the bottle and took his hand. The world spun, but only a little.

"Come on." CJ put a hand on my back and led me over to the horse. "Don't do that," he said when I reached out to touch Anarchy. "Have you ridden before?"

"When I was a kid at a birthday party. Does that count?"

"It does today. Climb up."

"I thought I wasn't supposed to touch her."

"She can't bite you if you're on her back."

"No, but she can throw me off."

"Not if I'm on there with you. Now get up on the saddle before you get deep-fried by the sun."

Anarchy let her displeasure be known by huffing in annoyance when I put my sneaker in the stirrup. I did a half-decent job at heaving myself up with what little energy I had left.

"Saddle's only made for one, so I'm going to sit behind it," CJ said as he threw his leg over and settled on Anny's back. "Hold on."

He reached around me and grabbed the reins.

"You know Ray's gonna chew your ass out about this, right?"

The thought of Ray anywhere near my ass made my spine turn electric.

"He's the one who told me to go on a walk."

CJ let a wry laugh slip. "Yeah, and he's the one who called me when you didn't come back after two hours and no one had seen you."

"Two hours?" I thought I had only been gone for the thirty minutes I told Ray. "I'm so getting fired for this," I grumbled.

"You're gonna get yelled at, but you're not getting fired. He likes you too much."

"He doesn't like me. He tolerates me."

"For Ray, that's the same thing."

Anny picked up her pace and delivered us back to Ray's house. He was sitting on the deck, scowling as CJ helped me down and marched me to my execution.

"Stay on the paths next time," CJ said before tipping his chin at Ray. "Mind if I use your tap to refill my water?"

Ray cocked his head toward the sliding door, and CJ took that as a yes.

Ray didn't say a word to me as I loped up the steps.

CJ passed me on his way back out. "Make sure you drink a lot. You're gonna be sunburnt. Don't forget what I said about staying on the paths."

"Thanks. I will," I said softly.

Silence hung between Ray and me as CJ rode away. "I'm sorry," I whispered as I stood in front of him like a kid getting scolded. "I went too far and I was trying to find my way back, but I didn't have service and then my phone died, and I—"

"I was worried." His stubbled jaw flexed with tension.

"CJ said you called him."

"I called everyone."

Guilt gnawed at me. "I'm sorry."

Ray closed his eyes and scrubbed his hands down his

face. Hurt was painted across his sharp features. "You've gotta be fucking careful out there. I can't come out and get you if you get hurt or pass out."

"I won't let it happen again. Promise."

Ray tipped his head toward the house. "Get inside."

I took my scolding and headed into the blissfully cool house.

"Sit on the couch," Ray ordered as he wheeled himself in after me and closed the sliding door.

Oddly specific, but okay.

I toed off my sneakers, sat on the couch, and waited. Ray made his way around the house, collecting things before coming back to the couch.

"Drink that," he said as he pushed a red sports drink into my hand. He tossed a bottle of lotion onto the couch, then eased out of his wheelchair to sit beside me. "Take your shirt off."

Hello, fantasy.

I set the drink on the coffee table and pulled my tank top off. I hissed as the straps scratched my burned skin.

Fantasy destroyed.

"Sit still and drink your drink," he said as he worked at the flip cap of the lotion.

I squealed when something cold touched my back.

"I told you to sit still," he snapped.

I turned to look over my shoulder at him. "You didn't warn me!"

Ray leaned forward, bringing our faces close. "I'm putting lotion on your back before you turn into a potato chip. Is that warning good enough?"

My eyes lowered to his mouth. "Uh-huh."

"Then sit still and do as you're told."

I closed my eyes as he worked the lotion over my shoulders and back, carefully sliding his hands under my bra straps.

I sucked in a breath when his fingers spanned my collarbone, working down toward my breasts. I was totally cool with it if he wanted to keep going, but he quickly moved back to my arms.

He worked more lotion around my lower back, even though it wasn't burned. His hands spanned my waist, trailing up, up, up until they were grazing the sides of my breasts.

I sucked in a sharp breath and cursed the fact that I was still wearing a bra.

I could feel the heat from his chest radiating against my back. I wanted to fall into him. To have those arms wrapped around me. To know what it felt like for him to work those calluses over my breasts.

The moment was shattered when he let go and squeezed more lotion into his palm.

I glanced at the bottle. "That's for tattoo aftercare."

"It works like magic on sunburns too."

"I like your tattoos."

His hands stalled on my biceps. "I, uh... I got 'em for the girls."

I peered over my shoulder. "For Bree and Gracie?"

Ray nodded. His touch shifted from simply smearing my skin with lotion to a massage. "I had a few when they were real little. After their mom died, I'd watch the girls for Christian and they'd color my tattoos in with markers. So, I kept getting tattoos. It was our thing. When..." He sighed. "When I'd compete in Houston or Dallas, I'd always come out here for a night or two, and they'd color my tattoos in for good luck."

"You really love them, don't you?"

His hands squeezed my shoulders. "Yeah. They were my girls as much as they were Christian's."

"Why won't you talk to them or let them see you?"

Ray's grip tightened. "Because I'm not their hero anymore."

"I don't know about that."

"Brooke—"

I turned on the couch and curled up beside him. "I don't think you were their hero because you were a rodeo star. You were their hero because you were there for them when they needed you. So, yeah. You're not their hero right now because you won't let them see you. You chose that. It has nothing to do with being able to walk or not."

I expected the anger to come, but it didn't. Ray's face never changed. "You know, you're the only one who can get away with saying that to me right now."

"Then I'll take that as a compliment."

"Don't push your luck, Sunnyside. I'll fire you."

I laughed. "I'm starting to think you just talk a big game about firing me." I let my hair down. "I think you like me."

"I don't hate you." But his dark eyes were twinkling like a starry sky. "But you are a walking disaster and a big pain in my ass."

"This is the best job ever. Even if my boss is a jerk sometimes."

Ray lifted an eyebrow and twisted one of my curls around his finger. "Yeah?"

I closed my eyes. "I love being out on the ranch. Your house is awesome. It's so quiet out here. Sitting by the pond is my favorite. That big tree out there reminds me of one I had in my yard growing up. I had a tire swing and I would spend hours out there pretending I could fly."

"Are you close with your family?" he asked.

I shook my head. "I don't have much family left. My parents passed away when I was about Gracie's age. They died in a house fire. I was at a sleepover," I said calmly, the same way I did every time I had to regurgitate the statement. Sadness lived inside of me. It always would. But it didn't control me. "I lived with my Grandma after that, but she passed away a few years ago. I have some extended family that lives in Missouri, but I've never met them."

People always got weird when I talked about my family, but Ray didn't. In fact, he didn't say anything. Instead, he passed me a new plastic bag of Sweet Tarts with the pink and blue ones sorted out just for me.

"Wanna watch a movie?"

I tossed my tank top onto the coffee table and grabbed the remote. "You can pick. I'll probably fall asleep halfway through. I think the sun sapped all my energy."

He picked up a pillow and dropped it on his lap. "Come on."

I curled up beside him and laid my head on the pillow as he flipped through the channels. When he landed on a heist flick, he set the remote down. Gentle fingers brushed my curls away from my face and combed through my hair.

"Sorry," I said with a yawn. "My hair's probably sweaty."

"I don't mind," he said gently.

And I didn't either.

14

RAY

It was official. I hated Saturdays. Granted, I hated most things these days, but especially Saturdays.

Brooke had left last night to spend the weekend at her house, and I wouldn't see her again until Monday. After spending every waking moment with her and every slumbering moment dreaming about her, it was weird for her to be gone.

The house was too quiet. I kept aimlessly wheeling around every few minutes, as if something would have changed between noon and 12:30.

It didn't.

I had tied thousands of knots. I had watered the plant. I had unloaded the three dishes that cycled between the cabinet and dishwasher. I did my physical therapy homework and took a few steps here and there. The hardware store in town made the delivery I asked for.

But, eventually, there was nothing left for me to do.

Now I was the one going stir crazy.

I never felt like that when she was here. Sure, I'd get tired of being around another person and retire to my room for a little space, but it wasn't because I was bothered by her. I was just used to being alone. Or at least I thought I was.

I looked at the text I had typed out but hadn't sent.

It wasn't fair for me to bother Brooke on her day off. She probably wanted the time away. I wasn't particularly exciting to hang out with.

It made me wonder if she had a boyfriend she was spending the weekend with. That thought made me want to put my fist through a wall, but split knuckles were the last thing I wanted to explain to my therapy team.

Saturday came and went, and Sunday dawned its miserable sunny self. I texted Cassandra to see if Christian was busy with the girls. I knew if I asked him for help directly, he'd drop everything and be down here in the blink of an eye. But weekends were sacred to him and his daughters. I didn't want to fuck that up.

My phone buzzed, and I picked it up expecting to see Cassandra's reply.

But it was Brooke.

> **BROOKE**
>
> Hey, I'm sorry to bother you on your day away from me.

My stomach churned. Was that what she thought? That I wanted her gone on the weekends?

Maybe at the beginning I did, but now I just missed her.

> **RAY**
>
> Not a bother.

> **BROOKE**
>
> Can I come back tonight? I promise I'll ignore you until tomorrow.

> RAY
> I don't mind.

A three-word response was the best I could do when I wanted to tell her that this was the first and only weekend I wanted her away.

Cassandra texted me back and said that she and Christian were cleaning their house, and that she'd send him out my way. I only needed him and his truck for a few minutes anyway.

When I heard the rumble of a diesel engine coming down my driveway, I wheeled out onto the front porch and pointed for him to pull around back. I headed back through the house and rolled down the ramp off the deck.

Pushing a wheelchair through grass was a bitch, but I didn't mind the burn in my arms and shoulders.

"Hey," Christian said as he slid out of the cab of his truck. "You okay?"

"Fine. Just need a hand, real quick."

"What's up?"

I had already tied the rope tightly around the tire, looping it over and securing it with a stack of stopper knots.

Drilling holes in the bottom of the tire had been a challenge. Getting the bit inserted was fine, but gripping the handle while it vibrated as I drilled through the rubber was more difficult than I thought it would be. But I managed to drill out enough spots for rain to drain through the tire.

"Can you back your truck up under that tree?" I pointed to the big one by the pond that Brooke liked. "I wanna hang a tire swing."

Christian lifted an eyebrow, but got back in his truck and did a neat three-point turn in my yard until the bed was situated under a heavy branch that stretched out over the grass toward the water.

While Christian hopped out of the truck and walked around to the tailgate, I locked my chair, bent over, and picked up the tire.

"Let me get that for you," Christian said.

"Don't worry about it," I grunted as I heaved it over my head and into the bed of his truck.

It landed with an echoing *clunk*. The long rope hung over the edge of the truck bed and coiled on the ground. I grabbed the bulk of it off the grass and threw it in after the tire.

"Damn," Christian said as he worked through the length of the rope to find the end that needed to go over the branch. "That's impressive."

I didn't respond because what was I supposed to say?

"So, you wanna tell me why you want a tire swing in your yard?" he asked as he pitched the end of the rope into the air. It missed the branch and slapped the metal truck bed.

I watched as he picked it up to try again. "Figured the girls could come down and use it if they wanted to." It was half of the truth.

Well, maybe a quarter of the truth.

Christian paused. "You mean that?"

I shrugged. "I guess Bree might be a little old for it."

Christian's brow furrowed. "No. She'll love it. I'll see if I can convince her to come down here and check it out."

"What do you mean?"

Christian threw the end of the rope at the branch, but missed again. "She's hurt, man. I kept them from seeing you when you were in the ICU. They lost their mom, and I didn't know what seeing you intubated would do to them. They wanted to see you when you woke up after the accident, but you wouldn't let them," he said, sighing and picking up the rope. "You moved back to the ranch and refused to see them for a year while you were up at the main house. Then you had this place built, and you still wouldn't let them see you. Then you just showed up at family dinner unannounced. They're hurt. They feel like you don't love them anymore, and they need time to work through that."

I scrubbed my hands down my face. "That's... That's not it."

"You know that, and I know that," he said, hitting me with a sharp look. "They don't know that, no matter how much I tell them you just need time."

I sighed. "I'll work on it."

He threw the rope again. The third time was the charm as it made it over the branch and slid down.

I grabbed the end of the rope and pulled until the tire lifted off the ground. "Hold it there," I said when I got it to the right height.

Christian held the tire, taking the weight off the rope so I could get the knot tied. When it was secure, he let go.

"Mind testing it out for me? I don't want the girls to fall."

Christian shrugged, braced one cowboy boot in the middle of the tire, and hopped on. The branch creaked under his weight, but the swing held strong. "Looks good," he said as he swung back and forth for a few seconds before hopping off.

"How's the lodge construction?" I asked as he shut the tailgate.

Christian leaned against the side of the truck and lifted his cowboy hat off his head to run his hand through his hair.

"Fine. The foreman said some tools went missing Thursday night. Cass is going through all the cameras we have at the gates."

Thursday? Why was this the first I was hearing about it?

"Why didn't anyone tell me?"

Christian shrugged. "Didn't want to bother you with it. You don't work for the ranch. Not your problem to deal with."

"I live here. You didn't think I should know someone stole shit off our property?"

Christian lifted his hands. "We don't know if it was theft. The site foreman said he's checking out his crew to make sure someone didn't take something home that they weren't supposed to. It used to be easy to spot someone who shouldn't be out here. If they weren't a Griffith or one of CJ's boys, it was a red flag." He sighed. "But there's all kinds of people coming out here every day. The construction crew. Inspectors. Investors. The energy company that rents the land where they put up that cell tower and the solar panels on top of the barns. Cass is about to get the equine program going, and that'll be a whole other thing. Random people coming in to ride or board their horses."

"CJ's gonna have an aneurysm."

Christian cracked a smile. "That's the truth."

We were all possessive of the ranch, but CJ took it to a whole other level. I was fully convinced that he would never leave the ranch if he didn't have to. He probably had a nice patch of dirt already picked out to be his grave when the day came.

"You wanna come up to the house for dinner?" Christian asked. "Cass is cooking."

Honest to goodness, I was half-tempted to. "Nah. I think

Brooke's coming back tonight. I don't know when she'll get in."

He cracked a smile. "You're sweet on her."

"Her car's a piece of shit. I just wanna make sure she gets here in one piece."

"You didn't deny it."

I shook my head. "She's too young for me."

"She's what—twenty-five?"

"Twenty-two."

He stroked his beard. "I mean, that's young, but she's not a kid. She's not even in college."

"I'm twelve years older than she is. That's too much."

He crossed his arms. "Same as our folks."

"It's not the same thing."

"Because you're in a wheelchair? So?"

I was done with this conversation. "Thanks for hanging the swing. Tell the girls they can come use it whenever they want."

"Ray—"

It didn't help that I did want Brooke in ways I shouldn't. It didn't help that every time I saw my nieces, I was reminded that having kids of my own was a bad idea.

Christian could hit me with all the well-meaning, well-adjusted, therapy-induced platitudes he wanted. It didn't change reality.

"Ray, stop."

"What?" I snapped as I headed for the ramp up to the deck.

"I don't think I ever said I was sorry for everything you lost."

I paused as Christian caught up to me. He went up the stairs and sat in one of the deck chairs while I took the ramp.

"I'm not saying I understand, because I don't. After what happened to Nate in Mosul and losing Gretchen, I coped by working and moving forward. I had the girls to think about, and I had to hold on to the good moments to deal with the downpour. And I'm sorry for putting that expectation on you."

I rolled it around in my head. "Did Cassandra put you up to this?"

He chuckled. "No. But she may have had a few choice words for me the other day and reminded me that she works through things by throwing knives."

"You sure you wanna marry that woman?"

He grinned. "Yeah. I love her. She keeps me on my toes. I have to make sure we always go to bed on good terms so I don't wake up with one of those knives in me instead of the target in the office."

"Probably smart."

"So," Christian said as he stretched out and crossed his ankles. "Wanna tell me how you went from firing anyone who set foot in your kitchen to paying an unqualified gopher to live with you full-time?"

"You and your assumptions can fuck off."

He laughed. "Yeah, I think my assumptions are pretty spot-on."

Like he was one to talk. He had Cassandra living in his house before she even tolerated him.

Christian pushed to his feet. "No judgment. I think she's a sweet girl."

"Just stop talking already."

He chuckled. "Momma loves her."

"Momma loves everybody."

"She's good for you," he said, shoving his hands in his pockets.

"She's not good for my truck. I need a new bumper."

"Trucks can be replaced. You can't," he said as he bumped my shoulder with his fist. "It's good to have you back. Holler if you need anything."

15

BROOKE

The sun was setting as I pulled into the gates of the ranch. A new "No Trespassing" sign had been posted at the entrance, warning people that they were being recorded.

I wondered what that was about.

Twilight hung over fire-lit skies. The plains glowed like embers as daylight turned to dusk. It was my favorite time of day out here. The land was enchanted. I felt myself drawn to it like a siren being called to sea.

I held out at the house as long as I could before packing my things and hurrying back to the ranch. I was miserable the second I left Ray's on Friday. I had a stomach ache as soon as I hit the road.

I tried to make it until Monday because I knew he wanted space from me, but I finally broke down and texted him this afternoon, asking if I could come back.

I had moved most of my stuff to Ray's house, but I spent the morning consolidating the rest of my belongings and stuffing them into my car. The bed and the dresser at the house weren't mine, and I didn't really care about the few things I hadn't taken with me.

Maybe I'd just get a hotel room next weekend.

The knot in my gut dissolved as I took the curving dirt road through the front part of the ranch to Ray's house. I let my hand hang out the window and surfed the breeze.

I had only been gone for a day and a half, but I missed it.

The ranch was a craving that just wouldn't go away.

But so was he.

I pulled down the driveway and parked beside his truck.

Huh. The front door was open.

The glass storm door was closed, but I could see through the kitchen and into the living room.

The lights were on, too. That was weird.

Maybe one of his brothers or Cassandra was over. Ray always kept the house locked up like Fort Knox.

I grabbed my bag and jogged up the ramp. The house smelled like food, but nothing was on the stove or in the oven. I slipped into the guest room and dropped my things.

"Ray?" I didn't want to bother him, but I didn't want to startle him either.

No answer.

His bedroom door was closed like usual, so I knocked. "Ray?"

Still nothing.

That was weird.

"Ray," I called out again. "I'm home." I heard the sliding door roll back, and looked over my shoulder. "Hey."

Ray looked absolutely sinful in a tight t-shirt, a pair of gym shorts, and sneakers. His hair was damp, and his scruff had been shaped up. I salivated at the sight of him.

"Hey, Sunnyside."

I laughed. "Why do you call me that?"

He cracked a smile. "Can't let you forget about those eggs you murdered, can I?"

I rolled my eyes like I was annoyed, but I wasn't. Not in the slightest. Because he was smiling today. "I was just letting you know I was here." I picked at my fingernails. "Thanks for letting me come back early."

He shrugged as he backed up his wheelchair so it wasn't blocking the door. "Have you eaten yet?"

The gurgle in my stomach responded before I could. "I forgot."

His brows knitted together, forming a deep valley above his aquiline nose. "Why?"

I shrugged. "Things were... a little crazy at home."

I didn't miss the way his jaw flexed as he ground his teeth together.

I lifted my hands. "I know our deal. I'll leave you alone."

Ray didn't argue, huff, or grunt. He didn't growl or groan.

There was a twinkle of mischief in his eyes.

"Come with me."

I looked down at my feet. "Are flip-flops okay?"

"Just fine. Come on."

I followed Ray out to the deck and pulled the door closed behind me. Mickey the cow was hanging out under the shade of the house, sporting a pair of pink and purple pool noodles on his horns.

"Did your car do alright leaving and coming back?" he asked.

"Surprisingly, it did," I said as I walked by his side down the ramp. "I am a little curious how the engine magically doesn't rattle anymore. Or how the oil magically got changed? Or how the sticker on my dashboard disappeared?"

Ray didn't even glance over at me. "Weird shit happens on the ranch. Could've been the cows."

"Uh-huh." I stopped at the bottom of the ramp. "And if I asked CJ how much work he did on my car, what would he say?"

Ray looked up at me. "He'd say he didn't do any work on your car."

"And what about Christian?"

"You think Christian has time for side projects?" He had a point, but I didn't miss the ghost of a smile at the corner of his mouth.

"Fair. What if I asked Nate?"

Ray didn't say anything.

Bingo.

I sighed. He must've done it the other day while we were at Ray's appointment. I hadn't said anything to Ray, but I had been a little worried about driving off the ranch by myself.

"Thank you. You didn't have to call in the cavalry. I could have figured something out. I always do."

Ray let a laugh slip. "Yeah. You figuring out car repairs is what I was afraid of. Close your eyes and follow me."

I shut my eyes. "Am I going to step in cow poop?"

He chuckled. "Maybe. Walk behind me and hold onto my chair. I'll make sure you don't. Are your eyes closed?"

"If you don't trust me, maybe you should blindfold me next time."

I heard him let out a quiet huff of air as grass swished under my feet. "Don't tempt me, Sunnyside."

I held onto the handles of his wheelchair as we walked. The gentle decline in the earth told me we were heading around to the pond.

"Eyes still closed?"

I laughed. "I'm starting to think closing them in the first place was a bad idea. What are you getting me into?"

"Open."

I squinted as the pond came into focus. But it wasn't just the sparkling water reflecting sunset colors. A tire swing hung from a thick branch. A quilt was spread out off to the side with a picnic basket on top.

"Ray..."

It was like stepping into the most idyllic painting. Crickets and frogs chirped a gentle love song as mist floated above the water. I wanted to run and leap onto the tire swing and feel weightless innocence.

I wanted to be carried away to a world where no one but Ray and I existed.

"Did you do this?" I asked.

He shrugged. "I had help."

I trailed my fingers over the bumpy tread of the tire, and the expertly tied knots wrapping around it and the rope. "So? I know this was you."

He looked down at his feet, a little bashful.

Stars glimmered over us like diamonds. The sun, in blazing orange, still peeked over the horizon, coating the pond in waves of fire. Somehow, standing between the heavens and the embers, he had created a hallowed place.

We walked through the brief moments granted between midnights, holding fast to the glimmers of elation and joy to ground us when anguish crashed in downpour. We were suspended in the tension between birth and death, chasing purpose and fulfillment.

And in this moment—in this place—I felt mine begin to bloom.

"Don't be humble," I said as I looked up from the tire swing with tears pooling in my eyes.

He shrugged again. "Figured you might like it when you don't wanna be in the house. You said you used to have a tire swing. It's probably stupid."

"Can I hug you?" I asked with a quivering lip. "I know you don't like being touched. I just... Thank you."

He hesitated, eyes shifting around. "Help me up."

I hurried over as he tucked his hands beneath his knees and lifted his legs out of the foot rests. When he was confident in his footing, he reached out for me. I held my arms steady as he pushed out of his chair and grabbed on to me.

The second Ray was sure he could balance his weight, his arms were around me.

"Thank you," I whispered, wrapping my arms around his waist, my head resting against his chest.

Ray cradled my head beneath his chin. He was taller than me, but not by much. It felt like we fit together like long-lost puzzle pieces. Maybe I dreamt it, but I could have swore he kissed my head.

Or maybe I simply wished it to be true.

"You smell really good," I murmured.

Ray laughed softly and motioned toward the picnic blanket. "I brought food down."

"Do you want me to walk with you?" I asked, hoping he would allow me to help him.

But Ray just shook his head and lowered back into his chair. "There's nothing to hold on to if I slip. I don't want to hurt you."

When he was settled, I slid my hand in his and squeezed. "Thank you. I mean it. That..." I looked at the swing again. "That was beyond thoughtful."

I settled on the blanket as he wheeled over and eased down. Ray pushed himself back until he could sit up against the trunk of the tree.

I opened the basket sitting between us. "What do we have here?"

"Frozen PB&Js," he replied with a chuckle. "Don't knock it until you try it."

"I'm trusting you, Griffith. What else is in here?" I pawed around and found a plastic container of cookies. Steam clouded the sides and they were still warm. "You bake?"

"Don't get your hopes up. It's cookie dough from a tube. I just know how to follow directions and use an oven."

A few pieces of fruit and a bag of chips had been tossed in for good measure. At the bottom, there was a bag of Sweet Tarts, specifically the pink and blue ones.

The thoughtfulness and simplicity of it all made my heart ache. Nostalgia was a slow-acting drug that had me tumbling further and further down the rabbit hole.

We ate in a comfortable silence. I had to admit, the frozen peanut butter sandwiches in the Texas heat were perfect.

"I'm glad I came back," I said as I leaned against the tree trunk and watched the sun set. "I felt bad about texting you to ask."

Ray looked down at me. His dark eyes mirrored the obsidian pond. "I'm glad you came back too." Our hands brushed, and he turned away with a deep exhale. "What's home like for you?"

I wavered about how much to share. Besides, it didn't really matter anymore. I stayed here most of the time. "I live about forty minutes away. I share a house with a bunch of roommates. It's... always lively. It feels like a college dorm, I guess. There's always someone around."

Ray licked his lips. "Does, uh... Does your boyfriend live with you?"

I laughed. "I haven't had a boyfriend in a dreadfully long time. My vibrator gets a seriously intense workout."

Ray chuckled. "I'll take a wild guess and say it's probably been longer since I've been with someone than you have."

Our laughter faded along with any lingering tension. This felt comfortable. Familiar. Easy.

"I don't like living at the house," I admitted under the sanctity of the night sky.

"Why's that?"

I sighed. "It was the only place I could afford. My roommates are really inconsiderate. They're always loud and throwing parties. I think they eat my food. One of them got arrested for possession a few days ago, and it was really tense when I came back Friday night. I always lock the door to my room, but it was unlocked when I got there. I just... I never feel safe. Not like I do when I'm here. I can actually sleep when I'm here."

Ray wrapped his arm around my shoulders, and I curled into his side. "Then don't leave."

I sighed and rubbed my temple. "I just need to figure something out. I can't stay forever. What would I even do?"

His eyes lowered. "Give me peace."

I sighed. "I know. I keep your family from bothering you."

Ray tensed, but didn't say anything. He just cradled the back of my head in his palm and gently massaged my scalp.

I melted into him. "Maybe moving out of the house isn't the right move. I guess the grass is always greener somewhere else. My grandma always said that. She could find the good in everything."

"You know what makes grass green?"
"Water?"

"Nope. Bull shit."

I laughed. "Is that what all the cowboys say?"

His smile was sad, but his arm around me tightened. "I'm not a cowboy, Sunnyside."

"I think you are." I took a chance, sliding around and straddling his hips so we could be face to face.

Ray slipped his hands around my waist and settled me on his thighs. I tried to keep my composure, but his touch electrified me.

"You're headstrong and stubborn to a fault. You work in silence because you don't need eyes on you. You just do what you have to do." I raked my fingers through his thick hair, and he melted. "You have this ardent work ethic that transcends your physical abilities. You're honest even when it hurts. It's honorable. You have grit and patience. There's not a single difference between you and your brothers. I see it every time I look at you, cowboy."

Ray's eyes lowered to my mouth. "Then you don't know my reputation."

"I don't need to know your reputation because I know you. People selling click-bait headlines see the falling star. I see the galaxy."

Ray's nose nudged mine. I tipped my chin up. Our lips brushed. Flickers of heat licked up my spine, and anticipation welled in my chest. His brows furrowed as he brushed his bottom lip across mine.

"Did you just admit to Googling me?" he whispered with a hint of amusement.

I grinned against his mouth and whispered, "I heard you did some underwear modeling. Color me curious."

Ray's devilish smirk melted me as he slid his fingers into my hair, keeping me close. "Did you like what you saw?"

All I could do was nod. The man in the black and white photos, who had miles of muscle and tattoos, hadn't stolen my breath.

The one in front of me had.

Ray's grin was bright and brilliantly fleeting as his mouth crashed against mine. I wrapped my arms loosely around his neck, pressing my chest to his as he pulled against my lips until I yielded. His tongue slid against mine in slow strokes.

I couldn't get enough. No matter how deep or how long we kissed, it wasn't enough.

I smoothed my hands up and down his chest as he palmed my ass with one hand. The other hand tangled and twisted in my hair, keeping my head right where he wanted it.

A whimper escaped as he sucked my bottom lip between his teeth. The sound made his cock thicken beneath his shorts. It pressed between my legs, teasing me with forbidden pleasure.

I rocked against his shaft, my clit throbbing as a deep groan echoed in his chest. "Brooke," he grunted.

But I just... needed... a little...

Ray stiffened. His hand shot up and shackled my throat. "Brooke—"

My name, uttered as an order from his lips, made me freeze.

"Stop, or you're going to make me come in my fucking shorts," he rasped, half in demand and half in desperation.

My breath hung on that desperation. I wanted him to want me as much as I craved him.

I swallowed as the heady rush of endorphins swam through my body, feeling the tendons along my neck constrict under his palm. Ray licked his lips and slowly released the pressure on my throat. His inescapable grip turned to a tender finger lifting my chin.

"Come here," he said softly as he drew my lips to his again. "I need one more taste."

16

RAY

"Ray?" Brooke's tired voice floated through my dreams.

"Hmm?"

Pressure shifted on my chest. "Were we out here all night?"

I rubbed my eyes, blinking and taking in the morning haze. Sunlight streamed through the tree branches, camouflaging us in waltzes of light and shadows.

Brooke and I were still on the picnic blanket, but we were lying down. I was stretched out and she was curled up into my side. Her chestnut curls were splayed across my chest. At some point during the night, she had slid her hand up my shirt, and it was resting on my stomach.

"I think so," I murmured as I pressed a soft kiss to the top of her head.

Jesus Christ, my back hurt. But I didn't say anything about it. She looked comfortable on my chest. I would deal with the repercussions later.

Reminders of last night filtered through my mind.

Her coming home. Showing her the swing. Eating a late dinner and watching the sunset. Talking.

Kissing her.

Brooke stretched like a cat, stiffening and curling her toes, then tucking back into my side. "Am I fired?" she yawned.

I chuckled. "Not today."

We lay there, slowly waking with the sun. She traced little circles on my skin, and I grazed my fingers up and down her spine.

"How is it possible I missed someone this much?" she said softly. "The moment I left the ranch on Friday, I started counting down until I could come back."

Something ate away at me like acid. "Sounds like you just missed the ranch."

We had kissed last night, but I chalked it up to something that happened in the heat of the moment. Brooke had a shitty weekend with her roommates and was just glad to get away. That's all this was, and I couldn't let myself forget it.

I was a steady paycheck, and she was a distraction.

I had almost leapt off the edge and jumped down the rabbit hole of despair and self-loathing when Brooke's eyelashes lifted, hitting me with a shock of blue. She gave a small shake of her head. "I missed you."

Her words pulled me back from the crumbling cliff, but I couldn't let myself dwell on them.

"How's the sunburn?" I asked, pushing her hair away so I could get a look at her shoulders.

Freckles dotted her tanned skin. It was still a little rosy, but the worst of the burn had faded quickly.

"Almost gone."

I traced a string of freckles, connecting them like a constellation. "I suppose the sun can't burn itself."

Brooke lifted her chin, bringing her lips in proximity to mine. I sifted my fingers through her hair, cupping her cheek.

The moment was shattered by the roar of a diesel engine.

"What are they doing up this early?" she murmured into my chest.

"Ranch life never stops, Sunnyside." I stroked her velvet cheek with my thumb. "But we better get inside before someone comes down here."

The light in her eyes dimmed, but she nodded. "Yeah." Brooke rolled off of me and sat up. Lines from sleeping on me streaked her arms and cheek. "I know you know how to get up by yourself, but do you want a hand?"

I fought back the urge to snap at her and tell her to get inside. It was an ingrained reflex from over a year of telling my family to leave me alone so I could figure things out for myself.

I appreciated that Brooke offered help, but also acknowledged that it was just that—an offer. She knew I could do it on my own.

I pointed at my chair. "Bring it over."

While Brooke scrambled to push it over, I pressed my palms to the ground and pushed up to sit against the tree trunk.

"Do you want it beside you or in front of you?"

"Beside me. Make sure it's locked," I said as I laced my hands behind my thighs and pulled them up so my feet were flat on the ground.

Brooke's eyes locked on mine and, in them, I saw kindness. Not pity. "Do you want me to go inside?"

"No. Give me a hand, will you?" I asked as I braced one hand on my chair and reached out to her with the other.

Brooke's palm was soft as she slid it into mine. "Tell me when you're ready."

Using my legs first thing in the morning was usually out of the question, but I needed to get inside. I counted down and pushed up against my wheelchair as she helped pull me up.

My knees buckled long enough for me to drop down less than gracefully into my chair, but almost immediately gave out. "Thanks."

Brooke squeezed my hand, then hurried to gather the blanket and picnic basket while I made my way up the ramp.

"Breakfast?" she asked when we convened in the kitchen. "What sounds good?"

Cereal sounded good. But after sleeping on the ground, my body was fucked up, and I didn't know how well I'd be able to use a spoon.

"I'm just gonna eat a granola bar."

There was a hint of doubt in Brooke's face, but she didn't question it. While she made herself some toast, I grabbed the power bar box from the lower cabinets. I blew my hair out of my face so I could see between the flavors, but it just kept flopping in my eyes.

"When was the last time you had a haircut?" Brooke asked as she spread butter over her toast.

I found a chocolate chip bar and shut the cabinet. "Been a while. I don't feel like going to a barber. I'm probably gonna just buzz it."

"Can I cut it?"

I almost laughed, but I held it in.

I liked Brooke and, with the exception of driving and cooking, I trusted her.

I did not trust her with scissors near my head.

I rubbed the back of my neck. "I'll just buzz it."

"Please," she begged, clasping her hands together. "I love cutting hair."

I lifted an eyebrow. "You've cut hair before?"

"Yeah! I did three semesters in beauty school before I switched to early childhood development, but the classes were so boring that I dropped out after a few weeks. I love kids, but I hated school. I even tried massage therapy since it was hands-on. I really loved that, but everyone said I talked too much and they couldn't relax."

And yet all I could think about was her hands on me.

I cleared my throat and turned away so she wouldn't see my shorts starting to tent. "So that's why you're waiting to go back to school? Until you know what you want to do?"

"Yep," she said, taking a bite of toast. "That, and I can't pay for it at the moment. But maybe I'll figure out what I want to do with my life between now and twenty-five. So can I cut your hair? I've done clipper cuts before. And if I mess it up, you were going to buzz it anyway."

I was going to say no, but she hit me with those fucking Bambi eyes.

"Please," she whispered.

I found myself in the bathroom with my shirt off and a towel around my shoulders, watching Brooke rummage through my cabinets. She found the clipper guard in a drawer under the sink, plugged it in, and hit the power button for a test buzz.

I already regretted everything.

Then she touched me.

"Ready?" Brooke asked as she stood behind me and ran

her fingers through my hair to get a feel for it. Her breasts pressed against the back of my neck as her fingertips glided along my temples.

I wanted her to keep doing that.

I mumbled something unintelligible.

She smelled like the outdoors. Like grass and sunshine and fresh air. One hand draped over my shoulder, her thumb stroking my neck as she scrolled through her phone.

"What are you doing?"

"Just a little refresher tutorial."

"I thought you said you'd done this before?" I growled. "You're cutting my hair using a YouTube video?"

Her laugh was melodic. "Just a *refresher*. It's been a while. I can always give you a mohawk." Her fingers combed through the shaggy length that brushed past the collar of my shirt. "Or a mullet."

"Just buzz it." *Or just keep touching it.* But I didn't say that part out loud.

"Can you lift your chin a little?" she asked, grabbing my comb.

I licked my lips and met her eyes in the mirror. "This is me sitting straight."

"That's fine," she said, running the comb through my hair. "As long as you're comfortable."

I wasn't, but it had nothing to do with my posture. It had everything to do with the fact that I hadn't been touched like this in a long time. It wasn't just the way we had kissed last night. It was her hands on me in simple touches that weren't meant to move me or fix me.

"I have a rod in my neck," I said, focusing on her fingers moving across my scalp. I closed my eyes and listened to her giggle.

"So, you're like the real-life Iron Man."

I chuckled. "Something like that."

Her body was soft and warm against my head as she leaned forward. "Is it okay if I touch your scar?"

Usually, I would have said no, but I wanted her to touch me more than anything. "Yeah, it's fine."

Two fingers pressed against the back of my neck as she worked the comb through a few tangles.

I missed the feel of her when she reached for the clippers. "Ready?"

"Just don't slit my throat, Sunnyside."

Brooke threw her head back and laughed. "I won't slit your throat. Promise."

"Don't give me a bowl cut either."

I sat still while she worked the comb and clippers through my hair. Her soft breaths made me melt as tufts of hair fell onto the towel she had draped around my shoulders.

The aches and pains from falling asleep outside didn't go away, but they did fade.

Far sooner than I wanted it to end, Brooke turned off the clippers and set them on the sink.

Her breasts pressed against the back of my head as she worked her fingers through the front of my hair to get it back where it needed to be.

"What do you think?" she asked, stepping back and laying her hands on my shoulders. I opened my eyes and caught her hopeful look in the mirror.

I had to admit, it wasn't half bad. It was a hell of a lot better than the shaggy mess I had been rolling around with, and more preferable than a buzz cut. A shower and a little hair gel, and I'd look like the old me.

Something about that thought didn't bring on the pang

of acid exploding in my gut that I used to get whenever I thought about the man who existed before the accident.

"Not bad," I said.

Brooke's face lit up as she carefully peeled the towel away so hair didn't fly all over the place. "Really?"

I caught her hip before she could walk out with the towel. "Thank you."

Her grin was infectious. "If you had a sink with a sprayer, I'd wash it out for you. Getting your hair shampooed is, like, the best part of getting your hair done."

I glanced at the shower and the handheld sprayer hanging from the cradle on the wall. The thought of her in the shower with me made my cock spring to life, but I couldn't. I didn't want to take advantage of her.

I could get in and out of the shower on my own, and she knew that.

But there we stood, crammed in the bathroom, with neither of us moving.

"Yeah," I said as I swallowed. "Having someone else wash your hair feels good."

She tipped her head to the side. "Is it hard for you to get your hair washed at a salon? You know, laying back with your head in the bowl?"

"Yeah."

A soft smile lifted her lips. "I'll wash your hair if you want. Everyone deserves to feel good."

"I don't want to take advantage of the situation."

She dropped the towel into the sink. "You're not taking advantage of me, Ray." She smirked. "Besides. I can run faster than you."

The laugh that ripped out of my chest was long and loud. I couldn't remember the last time I had laughed like that.

Brooke smiled as she nudged my shoulder toward the shower. "Get in and leave your shorts on. I'm gonna change."

I was sitting on the shower seat when she came back, and I nearly dropped my jaw. She had changed into a bikini top and a pair of athletic shorts.

God help me, Brooke was going to kill me.

"Ready?"

I kept my mouth shut and closed my eyes as she turned on the water and tested the temperature.

"Lean back against me so the water doesn't run into your eyes."

She didn't have to tell me twice.

Her stomach was soft and warm against my shoulders. The swells of her breasts felt like pillows.

Closing my eyes, I exhaled slowly. "Is this alright?"

"Perfect," she replied, dousing my hair and switching to the rain shower while grabbing my shampoo.

Steam enveloped us, providing warmth as she poured the shampoo into her hands and began massaging it into my scalp.

"*Fuck*," I softly groaned.

"Good?" she asked softly.

"Yeah."

Neither of us said anything else as she slowly worked the shampoo into my hair and grew it into a lather. Brooke kept a hand on my arm, her fingers tracing my tattoos as she rinsed it out of my hair.

I had a bottle of conditioner, though I never bothered using it. Brooke opened the bottle and squeezed a dollop into her palm, massaging it into my hair.

There was something about this moment that transcended the physical connection I was used to feeling during sex.

It was care, connection, intimacy, and tenderness. It made me feel human again. Like a man.

She made me feel like I could be wanted.

The hot water eased the tension in my shoulders and back, as her hands washed away my demons.

"Ray?" she asked quietly while rinsing out the conditioner.

"Hmm?"

"What's the scar on your spine from? The accident?"

"Kind of." I sighed. "Cass got me into this experimental human trial."

"I remember you saying something about that."

"A bunch of surgeons implanted electrodes in my spine to stimulate my muscles and nerves. It was really invasive, but it has given me some mobility back. More than I could have expected."

"How did she get you into the trial?"

I chuckled. "She knows people. And not many of them have the guts to say no to her. She probably keeps a blackmail file handy for when she needs to cash in favors."

Brooke's hand trailed down my back. "Are you glad you did it?"

I glanced at the water pooling at my feet. "At the time, I wasn't. I allowed myself to be used like a lab rat because I thought it was all I was good for."

"What about now?" she asked as she went back to spraying the little flecks of hair off my shoulders.

I caught her hand in mine. "Yeah. I'm glad I stuck around."

17

BROOKE

"Whoa, whoa, whoa," Ray grabbed the center console of the truck and held on for dear life.

I rolled my eyes as the truck shuddered. "Dramatic much? It was just a speed bump."

"That was a curb!" Ray shouted. "With people on it!"

I spotted a horizontal parking space along the sidewalk, slowed down to pull in, then thought better of it.

Ray let out a sigh of relief. "Thank god. We'd be late if you tried to parallel park."

"Has anyone ever told you that you're mean sometimes?" I said as I pulled around to the back of the physical therapist's office and snagged a spot right at the front.

"You've learned to tolerate it," Ray said, not denying my assessment.

"And you still have some serious groveling to do," I said as I grabbed the bag of Sweet Tarts he had sorted out for me and popped one in my mouth. "I'll grab your wheelchair out the back. Text me when you're done. I'll just be chilling out here. Think about what you want for lunch before we head back."

Ray paused. The banter we had been tossing around faded.

I worked my finger into a groove in the steering wheel. "Unless you just wanted to get lunch at home... Which is fine. I just figured you'd want something other than sandwiches."

He glanced at the building, then back at me. "Why don't you come in today?" He rubbed the back of his neck. "You know... with me. It's hot out, and I don't want you sitting in the truck that long."

"I'll keep the windows down, and I brought a drink." I picked up the thick insulated tumbler I had stolen from his house and gave it a shake.

His thick lashes lowered. "Will you come in with me today?"

"Look, if it's about the heat, I'll find a coffee shop or somewhere to hang out."

"It's not about the heat. I... I want you to come in." And like it pained him to do so, he gritted out, "*Please.*"

I squeezed his hand. "I'd love to."

Ray didn't say anything as we got out of the truck and went inside. By the time we made it through the automatic doors of the medical complex, my hair was stuck to the back of my neck. Sweat beaded across my forehead.

I followed Ray as he navigated the elevator and the maze of hallways, then pushed himself through a set of automatic doors. The physical therapy unit was brightly lit and cheery. Upbeat music played in the lobby, and a little sitting area with snacks and coffee had been set up for the plus-ones while they waited.

"I'll sit over there until you're done," I said as he pushed himself up to the front desk.

"You can come back with me."

My heart did an extra little pitter-pat. "Okay." I stayed a few paces back while Ray checked in with the receptionist.

When he turned around to wait in the lobby, unease settled in his eyes. I took the seat beside him and crossed my legs. "Ray, I can wait right here if you don't want me going back with you. I'll be fine. I promise."

Ray kept his eyes trained on the floor. "I haven't brought someone back with me before. They always waited outside or in the lobby. But I... I want you there. Other people bring their... people with them."

I rested my hand on the armrest of his wheelchair. Ray slid his hand around mine and our fingers intertwined. I tilted my head and rested it on his shoulder.

"Ray?" A woman wearing blue scrubs appeared in the hallway and smiled at him.

"Come on," he said to me as he let go of my hand and pushed himself toward the woman.

"Just tell me where you want me and what you want me to do," I said.

The woman looked between the two of us and beamed. "Are you going to make me ask, or are you going to tell me?"

Ray frowned, but there was a smile in his eyes. "Do I ever tell you anything?"

"Nice to meet you," she said. "I'm Callie."

"Brooke," I said as I shook her hand.

Callie raised an eyebrow at Ray. "And Brooke is your..."

"None of your business," he groused as he pushed past us and started down the hall.

Callie grinned. "Someone's in a good mood today. And you got a haircut. You don't look like a mop anymore."

"Yeah, and you're about to ruin my mood," Ray hollered as he lifted a middle finger.

"Are you coming back with us?" she asked me with a snicker.

"I think so."

Since Ray had left us in the dust, Callie led me back to a room where two other people were being put through their paces.

"How was your weekend?" she asked Ray when we caught up with him.

I wasn't sure where to stand. There weren't any extra chairs lying around or other people lingering in the corner. I parked myself beside his wheelchair and pressed my back against the wall so I wouldn't be in the way.

"Fine," he said as he tightened the laces on his sneakers.

Callie didn't seem bothered by his rancor. She pointed to the set of parallel bars in the middle of the room. "Start with the bars."

And then she walked away.

"Isn't she..." I looked around. No one else was coming to help. "Isn't she supposed to assist you?"

The parallel bars were about four feet away—just far enough that he didn't have anything to hold onto until he reached them.

"Who? Callie?" Ray shook his head. "No. Her style of PT is kicking a baby bird out of its nest over and over again until it flies. Give me your hand."

I stepped in front of him and held out my hands. Ray glared at me. "Beside me."

"Right. Sorry." I scrambled to his side and waited as he pushed out of his chair. "You gotta be more specific. Saying 'please' also helps."

I watched as he tried to lift his feet out of the footrests.

When he couldn't, he used his hands to pull them out and get them flat on the floor. Ray grabbed my hand and held tight as he pushed up to his feet.

My heart felt like it stopped as he took two shuffling steps forward. I held his hand even tighter.

"Thank you," he said quietly when we were halfway to the parallel bars. "And I'm... I'm sorry I snapped."

"You know, you wouldn't have to apologize as much if you just said things nicely the first time."

"We can't all be you, Sunnyside," he said with a pained groan as he reached out and snagged the bar with his free hand. A few more shuffled steps and he had both hands on the bar.

Callie came back with an armful of resistance bands and weights. "Oh good. You're ready to start."

"Is anyone ever ready to be tortured?" he grumbled as he stationed himself on the padded track between the bars.

She laughed. "I want five passes. Try to lift your feet today instead of dragging them. You can do your first pass holding your weight on the bars. After that, I want as much weight on your feet as you can. Focus on your hips. Keep them square."

While Ray went to work on his first trip down the bars, Callie sidled up to me. "So. Who are you? Sister? Girlfriend?"

"Oh, no. I just live with Ray. But not like that. I work for him."

"He hasn't brought anyone with him before. I've always wondered if he had help at home."

"He doesn't need it," I admitted. "I think we're just doing each other a favor. Me being there keeps people from pestering him."

Callie smirked. "I'd say it's probably more than that. He's

been different the last few weeks. More motivated. In the early months, he wouldn't talk to us at all. He'd just half-ass it through his session and go home. I wanted to think someone in the office had a breakthrough with him, but I think it's been you."

"You know I can hear you, right?" Ray shouted.

"Mind your business or I'll make you do more passes!" Callie shouted back.

I giggled.

Callie tipped her head toward Ray. "Hang out by the bars and distract him, will you?"

I gave her a salute. "Aye, aye, Captain."

Ray rolled his eyes when I walked over to the parallel bars and rested my arms on top of them.

"Don't scowl. You're the one who invited me up here."

"And I'm regretting it," he said. "You and Callie can't gang up on me."

I snickered and chewed on my lip. "Is that what we're doing?"

His eyes crinkled at the corners. "Put that look away, Sunnyside. You're distracting me."

"What look?"

He stopped in his tracks, and his gaze dropped to my mouth. One hand left the bar and cupped my jaw. "The look that's been on your face since the other night."

"Well damn. If I had known all it took to get you motivated was a pretty girl, I would have rush-ordered some cardboard cut-outs," Callie teased from across the room.

Ray flipped her off and went back to holding the bar

"You look good today," I said.

Ray smirked.

"I meant your gait."

He just shook his head and kept walking.

I lingered around the different areas of the office while Callie worked her magic. Ray was always exhausted after PT, and I could see why. She didn't take it easy on him, and she didn't coddle him.

He looked happy today. There was a fire in his eyes where I had only seen embers before.

I hung out in Ray's wheelchair while Callie helped him step up onto a balance ball. From the way she carefully explained how she wanted him to try the exercise, it seemed like it was his first time.

The half-ball was positioned between the parallel bars. He held on to them as Callie kneeled beside him, talking about the muscles in his knee and ankle. My heart raced as she scooted away and told him to give it a try.

Ray's eyes were laser-focused on the ball.

"Stop pushing on your arms," she said. "Use the bars for balance, but don't bear your weight on them."

"Easier said than done."

Ray lifted his right foot off the ground and leaned forward to step on the balance ball. His knee buckled, and he fell forward.

I let out a squeak and covered my mouth with my hands.

He tried to grab onto the bars, but his left hand slipped. Ray fell and swung around, gripping the bar with one hand as he swore loudly enough to silence the whole room.

My heart was in my throat. I could see the pain written all over his face. I wanted to rush over and wrap my arms around him.

Callie didn't touch him. She knelt down and exchanged a few quiet words. Ray's right hand turned white as he squeezed the bar and pulled himself back up.

Ray was going to be angry that I came to the appointment with him. I could feel it in the energy that radiated from him.

But instead of calling it quits, Callie made him do it again.

His arms strained as he held a bit more of his weight this time. Carefully, he lifted his foot and placed it on top of the balance ball.

I was mesmerized by his arms. By the ink that wrapped around thick straps of muscle. By the way his shoulders flexed and rippled.

I had woken up in those arms. I had laid against that chest. I had been cradled by those muscles.

The lips that were parted with each labored breath had kissed me and stolen mine.

Ray shifted his weight onto his foot and slowly brought the other foot to join it on top of the ball. When his legs buckled again, he tightened his grip and eased off, returning to the floor.

They exchanged a few words, then Ray looked over at me and signaled for his wheelchair. I quickly jumped out of it and pushed it over.

"Thanks," he said, breathless as he slowly lowered himself into it. Sweat glistened on his forehead. And honest to goodness, it was sexy.

"Are you okay?" I asked softly.

Ray retrieved his water bottle from the cupholder I'd attached to his wheelchair and took a long drink. "Tired as hell."

"You looked really strong up there."

His eyes softened as they met mine. "Thank you."

"Can I ask you something?"

He nodded and wiped the sweat from his eyes.

"What did Callie say when you fell?"

Ray took another drink, then closed his eyes as he rested. "For every time you couldn't get up before, get up now. And if you can't get up now, know that you will someday."

I placed my hand on top of his. "I'm proud of you."

I walked around the lobby while Ray had a quick hydrotherapy session and massage. An hour later, he was checked out, and we headed for lunch.

"What sounds good?" I asked as I parked in a strategic space in Temple's downtown district.

Ray glanced at the Mexican restaurant we usually grabbed takeout from. "There are spots on the patio."

I paused. Ray hated going out in public. Usually, I slipped in and got our food to-go. I couldn't tell if his comment was just a brief observation, or if he was considering sitting at the restaurant and eating.

"It's a nice day," I said. "And they don't look too busy. The food will probably come out fast."

Ray tipped his head toward the bed of the truck. "Mind grabbing my chair out of the back? I don't feel like going back to the ranch right away."

He looked wiped out, but stepped up onto the sidewalk by himself before easing down into his chair.

"You're getting there," I said as I shut the doors and locked the truck. "I'll be out of a job soon."

Ray sighed. "It's just maintenance at this point. This is as good as it's going to get. Little bursts of energy and my body working, and then the rest is shit."

"You know, there are adaptive driving modifications that can be made to your truck so you can drive it yourself. Hand controls for the gas and brake. Lifts for your wheelchair. Things like that."

"I know," he said. A teasing smile worked up to his sharp

cheekbones. "Maybe I just like the little hit of adrenaline I get every time you drive. It's like being back on a bull."

I laughed. "I'm not that bad!"

"Baby, I mean this nicely, but you're the worst driver I've ever seen."

Tingles danced up my spine.

"Yo, Stace—"

I froze mid-stride to the restaurant.

Ray paused and cut his eyes over his shoulder. "Who's that?"

"My roommate, Nick."

Ray's face contorted.

I knew should keep walking and head into the restaurant, but Nick would follow, and I would be cornered. I turned. "Hey."

Nick looked us both up and down. Two of my other roommates were with him. "Who's this?"

"Ray," I said.

Nick's gaze turned to Ray. "Right... The loaded rodeo star with that ranch job..."

I cleared my throat. "Ray, these are some of my roommates, Nick, Chandler, and Devin."

Ray didn't say a word.

Chandler's beady eyes turned to the truck. "Nice ride." There was something unsettling about the way he looked at Ray's truck.

"You owe me rent," Nick said.

"I moved my stuff out, and I already paid you for this month."

"Well, until we get someone else in the house, it's still on you."

"I was subletting."

"Still on you, Stacey. Pay up."

My stomach dropped, and my cheeks burned with embarrassment. I hated dealing with Nick, and I didn't want Ray to see this.

A hand slid into mine, and I looked down at Ray. But he was looking at Nick.

"Get fucked," he said, keeping a tight grip on my hand as he turned and guided his wheelchair with one hand into the restaurant.

18

RAY

My adrenaline was still pumping after lunch and the ride back to the ranch. Brooke was shaken, and I hated that with every fiber of my being.

The old me would have clocked that punk-ass kid across the face the minute he looked at Brooke. A little sidewalk brawl was fun now and then.

The man I was now couldn't. I was tempted to punch him in the balls, but I didn't.

Brooke was sitting on the couch, scrolling through her phone.

I made sure the doors were locked before wheeling into the living room. Something about the run-in on the sidewalk just didn't sit right with me. Those kids knew too much about me. I didn't like it.

I was used to people knowing shit about my life—especially around here.

I grew up in Temple, then went off and made a name for myself on the rodeo circuit. My accident was nationwide news for a week. When I finally woke up in the hospital, it ran the gamut of media outlets for three more weeks. I turned down interview requests by the dozen, even though I probably should have cashed in on them.

I never minded being famous, but I hated being infamous.

It wasn't absurd to think that Brooke's roommates followed the story of my accident, but I didn't think that's what was going on.

"You okay?" I asked as I made a neat turn around the corner of the sectional couch.

Brooke's eyes barely lifted from her phone. "Why wouldn't I be?"

"Your roommates are dicks."

She let out a soft breath. "Tell me about it."

"They're the reason you came back early over the weekend?"

She swallowed and didn't say anything for a long moment. "Yeah."

Instead of heading to my recliner, I pulled up in front of her. "Look at me."

She barely gave me a peek at her blue eyes.

"Brooke."

She sighed. "I'm sorry we ran into them."

"Why are you apologizing to me?"

"Because it's embarrassing! I got myself tied up in their mess because I was desperate for somewhere to live. Now they won't stop harassing me. I just want to be done with them."

"Then be done."

She laid her phone on her stomach and closed her eyes. "Can we just... not fight today? You can fire me tomorrow."

"Brooke, I'm not firing you."

"Right." She shifted, turning her head away from me. "Because you need a shiny little distraction."

What the hell was her problem? The sunshine that always beamed from her was completely shrouded by the clouds in her eyes.

"Help me up."

She peeled an eye open. "You... want me to—"

"I said what I said." I reached out for her. "Give me your hand." I clasped my hand around hers and eased onto the couch beside her. "Come here."

"I don't want your pity. I'm sorry we ran into them, and I'm trying to figure it out."

I wrapped my hand around her ankle. Brooke let out a squeak as I dragged her across the couch until her butt bumped against my leg.

"Will you just get over here and stop apologizing for shit that's not your fault?"

She huffed and sat up.

"Do you need to get out of here for a while?"

She looked away from me. "I don't really want to leave unless you don't want me around."

"I want you here," I tucked a curl behind her ear. "I just want you to stop blaming yourself for that run-in earlier."

"But I know it bothered you, and I'm sorry."

I chuckled. "It bothered me because I don't like seeing you shaken. I'm fine."

She looked up at me with doe eyes. "You sure?"

"Promise." For no other reason than the fact that I wanted to, I pressed a kiss to her temple. "Don't give it a second thought."

Brooke curled into my side. "Thanks." Her finger trailed along one of the lines of my tattoo sleeve. A single touch of her finger made my blood simmer.

My cock thickened when her hand brushed my thigh. I let out a slow breath to try and get it to calm down.

"What's the matter?" Brooke asked like the innocent devil she was. Her fingers skimmed the edge of my shorts.

"Nothing," I said between labored breaths.

"Really? Because it looks like you're—"

"I have to start wearing more than gym shorts around you."

"What? Why? You should wear whatever's comfortable. It's not like we're in an office or something."

The lines I had been trying so hard not to cross disappeared. I brought her hand to the front of my shorts and pressed her palm to my cock. "That's why."

Her lips parted as she looked down.

I gripped her chin and forced her eyes back up to me. "Don't look so surprised. You did this to me the night we kissed outside. Hell, you've done this every day since you showed up in my driveway."

"Ray—" Her breathless whisper of my name made my dick throb against her palm.

Brooke squeezed.

"Baby—"

A wicked smile tugged at the corner of her mouth, and she squeezed again.

"You're a fucking tease," I rasped as I breathed through the urge to come right then and there.

"Is it wrong if I want you?" Her breath turned ragged as she slipped over to straddle me. Her knees sank into the couch cushions. Our lips lingered a breath apart.

She leaned in, but I slid my hand up the back of her scalp, fisted her hair, and yanked down, exposing her throat.

"Yes," I growled. "It is."

"You're my... boss." She gasped when I latched onto her throat and sucked.

"That's right."

"And I... I signed... an..."

"You signed what?" I said as I kissed up her jaw.

She swallowed. "An agreement. That I... that I wouldn't..."

"Spit it out," I said as I licked up the shell of her ear. Her skin tasted like summer. I wanted to know what she tasted like everywhere.

"That I wouldn't have a relationship with a client."

I tightened my hand in her hair. "Who said this is a relationship?"

"Then what is it?"

I smirked against her lips. "This is just kissing, baby."

Her breath was warm and sweet. "Then let me kiss you."

But I wanted so much more from her. Things that I couldn't rightly ask for. I kept her mouth off of mine with my hand in her hair. "Hands behind your back."

She moved immediately, clasping her hands together.

I released her hair and took her in. Brooke's chest rose and fell in steady breaths as she panted. Her thighs squeezed against my hips as she tried to relieve the ache in her core. My cock tented my shorts and pressed between her legs.

She didn't make a move to grind down on me, though.

Brooke sitting there with her hands behind her back, waiting for direction, told me everything I needed to know.

She didn't want to be in control here.

She didn't want to make out.

She had the same hungry look I did.

The same craving.

I leaned back against the couch and stretched my arms

out across the back of it. The only part of our bodies that touched were her thighs on either side of mine.

"If you want this, you can have it. But we do it my way. You will do exactly what I say. No strings. And not a word to the agency you work for."

Brooke shifted. Her legs squeezed against mine, and she whimpered but kept her hands behind her back.

Still obedient.

My eyes flicked down to her shorts. "You're wet for me, aren't you?"

Her lips parted, and her eyes closed.

"Drop your shorts. I'll get you off. Get you feeling good."

"I want you," she whispered, arching her back and pushing her tits toward me. "I want your cock. Please."

It was the 'please' that did me in.

"I don't have condoms, baby. I hadn't thought about sex in a long time. And then you showed up wearing those fucking shorts that show off your little ass, and these tank tops that make me want to bury myself between your tits. And now it's all I can think about. I fuck my hand every time I'm in the shower because I can't stop thinking about you. And I shouldn't. You're too damn young for me."

Heavy lids lifted enough for her eyes to meet mine. "I'm a consenting adult."

"You're twelve years younger than me."

Instead of using her words, she widened her legs and dropped down on my cock, pressing it between her legs. "I'm on birth control. And I had a physical before I got this job. All my results were clear. And considering you've seen nearly every doctor in the state, I'll take a guess and say you're good."

She was trying to kill me. I was sure of it.

A thin strip of denim hid her pussy from me. I reached

between her legs and cupped her sex. "You want me to fuck this pussy raw?"

Brooke tipped her head back and whimpered. "Please."

I slipped a finger under the gusset of her panties. She was warm and wet and absolutely dripping for me. "My way."

"Yes."

"You can tell me to stop, but that's all. You don't get to dictate a thing."

Brooke tried to rock to get more pressure from my finger. "That's what I want. You. In charge."

I pulled my hand away. "Then go into my room, take all of your clothes off, and get on the bed on your knees."

She scrambled off the couch.

"And Brooke—"

She froze mid stride and looked at me.

A slow smile stretched up my mouth. "If you touch yourself before I get in there, I will make you regret it."

She bit her lip, fighting a smile, and clasped her hands behind her back.

"Good girl." I tipped my head toward the bedroom. "Go on."

When she disappeared through the door, I adjusted my dick and eased back into my chair.

I had thought about sex since the accident, but mostly in the context of realizing I'd never have it again.

But this... Her...

Brooke came out of nowhere.

She wasn't a buckle bunny, chasing me for clout and shiny things. She didn't pick me because I looked like an easy target.

Maybe I was overselling myself on the possibilities, but I had never thought about life after those eight seconds.

The mattress creaked as I rolled into the bedroom.

Brooke was kneeling in the middle of my bed, completely naked. Pert breasts were diamond-tipped in the chill of the AC. Her ankles were crossed, pretty as a picture, making her ass look like a heart.

My heart seized in my chest. All those motivational thoughts about taking that next step for myself went out the window. She was perfection—flawless in every way.

I didn't want her to watch me fumble around. I didn't want her to see me struggle to move my body.

I grabbed my sleep mask from the nightstand and placed it in front of her, raking my eyes down the front of her body. "Put that on.

"But I—"

"My way," I reminded her. "Do you want to do this?"

Brooke nodded and grabbed the mask.

"You can always say no. No harm. No foul."

"Your way," she said as she slid the mask over her eyes.

With her unable to see me, I stripped off my shirt and shorts. I reached into the nightstand drawer and pulled out the long rope I had been practicing with. I trailed the coil up the side of her hip and thigh.

Brooke shivered.

"Have you ever been tied up?" I asked as I found the end of the rope and shook out the loops to straighten it.

"No." She shifted her ankles. "But it... It turns me on. The thought of it. I want to try it."

"Do you trust me?"

She was quick to answer. "Yes."

19

RAY

"I'm not going to make it too tight, but you won't be able to move."

"I understand."

"It shouldn't hurt, so let me know if it does. Got it? I'll watch your skin color, but if your hands or fingers start tingling, speak up immediately."

Brooke nodded.

"Words, baby girl. I need to hear you say that you understand."

Her breath caught in her throat. "I understand," she whispered.

My arms were sore from PT, but I managed to pull myself onto the bed and sit in front of her. It took everything in me not to start touching—tasting—teasing. I wanted to bury myself in her.

She was like the sun. I wanted to get close, even if it meant getting burned. I wanted to be consumed by her again and again.

"You're so fucking beautiful," I said as I looped the ropes, draping them around the back of her neck like a scarf. They came together in a knot an inch from the top of her sternum.

My cock twitched against her leg.

"Do you feel what you do to me, baby?" I murmured as I wrapped the rope in bands around the tops of her arms, fastening them to her sides.

Brooke panted. "I want to feel your cock. Put it in my hand?"

"I love hearing those naughty things come from your perfect lips."

She gasped as I passed the ropes beneath her breasts. The tension pushed them forward, and I couldn't resist pulling one rosy nipple into my mouth. Brooke gasped again, struggling against the restraints.

"I'm going to tease you until your pussy is crying for this cock." I ran a finger through her slit, then coated her lips with her own arousal. "But I don't think you're wet enough yet."

I shifted on the bed until I was behind her. Taking my time, I secured the ladder of knots that ran down her spine. The rope tails had just enough length to loop them around the creases of her thighs, forcing her legs apart, trapping them in the tension between the ropes binding her arms.

I touched her fingers, squeezing them to check their color and temperature. "Wiggle your fingers for me."

She did, brushing them against my hand.

"Atta girl."

I admired my handiwork as I listened to her breathing. She looked like a goddess. A masterpiece.

"You look stunning." I hooked my hands into the bands of rope around her ribs and used it to pull myself up onto my knees. I pressed my chest to her spine. My cock pushed against her ass. "How does it feel?" I asked as I brushed her curls to the side and kissed the back of her neck. I looked over her shoulder at her breasts and thumbed her nipple.

Brooke gasped. "It... it feels..."

"Feels like what?"

"Safe," she whispered. "Warm. It feels like you're holding me, even when you're not." A high pitched whine escaped her lips when I slid my fingers through her pussy. "I feel like a statue. Like I can't move, but I want you to look."

I squeezed her tit. "You're breathtaking like this. Arch your back for me."

She had a little room to maneuver, so she pushed her ass against me, but not much more.

She let out a whimper with each scrape of the ropes. They were smooth, intended for bondage, but the fibers against her skin were a new sensation.

I had created a modified version of a dragonfly harness, hoping it would give me leverage and stability while holding onto her. I slid my left hand under the stack of knots along her spine and wrapped my fingers around them.

Brooke whimpered as it pulled against her breasts.

I reached between her legs and found her clit. She jolted and pulled against the restraints.

"You good?"

"I need to come," she pleaded.

"I know you do," I said with a teasing chuckle, massaging her clit. "This pussy is begging for me, isn't it? I know I won't last long once I finally get inside of you. So, I'm going to take my time, and you're going to enjoy it."

Her teeth sunk into her lower lip. "Please... hurry..."

"Come for me, baby girl. You don't have to wait. There will be more."

"But I—"

She couldn't finish her thought before I had her shattering on my hand. Her chest heaved against the ropes as she caught her breath.

I cupped both of her breasts, pressing her spine against my chest as I teased her nipples until they were swollen and hard.

"Needy little thing," I murmured against her neck. "So desperate that you're willing to be blindfolded, tied up, and fucked." Her legs started trembling again as I played with her nipples. "You'd look so pretty with clamps dangling from these tits and a toy in your ass."

She gasped and tilted her head back onto my shoulder. "Please," was the only word that escaped her mouth.

"Filthy girl."

"Only for you," she panted.

"That's right." I slid my hand between her legs again. "Just me."

My thighs trembled. I let go of her and turned around, sitting with our backs to each other before my legs gave out and I fell.

"Ray?" Worry filled her voice.

"Right behind you. I'm here. I just need to sit for a second."

"Okay," she whispered with a relieved exhale.

"I'm not leaving you," I promised as I laid on my back. "You're safe with me."

I reached over my head and grabbed her thighs. "Sit on my face, baby girl. I want to know what this pussy tastes like before I fuck it."

She didn't have to be told twice. Brooke shifted back with what little range of motion she had until her cunt settled on my mouth.

I swiped my tongue through her sex and groaned. "Fuck." I devoured her with another pass, teasing her clit.

"You're going to make me come from the way you taste." I fisted my cock. "You hear that sound? That's me fucking my hand." I sucked on her pussy until she was dripping into my mouth. "I can't help myself."

Brooke whined. "Oh my god... I need to come again."

She bucked her hips on my chin like she was riding a bull.

"That's it, beautiful. Get yourself off on my face. I want you all over me." I slid two fingers into her pussy and stroked her walls as I sucked her clit. "There you go. I feel you about to come. How tight you are. I can't wait to fuck this cunt."

Brooke let out a desperate moan as she thrashed against the ropes. Her thighs tightened around my head.

"Give me one more and I'll let you have my cock."

"Ray," she begged. Her thighs trembled.

I found her G-spot and teased it. The muscles inside of her constricted around my fingers.

Brooke fell forward as she came. She landed with her ass in the air and her face in a pillow.

I rolled onto my stomach and pushed up to my arms, giving her one long lick from her cunt to her ass. She squealed into the pillow and thrashed as I teased the tight rosette between her spread cheeks.

She tipped her head to the side and sucked in a deep breath.

"Every piece of you tastes so fucking good," I groaned as I grabbed the ropes around the base of her ribs and pulled myself up to my knees. "You owe me one more orgasm, baby girl."

Brooke's whole body was flushed pink as she caught her breath. The inside of her thighs were slick with arousal and saliva. My cock was leaking like a fucking hose as I lined up with her pussy.

"How are your hands?"

Brooke wiggled her fingers. "Good."

I held onto the knots down her spine with my right hand and dragged my cock through her entrance with my left. Without warning I pushed inside of her.

Brooke gasped, but I barely heard it over the roar of blood in my ears.

Fuck, I had missed this.

It was strange how something so simple made me feel more human than I had in over a year.

But it wasn't just the act.

It was her.

Brooke was radiant as she tossed her head back like a mare and groaned.

"You feel so fucking good, baby."

I had jacked myself off more times than I could count since moving into my house, but this was different. It was so much better. There was an energy pulsing between us that I didn't have on my own. A connection that bound us stronger than the ropes.

"Please fuck me harder," she begged.

Who was I to say no?

I held onto the ropes around her ribs and slammed my hips into her. Brooke cried out as I set a grueling pace, pleading for another orgasm.

I held on with my right hand, and used my left to rake my fingers up her scalp, fisting her hair at her root. I yanked her head off the pillow.

"Who does this pussy belong to?"

"You," she gasped, sucking in a deep breath.

I shoved her head back down into the pillow. "That's

right, baby girl." I thrust into her again. "Who are you going to come for?"

"You," she cried out into the pillow. Her fingers curled, scratching at the rope.

My balls ached to unload inside of her. My thighs shook and my knees buckled.

She let out a desperate whine. Her whole body shuddered as she came again. I collapsed on top of her spine as I broke apart, flooding her pussy with my release.

My body and mind were alive.

I pushed off of her and laid on my side as I untied the first of the knots and freed her hands.

Brooke let out a sigh of relief as the ropes loosened and slid off in a pile. Her body melted into the bed.

I shoved two fingers into her cunt and pushed my cum back inside of her.

Her toes curled. "Ray," she whimpered. "I can't. Not again."

"You don't have to come again," I murmured as I dotted her arms with kisses and gently stroked inside her pussy. "It helps ease you off that crash. Just breathe for me." I reached up and removed the mask from her eyes. "You're breathtaking."

Brooke's smile was soft and sated. Her eyes were dreamy as they found mine.

I eased up and kissed her forehead. "Thank you."

Her brow furrowed. "For what?"

"For bringing me back."

We spent a moment lying together, catching our breath. I knew I was fucked for the rest of the day. Between physical therapy and sex, my body was done.

I told Brooke to relax while I got dressed and settled into my wheelchair to go to the bathroom. When I came back after a quick pit stop in the kitchen, I found Brooke emerging from the bathroom, still naked.

She crawled back onto the bed and flopped down. "I don't think there's a single calorie left in my body."

I smirked. "Three orgasms will do that to you." I unloaded the snacks from my lap onto the bed and lifted the glass of water out of my chair's cup holder. "Eat something and drink that."

"No arguments here," Brooke said, sitting against the headboard and pulling the quilt up to her chest. "Thank you."

Trying to get back on the bed was less than graceful, but she paid me no mind. As soon as I was beside her against the headboard, I pulled her into my lap. "How do you feel?"

She leaned her head back onto my shoulder and closed her eyes. "Like I'm floating."

I chuckled. "Your shoulders will probably be sore tomorrow." I traced my fingertips around her shoulder joints and biceps. "Especially here." Bright red marks from the ropes streaked her skin. I ran my palm over each one, checking for any deep marks. She didn't flinch or react to my touch. "Soak in a bath before you go to bed tonight."

She let out a laugh. "I don't think I'll be able to get out of your bed."

I pressed a kiss to the back of her ear and wrapped my arms around her. "That's fine by me."

"Can I ask?"

"Ask what?"

"How did you learn all of this?"

I pressed my lips to her bare shoulder and smiled. "Well... I guess it's always been an affinity of mine."

"That's all I get?"

"You're forgetting that I've lived as an adult a lot longer than you have."

"Fair enough. But I'm just curious."

I kissed her again. "I traveled a lot in my twenties. It was a hobby I could learn on the road. I'd sit in hotel rooms at night and practice different kinds of knots and harnesses. Occasionally on a partner." I sighed. "And after my accident, I picked it back up to get dexterity back in my hands... without the partners."

Brooke released a yawn as she nodded.

"Tired?" I asked, brushing her hair away from her face.

She smirked. "I'm surprised you're not. You had PT this morning."

I laughed. "I won't be leaving this bed anytime soon."

Her blue eyes met mine. "Can I stay?"

I wanted nothing more than for her to stay and never leave. I shifted to lie on my back, pulling her down with me. "Make yourself comfortable."

Brooke nestled into my side and rested her head on my chest as if it were the most natural thing in the world.

And goddamn, it felt like it was.

20

BROOKE

"Thanks for the ride," I said to CJ as we trotted back into the barn. Each drop of Indy's hooves made me wince.

My *entire* body ached.

When CJ showed up at Ray's back deck with Anarchy and Independence tacked up, I couldn't refuse. But I also couldn't explain why I was walking like I had already gone on a miles-long ride.

Ray, the asshole, just sat on his back deck and smirked while I settled into the saddle.

At least it was a short ride. CJ took me out to the construction site where the lodge and restaurant were being built, around the paths that looped around the west side, then back to the south side of the ranch where Ray's house was.

Hopefully, I wouldn't get lost the next time I went out on my own.

"You did good," CJ said as he hopped off Anny and led her into a stall where food and water waited. "You're a natural."

I dismounted Indy and bit my lip, trying to suppress a groan. With each step I took, I could still feel Ray inside of me.

"Do you think you'll get Ray to come to family dinner again?" he asked.

An old, mottled cat peeked out from Indy's stall.

"Oh, hello there," I said as I bent down to pick it up.

The tomcat yowled as soon as I touched it.

"Aren't you a fluffy fellow." I brought the screaming cat to my chest.

CJ whipped around. "Brooke—no—"

It was too late. The cat swiped at me with a vicious one-two punch. Claws sank into my face, chest, and arms as it tried to scramble away.

"Hey, it's okay," I soothed despite the cat's hissing. "I'm nice, I promise."

CJ ripped the cat out of my hands and tossed it into a pile of hay. "Yeah, but Dusty isn't. That thing is an asshole, but she keeps the mice away."

He assessed the rips in my shirt, the scratches covering my skin, and the blood trickling down my body. "Ray's gonna fucking kill me. I said I'd bring you back in one piece."

"It's fine. It's just a little scratch," I said, waving it off. "I'll get her to like me eventually."

CJ chuckled and shook his head as he helped me remove Indy's gear. "You're an animal person."

I grinned as I started brushing Indy's gorgeous coat. "I love them. And plants. And kids. And old people."

He snickered. "I'd love to see you and Cass locked in a room together."

I shuddered. "She's terrifying."

"Yeah, that's what most people say." He paused for a moment. "How's Ray?"

"You should ask him," I chirped.

Ray never said it outright, but I knew it bothered him when people talked around him, about him, but not to him. Frankly, it was rude.

CJ raised an eyebrow. "You work with him."

"No, I work for him. Ray's my boss."

CJ paused. "Fair. Point taken."

I glanced at the old clock hanging on the wall. "I should probably head back to the house. What else do I need to do?"

"You're good. I'll finish up."

I left CJ with the horses and made my way back up the path to Ray's house. The moment I stepped back inside, I knew I had made a mistake.

"Jesus Christ, what the hell happened to you?" Ray shouted across the living room. "I thought you were going on a trail ride? Why the fuck are you bleeding? I swear, I'm going to kill CJ—"

"Ray, stop," I said, laughing. "I'm fine. I tried to pick up the barn cat and it got a little sassy with me."

Ray paused, huffed, and pinched the bridge of his nose. "You're going to give me blood pressure issues, you know that?"

I giggled as I took off my shoes at the door and opened the fridge. "You worry too much."

"I think it's justified."

I pulled a soda from the fridge door and cracked it open. Before I could turn and shut the door, hands were on me.

"What—"

Ray pulled me down into his lap. He pushed the wheels

backward and closed the fridge door. "You need to take better care of yourself, Sunnyside."

"It's just a few scratches."

"That barn cat has been around since high school. I've seen the people she's fucked up, and I've been one of them." Ray's hands roamed over my arms and shoulders, checking the scratches. He let out a soft exhale. "They don't look too deep."

"Told you."

Ray gave me a sharp glare. "Do you need help cleaning them up?"

"I was going to rinse off anyway. I smell like sweat and horses."

His hand curled around my hip. "You smell good to me."

I laughed and pushed his chest. "Weirdo."

He cracked a smile. "I'm just saying. It suits you."

Ray gave me a ride to the bathroom as I sipped my drink. He placed me in the shower before throwing a clean towel at me from the dryer. After I rinsed off and disinfected the cat scratches, I found him on the couch with his laptop.

Every time I saw him sitting on the couch instead of the recliner, my heart swelled. It was an unspoken invitation to join him. The recliner was his alone, but I was welcome on the couch.

"Whatcha doing?" I asked as I curled up beside him, working a wide comb through my water-logged curls.

"Nothing," he said quickly, attempting to close a video streaming app.

But he couldn't hide what he had been watching.

"Do you miss it?" I asked, staring at the paused thumbnail of a rider on the back of a massive bull.

His silence spoke volumes. The answer was evident in

the clenched flex of his jaw. "My old manager wanted me to watch this kid ride and send back some critique."

I snorted. "Sounds like he's slacking off."

The corner of his mouth lifted, but that was all.

"I miss it," he admitted. "I hate watching it from this fucking couch. I know I'm supposed to believe that there was a purpose for my accident. You know—all that positivity bullshit that Christian can spew at the drop of a hat." He sighed and closed his computer. "But I don't see the good in it. And I don't think I ever will. I still can't write my own damn name, and it's only three letters."

I curled into his side and rested my head on his shoulder. "I don't think you have to find the good in it. Sometimes there is no good to be found."

Ray looked at me curiously. "Did you fall and hit your head on that ride, Sunnyside?"

I laughed. "No. I just..." I sighed. "My parents died. My grandma died. I don't have a family. I have shitty roommates who kind of scare me, and I wake up every day just hoping to get through the next twenty-four hours so I'm one day closer to accessing my trust and having a life. There's no good in that. There's no good in you getting thrown off a bull and having your career end. You don't have to pretend there's some greater meaning in it all. Sometimes life just sucks."

"Is this where you tell me to enjoy the little things and be grateful for what I have left?"

I shrugged. "What you do with what you have is your business. I'm not saying you have to pretend your accident or your diagnosis was good. But I am saying that good things still exist."

Ray found my hand and squeezed.

I studied the contrast of black ink that danced across his

light skin. "Darkness and light exist together in the same moments. We find it in sunrises and sunsets. It's the clash that people trek across mountains to experience."

The house was quiet. Too quiet. Ray was jittery. Frankly, so was I.

"Let's get out of here."

He lifted an eyebrow. "Why? Where?"

"Who cares where we go? What else do we have to do? You don't have PT until tomorrow afternoon."

He blinked for a moment, and I could tell he was mulling it over in his mind. "Pack a bag. We're leaving in twenty minutes."

∼

"Take the next right and get on the highway."

The truck engine growled as we sped through town without giving anyone on the ranch a heads-up that we were leaving.

"You gonna tell me where I'm driving us?" I asked as I fiddled with the radio.

Ray swatted my hands away. "Ten and two, Evel Knievel." He found the station I was looking for and turned up the volume. "And no. You get directions, not a destination. You'd just get lost anyway."

I rolled my eyes. "Ye of little faith."

"I'm making educated guesses based on previous patterns of behavior." He slid his hand down my arm and peeled my hand off the steering wheel when I settled into the right lane on the highway. Ray wrapped his hand around mine. "We're going east."

"Alright, Lewis and Clark. What are we going to do out *east*?"

The heat in his eyes was positively carnivorous. "Getting out of town for the night."

I squeezed my thighs together. "How much rope did you bring?"

Ray let out a loud, long laugh. It was a sharp contrast to the haunted man from earlier who had been contemplating the trajectory of his life. "I didn't bring any. Sorry to disappoint."

"I'm not disappointed," I blurted out.

Oh my god. It was so obvious that I was actually disappointed.

Ray snickered.

"Okay, fine. Maybe I'm a little disappointed." I briefly took my eyes off the road. "Is a repeat of yesterday on the table?"

He licked his lips. "Eyes on the road, Sunnyside."

I huffed and focused on driving.

"Is that... something you want? With me, I mean."

"Sex? Um. Yes, please? I thought that was pretty obvious."

"It's not."

"Obvious?"

Ray clenched his jaw, and his stormy expression returned. "I'll give you what you want. I just need to know what it is."

Him. I wanted him.

The thought startled me with its immediacy. "What do you want?" I countered.

Ray shook his head. "That's not what I asked. Take the next exit."

Did he seriously just give me directions? He was being so nonchalant about a conversation that should have been highly intimate.

If he wasn't going to be brave, I would be. "I like you," I confessed. "A lot. And maybe that's weird since I work for you and we don't have much in common. But I like hanging out with you. And I'm pretty sure you're the sexiest man I've ever met in person."

Ray raised an eyebrow. "In person?"

I shrugged. "I mean, Ryan Reynolds exists."

He cracked a smile. "That's fair."

I held his hand a little tighter as I exited the highway and made the left turn he pointed out. "I don't want to get my hopes up because I know you probably don't want what I want. So if you just want sex, that's fine."

"What do you want, Brooke?"

"I want to be with you. To see where things go. And if it doesn't work, it doesn't work. But at least we tried."

"You want to date me?"

I hated his tone, as if it was strange to want to date. He could probably have any woman he wanted.

"You don't have to sound so appalled."

"I'm not appalled." Ray sighed. "The end game of dating is marriage, and I'm not the marrying kind."

"Says who?"

"Says me."

"Why? Because you don't want it?" I laughed. "I'm not walking down the aisle any time soon. I didn't pack a white dress and I'm not driving us to the courthouse."

He let go of my hand and raked his fingers through his hair. "Don't play this fucking game with me. I thought you were better than that."

"What game?"

"The thing people do where they pretend like I'm not paraplegic. I am. That's not changing. The game where people pretend like it doesn't affect everything. I can't drive you on dates. I can't walk beside you and hold your hand. I can't dance with you at a wedding. I can't be the one to take you to the hospital when you're in labor with our babies. I'm not putting someone I love through that. I'm not going to make you take on a dependent when you should have a partner. I'm not going to be selfish, no matter how much I want to be."

Oh. He... He said a lot of things.

I veered into a fast food parking lot and slammed on the brakes. "Did you just say you love me?"

Ray pressed his head against the headrest. "Really? That's what you got from all of that?"

"Yes or no."

"It doesn't matter."

"It matters to me. Isn't that something people promise to each other? For better or worse? In sickness and in health?"

He stared out the window. "They promise those things before they happen. It's a frivolous insurance policy that doesn't apply to pre-existing conditions."

I pushed the gear shift into park and turned in the seat. "Ray..."

"You know, I was excited to retire in a few years," he admitted with a heartbreaking crack in his voice. "I wanted to settle down and have kids. Taking care of my nieces when they were little and needed someone put that fire in me. I wanted to have the kind of family I had growing up."

"You can still have all those things. You're the man who figures it out and makes it work. I'm not saying it would be with me. Hell, we might hate each other by the time we get home tomorrow. You're forgetting that you don't need me. Remember?"

His eyes were soft and glassy. "I think I was wrong."

21

RAY

We pulled out of the parking lot in silence, but Brooke never let go of my hand. Even when she drove over the curb.

I had never admitted any of that to anyone, not even before the accident. My public persona was built on being the carefree, unattached wild child. My sponsors didn't want the doting uncle. The brother. The kid from the ranch in Temple, Texas, who wore his heart on his sleeve.

They needed the guy who rode hard, stripped down for photoshoots, and partied.

So, I put the kid I used to be away.

Without the cameras, the lights, and the glory, all that was left was torn skin and broken bones. My body gave up on me before I was ready to quit.

I used to think about what I would do after I was finished with the rodeo circuit, but I never made a plan. I considered going back home to Colorado, packing up my life, and traveling for a while. Maybe going further West to California or North to Wyoming.

Once, I even threw darts at a map, hoping to decide where I would end up. But sinking those little silver tips into Laramie, Wyoming, Marion, Iowa, Saskatoon, Saskatchewan, and Wilmington, North Carolina didn't bring any clarity.

I never expected to be back on the ranch for good. I liked visiting and I missed it, of course. I missed my brothers, parents, and nieces. But coming back when I had finally gotten out wasn't part of the plan.

And now, I was leaving again.

Except for a few supervised trips to see specialists in Dallas, I never left the ranch or my town anymore.

Leaving this afternoon with Brooke was different. We were getting away just for the hell of it, and it felt so fucking good.

I wasn't accustomed to this feeling. But recently, I had been feeling really good. It was all because of her.

The sex was incredible. But it was also the comfort and ease I felt with her that truly mattered. I didn't have to pretend or put on a show.

Brooke didn't look at me the way my family did—with pity. She didn't treat me like the buckle bunnies who latched onto riders every season to be their meal ticket. She looked at me like I was the one she wanted to spend every moment with.

As Brooke pulled into the lot of the Maren Motel and parked in front of the office, memories flooded back. I had stayed here before. It was a simple place, but clean and well-maintained. But those memories felt like they belonged to another man in another life.

While she went inside to book a room, I sat in the cab and worried about everything that had spilled out of my mouth.

Talking about going on dates. Holding her hand. *Our* wedding and future children.

I ran my hands over my face in frustration. Why had I said all that shit out loud?

She was going to think I was trying to pressure her into something she wasn't ready for.

The last thing I wanted was for Brooke to feel obligated to stay.

I watched through the window as she skipped out of the office with a room key in her hand.

She was wearing another pair of iconically short denim shorts. Her tanned legs were a fucking dream. A sliver of her stomach peeked out of the bottom of her tied-off tank top. Her thick hair was in a bun on top of her head. She had the most graceful neck and delicate jawline.

Brooke tapped on the window, and I rolled it down. "3A is ours. They only had one accessible room left, so it looks like we got here just in time."

Room 3A was neatly furnished with a standing shower, a mini-fridge, a microwave, a TV, and a single king-sized bed.

"Do you mind sharing? I can sleep on the floor if you want the whole thing. It won't bother me at all," she said.

I chuckled. "It's fine. We can share."

It was more than fine.

"So," Brooke said as she tossed a duffle bag onto the chair by the window. "You seem like you know this town. Is there stuff to do around here?"

"There's a bar not too far from here," I said as I parked my wheelchair beside the bed and locked the brake. "They've got good live music."

"That sounds fun. Do I have time to change?"

I eased up onto the bed, sat against the headboard, and laced my hands behind my neck. "Yeah."

Brooke was bent over, digging through her bag. She looked up and raised an eyebrow. A sly smirk slid across her face. "And you're just going to watch?"

I licked my lips. "You gonna give me a show?"

Her cheeks flushed a sunset pink. Brooke bit her lip as she unbuttoned her shorts, unzipped them, and wiggled them off her hips.

I adjusted my cock as I looked at the pair of light blue panties that barely covered her ass. "Goddamn, you're a sexy little firecracker. Keep going."

Brooke lifted her loose tank top over her head and tossed it into her bag. The bra she wore had been teasing me through the low-cut arms of her tank top during the drive out here.

"You look good in lace, baby girl. Hands behind your back. Let me see you."

She looked bashful, tipping her head to the side and rocking her shoulders back and forth as I enjoyed her breasts.

I patted my thigh. "Come here, pretty girl."

Brooke hurried to the edge of the bed, then slowed. The mattress sank as she crawled up, prowling toward me. Her tits hung heavy in front of me, cradled by the lace.

I could still smell her shampoo—floral and light. It made my dick stand at attention.

She straddled me, smoothing her hands down my chest. I reached up and found the elastic she used to tie her hair up. My blood pressure started to simmer when I couldn't get a grip on it after three tries, but Brooke paid my frustration no mind.

Her mouth was warm and soft against my throat as she kissed up to my jaw. Her soft pants against my skin made my cock rock hard. Finally, I got my finger around the elastic and pulled it out.

I dug my hands into her hair and brought her mouth to mine. Brooke let out a soft sigh and melted against my chest. I kept one hand in her hair and palmed her ass with the other. She slid her tongue into my mouth, letting desperate, depraved sounds float between us.

A whimper escaped her lips when I pulled her bra straps off her shoulders and flipped the cups down. I pulled a pebbled nipple into my mouth and sucked.

Brooke threw her head back and moaned. "Oh god, yes—Ray—" She gasped as I teased her pussy through her panties. "Make me come."

I chuckled and released her tit. "It's funny that you think you call the shots around here." I cupped her cheek and wiped the sheen of saliva off of her lips with my thumb. "Now get dressed."

The lips that had been praying my name turned to a frown. "But—" She sunk down and rolled her hips, teasing my cock with her pussy.

"We'll finish this tonight. Maybe I want to watch you listening to the band, drinking a beer, and know you're already wet for me."

Brooke bit my lower lip and sucked on it, teasing me as she worked herself against my dick. "You're mean."

She had the words, but didn't have the music.

I cupped her pussy to stop her from edging any closer to an orgasm. "And if you come right now, I won't let you come for a week."

∼

Brooke grumbled under her breath as she followed my directions to The Silver Spur. Watching her get ready had been a bigger tease than making out. It was as if she was trying to get in my head by deciding she wanted a different bra and pair of panties.

Watching her strip down was a tease; seeing her get dressed was agony.

I let my gaze wander over the shredded denim shorts and busty tank top she was wearing. The front was low, the sides were missing, and the back started and ended at her waist.

It was going to be a long few hours of keeping my hands mostly to myself, but the idea of hanging out at a bar for a few hours and watching a set wasn't half bad.

It felt... normal.

Brooke pulled into the parking lot and turned off the engine. "Do you know the layout inside?"

I wracked my brain. "It's been a few years since I've been here, but it's pretty tight. Lots of tables. I think they have a ramp in the back."

Her pretty features twisted into a look of disgust. "That's ridiculous."

I shrugged. "It is what it is."

"Want me to go scope it out and grab a table?" she offered as she unbuckled her seatbelt.

I opened my door. "Nah. Let's just bite the bullet together."

I waited until she pulled my wheelchair out of the truck bed before I spoke up again. "Besides, you in those shorts? No way in hell I'm letting you walk in there alone."

Brooke blushed. "Sounds like you're staking your claim."

I settled into my chair and slid my hand up the back of her thigh, squeezing her ass. "Yes, ma'am."

I clenched my teeth as she helped me navigate the wheelchair over the lip of the sidewalk, but tried my best not to snap at her.

While Brooke got carded at the door, I peered inside and planned my path. It was crowded, but not too packed. We made it inside just as the dinner rush began, seconds before it became wall-to-wall with people.

"This place is such a vibe," Brooke said as she walked behind me, taking in the neon signs, stage, and mechanical bull. "I'm obsessed. Do you know the band?"

"No," I said as I spotted an empty high-top table. "I need a hand."

Brooke's palm felt soft as she slid it into mine and helped me up. I grabbed the edge of the table and stretched to my full height before settling backwards onto the tall chair. She folded up my wheelchair and stowed it between my seat and the table, keeping it out of the way until I needed it.

I'd probably stay in this seat all night, but it felt good. Normal. Something I hadn't felt in a while.

"I'm gonna grab some drinks," Brooke said before heading to the bar.

From the high-top, I had a clear view over the heads of the bar patrons. I could watch people play pool and darts. I watched the musicians fiddling with the amps and instruments on stage. A woman was at the padded ring where the mechanical bull was set up, sweeping and making sure it was clean.

A lump formed in my throat. The old me used to love coming here when I was nearby and had time off.

"Excuse me," a feminine voice said, but it wasn't Brooke's.

I looked over my shoulder at the redhead who was

hanging off the back of my seat. She had big green eyes, a blinding smile, and something mischievous in her gaze.

Her tone was sugar-sweet as she laid a manicured hand on my thigh. "This is going to make me sound crazy if I'm wrong, but are you Ray Griffith?"

Her serpentine posture made it very clear that she knew exactly who I was.

I kept my eyes on Brooke. Her back was arched as she leaned on the bartop, waiting for our drinks.

"I used to be."

She slinked closer. "The tattoos give it away. I watched your last ride in Houston. I've always been a big rodeo girl. What are you doing these days?"

Brooke's hips swung as she grabbed two beers from the bartender and elbowed her way back to the table.

The redhead looked Brooke up and down when she sidled up to the table and placed a beer in front of me. "Still pulling buckle bunnies, I see..."

I was about to tell the woman to get lost when Brooke's smile lit up the room. "Oh my god. You're the sweetest. Thank you."

The woman sneered. "That wasn't a compliment, honey."

"Oh?" Brooke plucked the woman's hand off my thigh, promptly removing it before coming to stand between my parted knees. "Because it sounded like you think I'm hotter than you are. So, yeah. If being hot and getting laid by a bull rider who fucks like a god makes me a buckle bunny, then give me a belt and some rabbit ears, sweetie."

I... I had hallucinated that, right?

Brooke slid her hands up my chest and draped her arms around my neck. She looked over her shoulder at the gaping redhead. "Feel free to pick your jaw up and leave when you're done staring at my ass."

And with that, she tilted her head to the side and kissed me as she raked her hands through my hair.

I barely noticed the woman stomping off. "You are something else," I murmured against Brooke's mouth before going in for another kiss.

Her grin was feline. "No one touches my man."

It had been a while since I'd fallen. But this time, I didn't mind. My gait and stability were no match for Brooke. Because just like that, I fell.

22

BROOKE

The band was incredible. The beer was half-decent. The food was great. The company was bar-none.

I stood between Ray's knees with my bottle in the air, screaming the words to an old Travis Tritt song. His hands were warm and strong against my waist as he moved with me.

Ray looked absolutely sinful in a tight black t-shirt, jeans, and cowboy boots. He usually wore sneakers, but the boots did something to me. It was like seeing him in his natural habitat.

"You gonna get another drink?" he asked when I finished off my beer.

I shook my head. "No," I shouted over the band. "Just one for me so I can drive us back to the motel. Do you want another one?"

"Nah. I shouldn't drink that much with my meds."

As great as the band was, I was still unfairly horny from him teasing me before we left for the bar. "Do you want to go?"

He smirked. "Not yet. I like watching you."

I leaned up on my tiptoes. "You could watch me naked back in the room."

Fingers slid across my bare midriff and ghosted over my sides. "I like watching you here."

The lead singer on stage announced they'd be taking a break, and the lights switched over to the padded ring where a mechanical bull sat in the middle. I felt Ray stiffen behind me.

"You sure you want to stay?"

"I'm fine," he grunted.

I didn't quite believe it, but I didn't have the right to argue with him either. If he was fine with watching some mechanical bull riding, then I had to trust that he was.

I leaned backward, and Ray slid his arms around me. "Did you ever ride mechanical bulls or just the real ones?"

He chuckled. "Only when I was really, really drunk."

I laughed. "I get the feeling you were the wild child of the Griffith brothers."

"I used to be."

"Is it different? Riding a machine rather than an animal?"

"Yeah. Same mechanics. Different applications. Different stakes." His mouth grazed my ear. "But, uh... bull riding here is a little different."

"What do you—"

One of the bartenders had grabbed the microphone, drawing everyone's attention to the ring. A silhouette sat on top of the mechanical bull. Her head was tipped back with long hair spilling down her spine.

Spotlights danced over the rider's body. Slowly, they focused on her as the music grew, and the bull started to rock.

"Oh my god," I whispered. "She's hot."

Ray chuckled from behind me. "Topless bull riding is a tradition around here. It's been going on for decades."

That's when I realized there was nothing but a thong beneath her chaps. Her ass and tits bounced with each swing of the bull. Her chest was mostly hidden—for now—beneath an open leather vest.

"You mean she's going to—"

Ray's hands were steady as he skated them down my arms and laced our fingers together. "We can go if you want."

I whipped around. "Are you kidding? I want to watch."

"You sure, baby?"

I was fairly sure I nodded, but my focus was fixed on the rider. She grabbed a rope hanging from the ceiling and pulled herself up to stand on top of the bull, skillfully surfing it as it rocked and spun. She shook her ass as people cheered and made it rain dollar bills.

"She's so good." I gasped when the bull slowed and she did a backflip.

Her boots slammed into the back of the bull, and she dropped down to straddle it again. The bar erupted with applause when the vest fell open and her breasts bounced free.

"How does she stay on like that?" I asked when the woman operating the control panel made the bull whip around, changing its direction halfway through the turn.

Ray wrapped his hands around my waist and gently lifted me, placing me on his lap. "Close your eyes."

I let the music and the feeling of his chest against my back transport me away from the chaos and cheers.

Two fingers ran down my spine. "Focus right here." He trailed them across the back of my hips. "And right here. Move them in two different directions. Your hips go with the bull. Lean into the tilt. Your spine and shoulders counterbalance it."

His hands wrapped around my thighs, gently parting my legs. Heat surged down my spine and pooled in my core.

"Tight legs. Loose hips." He slid his hands down the inside of my thighs. "Tighten these muscles right here."

I clenched, feeling his hand slide higher and higher up my thighs.

My lips parted, and I tilted my head back against his shoulder. Ray placed a hand across my stomach, pressing me against his chest as his fingers grazed along the thin fabric between my legs.

I sucked in a sharp breath.

"Right here," he murmured, his thumb pressing into the crease of my thigh and pelvis. "That's where you squeeze the hardest. Your knees and your adductor muscles."

"How does this not turn you on?" I whimpered. It felt like we had gone through hours of foreplay, but all he had done was point out muscle groups.

Ray's chuckle was dark. "It's a little more sobering when there's a two-thousand-pound animal under your ass trying to kill you."

"It feels like you're trying to kill me," I gasped when he pulled me back further, pressing his erection into my backside.

His mouth was warm on the back of my neck. "Does watching her ride that bull turn you on, baby girl?"

I nodded. Each press and suck of his mouth against my neck made me tumble further and further down the rabbit hole. I was three sheets to the wind, drunk on lust.

I rocked my ass against his cock.

Ray chuckled. "You enjoy putting on a show, don't you?"

I nodded. "I want you to see me."

He cupped my jaw and turned my face, leaning in to brush his lips against mine. "You're pure sunshine. There's no way I could miss you."

The crowd erupted in applause as the rider finished her performance."Let's hear it for Jo Reed!" the bartender announced into the microphone.

My vision was blurred as Ray pulled away from the kiss so we could clap for her.

"The ring is open. Automatic cash prize if you last more than thirty seconds, and a generous crowd ready to tip for a good show, if you catch my drift."

I chewed on my lip and peered at the empty ring.

"You gonna try it?" Ray asked, running his hands up and down my legs.

I wanted to. It looked so exhilarating and carefree. I'd never tried anything like it before. The way Jo—the first rider—looked when she was up there was something I wanted.

To feel powerful.

"I'd probably fall off," I said.

"I think you want to," he murmured. "I can watch you from here."

"I can't do backflips. I'd break my neck."

Ray chuckled. "Yeah, I don't recommend breaking your neck. It sucks." His stubble brushed against my skin as he kissed behind my ear. "But if you want to try, there's nothing stopping you."

"You're okay with me taking my top off in front of a crowd of strangers?"

"I'm fine with you doing whatever makes you happy. Life is short. Shake your tits and have a good time."

I leaned into him, soaking up his strength.

"Can I give you a piece of advice?" he murmured. "Don't count. Just breathe."

My body felt numb as I pushed my way through the crowd and flagged down the bartender. She whisked me into a back room where Jo, the girl who had ridden first, helped me put on a pair of chaps. I looked over my shoulder at the mirror on the wall and studied the way my butt peeked out of the assless chaps.

"Oh my god, you have an amazing body. You're gonna kill it out there."

I pressed my hand against my bra. "I feel like I'm going to throw up."

She grimaced. "You haven't had a lot to drink, have you? If you vomit on the mats, you'll have to clean it up."

"Just a beer."

"That's perfect. A little buzz is good. Tequila shots, not so much."

"Solid life advice."

"You gonna show your tits or keep your bra on?" Jo asked as she held out the vest.

I looked at the vest. "What would you do?"

She tossed her hair over her shoulder. "I pay my bills this way. There's no shame in going all the way or just dipping your toes in the water. It's your body, your decision."

Fuck it.

I pulled my bra off and slipped my arms into the vest. "Let's do this."

"Hell yeah!"

Jo led me through the narrow corridor. The bar noise grew the closer we got to the ring. "Is that your man over there?" she asked as she pointed to Ray.

My body was electric with nerves. "Yeah."

She smirked. "I'll get Jenny to give you a good song to drive him crazy. Good luck out there."

And just like that, I was on my own.

My heart was in my throat. Blood rushed in my ears, drowning out the roar of the crowd. Was this what Ray felt every time he got on the back of a bull?

It was terrifying and exhilarating all at once.

Sure, he did it fully clothed. But he also performed in front of arenas packed with thousands of people.

Holy shit. He was so brave.

Somehow, I managed to get up onto the back of the mechanical bull. But when I looked up, I couldn't find Ray in the crowd.

A sharp whistle pierced the air. I looked over and gasped. Ray was leaning against the side of the ring. His knuckles were white as he held on. A man in a cowboy hat carried a tall chair over so he could sit.

"Don't worry," Jo said from the controls as she stood beside Jenny. "Ryman's got your boy." She winked. "Give him a show."

Spotlights swirled around, and the music started. I tried to copy what Jo had done, pushing my ass out and arching my back, but it felt awkward and disjointed.

I closed my eyes as the bull spun, squeezing hard with my legs.

It was like I could feel Ray's hands holding me to the machine. His thumbs pressing into my spine, telling me to separate it from my hips in my mind.

Cool air danced across my chest, and the bar cheered.

Oh my god. They could totally see my boobs.

I caught Ray's eyes when the bull turned and shuddered. I slid down the front with my ass in the air and held on tight as it shook back and forth. I recognized that whistle and holler. It was Ray's.

It made me sit taller. Swing my hips more. Smile brighter. Throw my head back and laugh.

I wanted his gaze. I wanted his approval. I wanted him. All of him.

Somehow, I managed thirty seconds on the back of the bull before I was flung off. I landed in a pile of limbs and leather against the padded wall where Ray was seated.

"Brooke!" Worry and panic raged in my name as he leaned over the partition. "Baby, are you okay? Look at me. Are you hurt?"

I laughed, rolling onto my back and holding the vest closed. "I'm so good."

I opened my eyes and watched the storm clouds break in his gaze. Ray let out a scared breath. "Fuckin' terrified me," he said quietly.

I scrambled up to my feet and pressed a kiss to his mouth. "How'd I do, champ?"

He reached over the wall and palmed my ass as he kissed me. "Like a firecracker, baby."

Ray was waiting for me at the table when I came out of the dressing room with my clothes back on.

A thick white envelope was in his hand. "Looks like everyone else thought you were a star too."

I laughed as I peeked inside, then almost choked at the stack of bills. "Damn."

"You want to hang out and watch the band?"

I let out a heavy sigh. "Honestly, I'd rather get out of here."

Ray kissed me long and hard. "I was hoping you'd say that."

I hadn't started a tab, so we gathered our things and

headed out to the truck. I was grateful that the drive back to the motel was short.

The motel room door slammed like a bomb exploding. The deadbolt echoed like a gunshot. I froze, knowing Ray was behind me.

"I don't think I'll ever forget seeing your ass in those chaps..." The footrests on his chair knocked against the back of my ankles. "Shorts off," he said.

"Are we finally going to finish what we started?"

"Are you going to stop talking back to me and do as you're told?"

I shimmied my shorts off, standing in front of him in my panties and tank top.

"That's my good girl," he murmured as he tugged my underwear down to my knees. "Bra off and touch your toes."

I yanked my shirt and bra over my head and slowly bent over. It was like an unseen force took over my body when he spoke to me in that deep, gruff voice.

It felt like being hypnotized. Out of control, yet desperate.

"Already wet or still wet?" he asked as he slid a finger through my pussy.

"Still," I whispered. "Still wet."

"Poor thing," he said with a depraved chuckle. "It's been hours."

I shook my head. "It's been weeks."

"Weeks, huh?" Ray slid two fingers inside me. "Sounds like I need to take care of some business, then."

"Please," I begged. My back ached and my arms trembled. "Please."

He curled his fingers, stroking inside me. "I loved watching you ride that bull. Did it make you wet? I liked knowing all those people were watching my girl. Knowing every single one of them wanted what only I get to touch."

"Yes," I rasped.

"You're gonna get on that bed and ride me, baby girl. It's time for my show."

I scrambled onto the mattress while Ray got undressed and settled against the headboard.

His cock was thick. An angry, swollen color flooded the head as he stroked it.

I crawled toward him, moving up his body. My slit grazed his shaft as I straddled him.

"Is this what you've been missing?" he murmured against my chest. "My cock in your pussy?"

I nodded.

"Go on then. Drop down on me. Let me feel how tight you are. How ready you are."

I dug my fingers in his thick hair, holding his head against my breast as he sucked and bit my nipple. With each pull of his mouth, I sank further and further onto his cock.

It was only when I was fully seated with him inside me that I took a breath.

He laid back, allowing me to brace against his chest as I eased off him, then slammed back down.

I gasped for air. After what felt like ages of foreplay, I needed it rough. "*Please, daddy*," I begged. "Fuck me hard."

His eyes flared and darkened as he growled, his fingers digging into my skin. "Say that again."

"Fuck—"

"No. Say *all* of it."

I gasped as he teased my clit. Whimpering, I choked out, "P-Please fuck me, daddy."

Ray pulled his hips back into the bed, then thrust into

me. My tits hung in front of his face, brushing against his cheek with each push.

"This is heaven, baby girl. You're my heaven," he grunted, using his other hand to play with my clit.

I wanted to live between his arms. I wanted to be consumed by him.

Fire raged inside of me, flashing like bolts of lightning with each touch of his hand, each push of his cock, each pull from his mouth.

"Ray," I keened when he grabbed my hips, holding me against him as he slammed inside of me, grinding our bodies together. "I-I can't stop it. I need to—"

I couldn't get the words out before my world shattered.

Strong arms caught me as I collapsed. Warmth flooded my core as he shuddered, coming violently inside of me.

Ray pressed his lips to my temple. "How was that?"

Our chests stuck together, fused by sweat, adrenaline, and comfort. "Like I'd wait lifetimes for you, if only to find you once."

23

RAY

"Morning, beautiful," I murmured, tipping my chin down and pressing a kiss to the top of Brooke's head.

She yawned and burrowed into my side. "Is it morning already?"

I chuckled. "It was morning when we went to bed."

"That's your fault," she mumbled into my chest. Her brows creased. Morning was the only time Brooke was remotely unpleasant. Even then, she wasn't ill-tempered. It just took her more than a few minutes to wake up.

It was pretty fucking cute.

"Pretty sure you were the one begging me to keep going," I said, slipping my hand up the shirt she had stolen from my bag to sleep in. I grazed her ribs. "Something like, *'Please, daddy, fuck me harder.'*"

I chuckled as she groaned and buried her face in the covers.

"Oh, God."

"Yeah, you said that too. A lot."

"Stop teasing me. People say way weirder stuff than that during sex."

I brushed her hair away from her face and peeled the covers back so she couldn't hide from me. "Hey, you don't have to be embarrassed around me. Okay? I liked it—a lot. You liked it. What's there to be bashful about?"

Her eyelids fluttered shut. "Promise?"

I pressed a kiss to her forehead. "Promise."

We dragged ourselves out of bed, packed up, and loaded into the truck for the drive back to the ranch. It wasn't until Brooke pulled the truck through the property gates that I let go of her hand.

"So, did you have fun?" she asked, turning down the dirt road that circled the barns.

"Yeah. I, uh... I did."

Brooke beamed, and damn it—I grinned back.

"Thanks for suggesting it," I said. "It's not something I've really thought about since I came back here. Leaving, I mean."

Her smile was infectious. "It's kinda lame to do a spontaneous trip by yourself. Way better with a friend."

Something stung me when she said that. Brooke wasn't my friend. I didn't want her to be.

As much as I wanted to force myself to believe that I didn't want more, I wanted more.

But wants and wishes didn't miraculously give me more to give her.

A figure was sitting on my front steps when Brooke pulled through my grove of trees.

Her smile grew. "I haven't seen your mom in forever."

Sure enough, my mom sat on the front steps, holding a pan covered in tin foil.

She stood when Brooke parked the truck and hopped out. Instead of getting out, I sat and watched.

Brooke threw her arms around my mom and gave her the biggest, tightest hug. My mom's eyes crinkled at the corners as she hugged her back. Brooke hurried back to the bed of the truck to get my wheelchair out. I popped my door open and lowered down.

"Hey, mom," I said, releasing the brake and pushing the wheels backward to shut the truck door.

She dabbed her eyes on the shoulder of her t-shirt. "Hey, honey." A heavy breath escaped her lungs. "Wow. I haven't ever seen you get out of a car that fast. You're looking good."

"I'll let y'all catch up," Brooke said, grabbing our overnight bags out of the back.

"Here, sweetheart," Mom said to Brooke. "I started baking and just couldn't stop. Thought you all might enjoy some banana bread."

Brooke peeked under the foil. "Oh my god, this looks amazing. Can you teach me how to make it?"

Mom's cheeks turned pink. "Well, of course. Just come up to the house anytime. I'd love to spend some time with you."

Brooke threw her arms around my mom's shoulders again. "Thanks, Momma. I can't wait!"

Mom gave me a pleased smile and a knowing look as Brooke made her way up the ramp with our things.

"Seems like you two are getting along." She glanced over her shoulder. "I like her. I hope she sticks around."

Yeah, I did too.

"Where were you two off to?" She checked the time. "I thought you'd be home since you don't have PT until this afternoon."

I rubbed the back of my neck. "We, uh... We got out of town for the night. Went to see a band play in Maren."

Worry flashed across her face, but it quickly turned into surprise. "Oh. Well, that's good. I'm glad you got out and had some fun." She squeezed my shoulder. "And Brooke was with you?"

I looked at the sky and let out a wry laugh. "Don't overthink it, momma."

"I'm not overthinking anything." She smirked and raised her hands in defense. "It's written in plain ink, honey."

"Momma—"

She chuckled and patted my shoulder. "Holler if you need anything."

I opened my mouth, but froze when I heard Brooke call out.

"Ray?" Panic flooded her voice. I had never heard her sound scared before.

I turned around and rushed up the ramp like my wheels were on fire. Mom's footsteps thumped up the wooden slats behind me. As soon as I rolled over the threshold, I stopped and looked around.

Brooke stood frozen in the kitchen. My house was in shambles.

Cabinets were open. Couch cushions were askew. Every bedroom and closet door was wide open. Dresser drawers were pulled out.

The strange thing was that my TV was still mounted to the wall and my laptop was sitting on the coffee table, right out in the open.

There were no signs of forced entry. Then again, I couldn't remember if I had locked the door.

I had stopped locking up when people stopped dropping by unannounced, thanks to Brooke. Frankly, nobody on the ranch bothered to lock anything. Not houses. Not vehicles. Not sheds or warehouses.

But we were entering a different era. It wasn't just our family and ranch hands on this land anymore. There were droves of people coming in and out of the gates every day to work on the revitalization projects.

If it wasn't construction crews, it was the renewable energy company or cell company leasing part of the land. If it wasn't them, it was investors, inspectors, and nosy folks.

We had fences surrounding the property, but they were meant to keep cattle in, not to keep people out.

"Don't touch anything," I said as I came up behind her, taking the banana bread out of Brooke's hands and setting it on the kitchen counter. "Come on."

Our overnight bags landed with a thump.

"I'm calling the police," Mom said from the door.

I steered with one hand, keeping the other on the small of Brooke's back, leading her out to the deck.

"Breathe," I said to Brooke while half-listening to my mom on her cell phone.

Brooke nodded, but she was still shaken.

"Hey," I said, pulling her down onto my lap. "You're okay. I'm okay. It's creepy as fuck, but we're fine. It's probably good that we were gone."

Brooke swallowed and stammered until she finally found her words. "You brought your pill organizer to the motel, not the prescription bottles, right?"

I cocked my head. "Right..."

She let out a shaken breath. "The prescription bottles you keep on the kitchen counter are gone."

I froze. "What?"

Brooke nodded. "All of them."

Some of the pills I kept on hand wouldn't be worth much, but there were a few narcotics that would probably fetch a good price on the street. And those had just been refilled.

"Okay."

"It-it's not," she whimpered.

I cupped her cheeks. "Baby, breathe for me. It's fine. I'll call the doc and get him to send in new prescriptions. The cops will come out and check it out and write up a report. We'll start locking up, and I'll order one of those doorbell cameras. It's going to be okay."

"Drugs going missing... I could lose my job," she whispered.

"They didn't go missing. They were stolen. A police report will prove that. Besides, you were with me the whole time, and there's a lot of witnesses who can place you at the bar—"

"—Yeah, riding a fucking bull with my tits out in front of my boss before we went back to a motel and fucked like rabbits," she hissed.

I grinned. "It was a pretty great night."

Brooke was grinding her teeth down to nothing, so I wrapped my arms around her and let her tuck her head into my shoulder.

"You're not getting fired today, Sunnyside," I murmured as I rubbed her back.

Brooke leaned back and wiped her eyes as she crawled off my lap. "Sorry. I probably shouldn't have done that in front of your mom."

"She knows."

"I'm sorry—she knows *what*?"

I shrugged. "Momma knows everything."

It wasn't long before cop cars flooded the ranch. Half of

the officers combed through my house, while the other half questioned every living being on the ranch.

I wasn't surprised when my brothers and their women showed up on my lawn. Blue lights had a way of doing that.

Brooke and I were sitting on the deck, finishing up talking to an officer when Christian burst through the back door. "Y'all alright?"

I kept my hand on Brooke's back. "We're fine. You didn't have to come down here." I could hear Cassandra yelling at people from inside my house. I sighed. "Tell her to leave the cops alone."

Christian chuckled. "You tell her."

"Hell no. I'm not stupid."

His gaze shifted to Brooke. "You okay, sweetheart?"

Brooke leaned closer into my arm. "Just fine. Thanks."

For Brooke to say she was 'fine' was a red flag. Not once in her life had she ever been fine. 'Fine' for her was probably close to rock bottom.

"Uncle Ray!" Gracie, Christian's youngest, darted through the house and threw her arms around me.

Tears welled up in my eyes.

I'd been a dick to them after my accident, and I knew I had some groveling to do. But honestly, I didn't even know where to start.

"Hey, squirt." I squeezed her tight. "You came all the way down here just to see me?"

Gracie wiped her eyes. She looked so much older. Like a young lady, rather than the kid I remembered. "We came to see you a lot. You wouldn't let us in."

I sighed. "I know, kid. I'm sorry."

She hugged me again. "Can we hang out when the cops are done?"

I glanced at the time. "I've gotta head into town for physical therapy in a little bit. But how about you and Bree come down tomorrow? I'll be here all day."

Gracie chewed on her lip. "I don't know if Bree wants to."

I peered through the open sliding glass door and spotted Bree pressed to Cassandra's side as they talked to my mom. "I've got some apologizing to do, don't I?"

Gracie nodded. "Yeah. You should probably apologize with presents."

I chuckled. "You got it, munchkin."

She rolled her eyes. "I'm thirteen."

"Yeah, I need to yell at your management. I specifically told them not to let you become a teenager."

Gracie hitched her thumb over her shoulder at Christian and Cassandra. "You'll have to take it up with dad and my evil stepmother."

Nate, Becks, and their toddler, Charlotte, arrived on my deck.

"Have you seen the tire swing your Uncle Ray put up?" Brooke asked Gracie.

"No?" Gracie popped up on her tiptoes, then smiled. "Can it hold me?"

I chuckled. "Your dad gave it a test ride. Go crazy."

"I'll go with you," Brooke said to Gracie. "I love tire swings."

Bree slipped out the sliding door and hurried past me without so much as a hello before joining Gracie and Brooke at the tire swing. Charlotte had wiggled out of Becks's arms and waddled over to her cousins.

I watched as Charlotte reached up to Brooke with gimme-hands. Brooke scooped her up and propped her on her hip while Gracie jumped on the tire swing.

My heart knotted in my chest. Goddamn, she looked so natural at it.

"I know that look," Nate said as he and Becks settled in the chairs across from me.

I pulled my attention away from Brooke. "Shut up."

"Oh good. We're teasing Ray about his little crush. I thought I was going to have to be the one to bring it up," Cassandra said as she stepped out to join the group.

"Are you done harassing public servants?" I asked.

Christian chuckled.

CJ joined us on the deck. "What the hell happened?"

"Someone broke into my house and stole my pills. We think it was Brooke's roommate."

CJ cracked his knuckles and turned to head out. "Give me an hour."

Christian grabbed the back of his collar and forced him to stay put. "Don't go and do something stupid just because you're itching to punch someone. You don't get to lose your shit."

CJ was seething. I could see it in his eyes.

Where Christian and I shared our dad's dark hair and eyes, Nate and CJ favored our mom. Unfortunately, Christian was the only one out of the four of us who had a lick of their patience. That usually meant he was the one keeping the three of us out of trouble.

Cassandra looked around. "Well? Are you going to tell me their names or not? I'll have this wrapped up before the cops can get off the property."

I huffed. "Let the fucking cops do their job. Jesus, you people are insane. Between you and CJ, people are starting to think we're the cowboy mafia or some shit. I'm fine. Brooke's fine. She's a little shaken up, but fine. Nothing else was taken. We weren't even here when it happened."

"Yeah, let's talk about that," Becks said with a nefarious grin.

"Let's not," I countered. "You're a journalist. I'm not talking to you."

Becks scoffed. "You guys are no fun. Who told you not to talk to journalists?"

"A really annoying publicist who likes to show up in my kitchen and throw mail at me."

Cassandra smirked.

"Seriously. Where'd you guys go?" Becks asked. "I saw your truck leave yesterday and didn't think anything of it until you didn't come back."

I knew they wouldn't leave it alone, so I decided to throw them a bone. "Got out of town for a change of scenery. Went out to that bar in Maren and listened to some music."

"Wait." CJ's eyes lifted to Brooke, who was now on the tire swing with Charlotte safely perched between her legs. "You took her to The Silver Spur?"

"Get that picture out of your mind before I beat it out of you," I growled.

CJ raised his hands in surrender.

Nate and Christian tried to hide their guilty smirks. Before Cassandra knocked Christian on his ass, he made plenty of trips out there to blow off some steam. Nate, not so much. But he knew what went on at the bar.

Becks and Cass exchanged a look that was loaded with telepathic thoughts.

I hated that.

"Whatever you two are thinking, stop," I said.

Becks looked innocent. "I have no idea what you're talking about."

Cassandra inspected her manicure. "We're gonna kidnap your girlfriend this weekend. Deal with it."

"Leave her alone."

"Saturdays are her day off, right?" Becks said with a smirk.

"Yeah," Cassandra chimed in. "You can deal with not fucking your employee for a few hours."

Christian broke out into an involuntary cough to hide his discomfort.

Nate pointed between Chris and me. "Pot, let me introduce you to kettle."

I pointed at him. "You fucked Becks when you were deployed. Together."

Becks pointed back at me. "Technically, I didn't work for Nathan. We were embedded together. Not deployed together."

"Am I the only one not fucking someone I work with?" CJ asked.

"You work with cattle. I'd be concerned if you were fucking them," Cassandra said.

"Glad you're fine. I need to get laid," CJ grumbled as he stomped out.

Christian took a seat, and Cassandra slid onto his lap. "Did y'all have a good time?" he asked.

I was distracted by Brooke again, watching her laugh with my nieces, and barely heard him. "Yeah. It was the most normal thing I've done in a while."

As the chaos inside the house began to die down, Nate and Becks declared it to be Charlotte's nap time and headed back to their house.

Christian looked like he had the weight of the world on his shoulders. Fortunately for him, he was about to marry a woman who had no problem relieving him of that burden.

Cassandra got straight to the point. "Have you thought about what's next? Or are you just going to keep her trapped in your house like Belle?"

Christian raised an eyebrow at her.

"What?" she snapped. "The girls and I had a movie marathon. We watched the classics." She huffed and turned back to me. "When you want to discuss your offers, come down to the office and we'll have a chat."

That made me pause. Marty hadn't mentioned anything about offers. Then again, I hadn't exchanged more than a few sentences with my old manager since I told him I didn't need him anymore.

"What offers?"

Cassandra let out a bitter laugh. "You really don't know? I've been fielding phone calls and emails every day. Teams wanting you to coach other bull riders. Companies wanting you to be the face of their brands. Some public speaking gigs. A docu-series. Interviews. A book deal. You name it. Since you broke up with Marty, they've been flooding the ranch's inbox and answering machine."

I couldn't wrap my head around it. "And... You didn't tell me earlier because...?"

Cassandra leaned forward. "Rebranding means pivoting. It means going from what you were to who you are now. But that's not what you have to do. You have to build something new from the ground up. We're revitalizing the ranch. Honoring the past and confidently moving into the future with new ventures. And when you're ready, you get to do the same. You just have to decide what it looks like."

24

BROOKE

Three pairs of eyes stared at me from across the table. Their gazes made me hesitant to reach for the shared basket of chips and bowl of salsa.

Becks had a mostly pleasant smile on her face, but it could have been fake. She was accustomed to faking it on TV. Cassandra didn't bother putting on a polite smile. She seemed to be contemplating whether I was small enough for her to dig a hole by hand to bury me in, or if she'd have to borrow a backhoe from the ranch.

Charlotte—or Charlie as most people called her—was unusually quiet for a toddler.

Becks nudged Cassandra. "Well?"

"Well, what? What do I do with her? Can she even drink?"

Becks laughed. "You hang out with Bree and Gracie all the time."

"I'm used to them!" Cassandra said.

"And of course she can drink," Becks said, then paused. "Wait. You can drink, right? We usually have margaritas and talk shit."

"I can drink," I squeaked.

"See?" Becks said. "Ray wouldn't... whatever you guys are doing with someone that young."

Cassandra let out a relieved sigh and gestured to the waiter. "I'm going to need tequila to get through this lunch."

We filled the uncomfortable silence by munching on warm tortilla chips while the waiter took our orders. Charlotte had found the perfect triangle chip, then proceeded to smash it to smithereens as she let out a mischievous giggle.

Finally, margaritas were doled out to each of us. Cassandra grabbed hers and sucked down half of it.

"Dramatic much?" Becks said, licking the salt rim and taking a sip.

"You know I don't like people," Cassandra said.

I wished I could disappear into the vinyl booth. The music playing overhead felt far too cheerful for the level of awkwardness I felt with the two Griffith sisters.

It felt like a job interview that I was woefully unprepared for.

Becks and Cassandra were stunning and sophisticated and mature and everything that I wasn't.

Hell, Becks was probably old enough to be my mom. Or at least close to it.

"Just ask her a question to get to know her," Becks said as if I wasn't sitting across from them. "Start with something easy. That's what I do when I'm interviewing people."

Cassandra took another sip. "So, are you fucking Ray?"

Becks choked on her chip. "Not that!"

"Well! You said to ask a question."

Becks rolled her eyes. "Yeah, but we already know they're sleeping together."

I had just taken a long drink of my margarita and

choked. I sputtered into my napkin as the tequila and salt burned my throat.

"Great," Cassandra deadpanned. "We took her out once and killed her. Ray's gonna be pissed."

Charlie crawled out of her mom's lap and ran around to my side of the booth. I was grateful when she climbed into my lap and giggled. I loved spending time with kids. They weren't judgmental.

Cassandra leaned back in the booth. "Alright, little miss fairytale princess who loves children and talks to animals, what's your deal?"

Becks giggled. "I think that's just called being a normal person."

"My deal?" I squeaked.

"Yeah," Cass said. "How'd you turn Ray from the beast in the castle to a normal person who voluntarily socializes?"

While I went out to lunch with Becks and Cassandra, Ray was spending his Saturday with CJ and Nate, overseeing a delivery of horses for the equine program that was coming to the ranch.

I had heard bits and pieces about it from CJ and Ray, and it sounded amazing. They would be hosting kids camps, running therapy programs, training, and boarding.

The ranch was a paradise. I loved being secluded from the world—blissfully unaware of the chaos and hustle and bustle. But I also loved watching the ranch grow and come to life with each new project development.

"I dunno," I said as I grabbed a chip and dipped it into the salsa. "We get along, I guess."

Cassandra's hand floated up and down in my direction. "I mean, you're hot. So you've got that going for you."

I choked again. "Um. I'm going to be honest, I don't

know how much I'm supposed to say. You know ... client confidentiality and all that."

Becks snickered. "Trust us. We know how to keep our mouths shut."

They exchanged a look that said as much.

Becks turned back to me. "Besides. I have a feeling you'll be sticking around. Us ranch ladies have to stick together, otherwise the testosterone will run rampant. How are things going with him?"

"Good," I evaded.

"You two went away for the weekend," Cassandra said.

"We did..." I looked around. "Am I in trouble? I've never been interrogated with margaritas before."

Becks snickered. "We're just trying to get to know you, that's all. I know I'm not around much these days since I'm traveling a lot. But it's obvious that everyone loves you. Momma Griff hasn't stopped talking about you."

Cassandra snorted, and Becks elbowed her.

"She's just jealous because everyone loves you," Becks said.

I smiled nervously at Cassandra. She was the woman around the ranch the most, so it just made sense to try and get on her good side. "Ray speaks highly of you. He told me you were the one who got him into that clinical trial."

Her eyes softened just a tad. "I know people. Sometimes it's nice to remind my contacts that I'm still waiting in the shadows and will use them when it suits me. Especially since I'm dealing with fucking horse auctions these days. I miss Manhattan."

Becks laughed.

I handed Charlie a chip and watched her munch on it with her brand new teeth. "I can't wait to see the new horses. I love going on rides with Indy and Anny."

Cassandra laughed. "You mean CJ's horse lets you get near her? That thing tried to bite me. I stay at least ten feet away from her at all times."

Becks grimaced. "Yeah. Anny hates me too."

"Really? She's a sweetie. You just have to get to know her," I said as I relaxed a little.

Cassandra snorted. "See? She's an animal-whispering fairy tale princess."

The waiter returned with our food and filled the table with plates. Charlie scurried back to her mom's lap and munched on an avocado wedge.

"And that's what happened with Ray, too?" Becks asked. "You just got to know him as well?"

I started feeling the subtle buzz of the margarita. "We have an agreement. I don't get fired, and I only help him when he asks for it. And I'm supposed to ignore him. But that didn't last long. I also kind of got lost on a walk, and CJ had to come find me, and Ray went ballistic."

Cassandra smirked. "Yeah, I heard about that. CJ told Christian. I stopped him from going to Ray's house to check on you." She pointed her fork at me. "I figured I'd let Ray have you all to himself. You're welcome."

My cheeks flushed at the memory of him telling me to take my shirt off so he could apply salve to my back and shoulders.

"Look," Becks said with a mouthful of food. "No judgment. Especially not from us. Nate and I had a fling when I was assigned to his unit in Afghanistan. Literally hooked up in his bunk. Sand everywhere."

I giggled.

Becks nodded toward Cassandra. "She started working at the ranch and hooked up with Christian. Apparently, it's a very relationship-friendly workplace. You know, the fence behind my house is still wobbly."

Cassandra didn't look up from her plate. "Huh. No idea how that happened."

Okay, maybe I shouldn't have downed an entire margarita on an empty stomach.

I shoveled a forkful of rice and beans into my mouth, attempting to soak up the alcohol. My head was spinning, but it felt nice. I loved girl talk. Being with them was fun.

"So, are you and Ray official or is it just a casual thing?" Cassandra asked. "The girls want to know if they're getting another aunt."

My stomach churned, and the margarita threatened to resurface. "I don't think it's serious."

My inebriated head swam with memories of all the "ours" that Ray had mentioned in the heat of an argument. Our dates. Our wedding. Our babies. Our life. Us.

"He's said ... things. But he's also said that he doesn't want anything serious. So, we don't really see eye-to-eye there. I guess it's just temporary."

Temporary like most things in my life.

But honestly, I was starting to tire of all the fleeting things. I had been holding on to the dream of making it to twenty-five. But what if I wanted to live in twenty-two, twenty-three, and twenty-four and truly enjoy them?

I felt like a potted plant sitting on a windowsill, waiting for brief moments of sunshine to keep me going, when all I wanted was to put down roots.

"Give it time," Cassandra said. "Ray and I usually see eye-to-eye, which means he's a stubborn asshole and takes a lot of convincing to change his mind."

"And that's what happened with you and Christian? He convinced you to stay?"

Something softened in Cassandra at the mention of his name. "Yeah, Christian and the girls did. I was ready to leave because I was scared to stay." She huffed and put on her armor of sass and sarcasm. "If it's meant to be, he'll come around. Because the alternative is him getting his way, but not having you. Sometimes being wrong feels really good."

After lunch, Becks and Cass updated me on some town gossip, shared stories about the ranch, and gave me a few tips on how to handle the Griffith brothers. Apparently Ray wasn't the only Griffith brother to have a reputation for being ornery and mule-headed.

When the drinks were empty and the chips were reduced to crumbs, we got into Becks's SUV and drove back to the ranch.

"Are you and Ray coming over to Claire's house for family dinner?" Cassandra asked from the front seat.

"Oh, I'm not sure. I'll have to see what Ray wants. He might go, but I'll probably stay back. It's my day off, and I don't want to intrude on family stuff. I'm supposed to be back at the house I rent a room in, but it's not the best place to be."

Especially since the cops couldn't pin down my roommates to question them about the break-in at Ray's house.

"Ray wasn't too thrilled about me leaving the ranch this weekend," I mentioned.

Becks grinned. "Because he's protective of you."

"I think you'll be sticking around for a lot more weekends," Cassandra said.

"I'd like to stay," I admitted as Becks maneuvered the winding dirt road. "But eventually he won't need me. Ray doesn't really rely on me anyway."

Cassandra hummed something vague under her breath and began typing a note on her phone.

"Do you want me to drop you off at Ray's house, or do you want to walk?" Becks asked.

I chose to walk. I wanted to enjoy the fresh air and sunshine. It would feel good to stretch my legs. I liked snooping around all the barns to see what the ranch hands had been working on. Lately, they had been renovating and expanding the stables to accommodate the new horses.

I waved at Gracie and Christian as they relaxed on their porch while Gracie painted her nails. I passed by the main office of the ranch and paused to hug Mickey the cow. I slipped into the stables and gave treats to Libby, Indy, and Anny.

Anarchy nuzzled her long black nose against my hand. She was a gentle giant. Fierce, sassy, and scary as hell, but soft with those she trusted.

I offered her an extra treat to stay in her good graces, then quietly left the stables to make my way back to Ray's house.

I waved at a group of ranch hands I recognized but didn't know by name.

This place felt like family.

It felt safe.

It felt like home.

25

RAY

I had just gotten out of the shower and thrown a clean pair of shorts and a shirt on when I heard the knock at the door. It wasn't Brooke. I knew that much.

She was out with Cass and Becks, and she didn't knock anyway.

I had just left CJ and Nate after the horse transport came, so I figured it wasn't them either. Christian always spent Saturdays with his daughters.

That just left my parents.

I had told my mom that Brooke and I would come up to the house for dinner tonight, so I wasn't sure why she'd be at my door just a few hours before.

"Door's unlocked," I hollered as I finished toweling off my hair and tossed it into the hamper. Maybe Brooke had forgotten to grab her keys and she was back early.

The front door opened and closed, and soft footsteps echoed in the kitchen.

It definitely wasn't the heavy boot thuds that signaled my brothers.

I turned my wheelchair and pushed out of my room and into the kitchen.

Bree, my oldest niece, stood in the kitchen with her hands clasped behind her back.

I froze.

She had completely ignored me the other day. Not that I blamed her. I was a little more than surprised to see her in my kitchen.

Bree was so grown up now. Gone was the toddler who used to only sleep if she was being held. She was a young lady and looked just like her mom. Christian's genes had surpassed her almost completely. It was like looking at a younger version of Gretchen, Christian's late wife.

"You said to come in, so I did," Bree said. There was no happy-go-lucky, giggly girl left. Her jaw was set and she looked angry.

I remembered how that anger felt. Like the world was at fault for everything. But I hadn't felt that way in a long time. I would always be angry about my accident, and I refused to feel bad about that.

But my anger towards the world had slowly dissipated ever since Brooke arrived at my house with skinned knees and a Cheshire smile.

But I had a feeling that Bree's anger wasn't directed toward the world. It was because of me.

And I deserved it.

"I'm glad you did," I said.

Her eyes darted from side to side. "Dad said I could come talk to you."

"Okay," I said as I rolled to the fridge. "Whatcha wanna talk about?" I opened the freezer and pulled out a box of popsicles.

Bree's eyebrows furrowed. "Why do you have those?"

"I asked Brooke to pick 'em up. I was hoping you'd come down to see me, and I wanted to be prepared if you did."

I pulled out two red, white, and blue layered popsicles from the box and handed them to her. "Can you take them out of the plastic for me? Kinda hard to do that these days."

Bree didn't say anything as she pinched the plastic packaging and opened it.

"What'cha wanna talk about, squirt?" I asked as we went out onto the deck.

Bree closed the sliding door behind her. "I dunno. It's been a while since I've seen you," she mumbled. Her eyes softened as she sat in the deck chair across from me and stared at her quickly melting popsicle.

I took a bite out of mine before it turned into a slushy. "Don't tell me you don't like 'em anymore. You can't be too old for popsicles."

Bree caught a drip of red syrup on her thumb and wiped it on her shorts. "After mom died, you'd always let me have a popsicle when I was sad."

"Yeah, your dad still doesn't know how much sugar I gave you two minions. So let's keep that between us."

Her eyes were watery as she looked up at me. "When I saw you on the ground in the arena, all I wanted was a popsicle. And you weren't there to give it to me."

"Bree—"

Tears streamed down her cheeks. Suddenly, she wasn't the fifteen-year-old who was learning to drive and the young lady who was rumored to have a boyfriend. She was the broken-hearted three-year-old who I'd sneak a popsicle to when she was crying for a mom who wasn't coming back.

When things returned to some version of normal after Gretchen's death, Nate came home from his deployment and I left my girls. I convinced him to keep popsicles at his house, just so the girls would know I was still thinking of them.

"Why didn't you let us see you?" she whimpered. "I ... I watched it happen. Dad wouldn't let us go to your hospital room until you woke up, and then when you did—"

"I'm sorry."

"That's not good enough!" she yelled, throwing her popsicle down on the deck slats. It broke into pieces, melting almost instantly in the mid-summer sun. "You promised to be there for us when we needed you. That we could always talk to you, even when you were on the road. And you lied."

Regret and anguish boiled inside me. It was like being thrown back into that hospital bed, unable to move. "I didn't want you to see me like that."

"I don't even know why I came down here," she muttered, storming back to the door.

"Bree, stop." I never raised my voice with Christian's daughters, but I needed her to hear me.

She froze with her hands balled in fists. "I never got to tell you about Cass. I mean *really* tell you about her. And when you moved back to the ranch, I wanted you to talk to her and Dad because there's a boy in the grade ahead of me that wants to take me on a date, but Dad won't let me because he can drive and I can't. And I wanted to sit and watch movies with you like we used to. And I wanted to color your tattoos. And I know it sounds stupid because I'm gonna be an adult in a few years, but—"

"It's not stupid," I snapped. "I missed every single one of those things too."

"Then why didn't you let us come see you?"

"Because I was stupid. Because I was a coward. Because you and Gracie have always been the most important people to me. And I mean it." I threw my popsicle down to melt beside hers. "You've always been more important to me than your dad. Than your Uncle Nate and Uncle CJ. The ranch. All of it. The only reason I ever came back was for you two. Because in some stupid way, I thought it was better for me to not be there for you at all, rather than being there as I was. As I am."

Her lip trembled. "It hurt."

"I know. And there's not much I can do to apologize and make up for it. But I'm going to try."

Bree crossed her arms. "Dad made us go to therapy when we lost Mom."

"I know. You've got a good dad."

"So, if you think you've lost yourself, then you need to go to therapy," she said. But this time, she didn't sound like a miniature version of her mom. She sounded like Cassandra.

"I go to therapy three times a week."

"Not physical therapy, smart-ass."

I let out a bark of laughter. "Excuse you, fifteen-going-on-twenty-five. Who said you're allowed to swear?"

She rolled her eyes. "It's barely a cuss word."

I sighed. "I'll think about it."

Bree's voice was soft. "If you won't do it for me, do it for Brooke."

I cocked my head. "What are you talking about?"

Bree shrugged. "You like her, don't you?"

I raked my hand through my hair, hoping it would ease some of the tension. But it didn't. 'Like' didn't even begin to cover what I felt for Brooke.

"Yeah. I do, squirt. A lot."

"She's really nice."

I nodded.

"And pretty," Bree added. "And she obviously likes you. Do it for her."

The sliding door rolled back and, speak of the devil, Brooke appeared. She was wearing a pair of short denim cut-offs and a flowing tank top that dipped between her breasts. Her hair was down in thick ringlets today. Her skin was flushed pink, probably from walking all the way from Becks's house.

"Hey, girlie," Brooke said with a smile as she wrapped her arm around Bree's shoulders and squeezed. "I didn't know I'd get to see you today." One look at the tears that were slowly drying on Bree's cheeks and Brooke's expression shifted to concern. "What's the matter?"

Bree wiped her cheeks with her fingers. "Nothing. We were just catching up."

Brooke's eyes fell on me, then on the puddle of popsicles. She lifted her eyebrows. "Okay. I see a dessert crisis. Nothing that can't be fixed. I'm sure we have more. I got, like, three or four boxes."

"It's fine." Bree wiped away the rest of her tears. "I'm not really in the mood for a popsicle anyway."

My stomach clenched.

"You sure?" Brooke asked.

"Yeah. I feel better." Bree looked at me. "Are y'all coming up to Grandma's house for supper with everyone?"

I let out a breath. "Yeah, squirt. We'll be there."

Bree said goodbye to Brooke and slipped through the house and out the front door.

"Hey, how was going out with Becks and Cass?" I asked as I wheeled over and bent down to pick up the popsicle sticks from the puddle of syrup.

Brooke let out a light laugh. "I think I got interrogated, and then I burned off my tacos and margarita with the walk back to the house. How long do we have to wait until supper?"

I chuckled and went inside with her. "Not long. What'd they interrogate you about?"

Brooke slid onto my lap and wrapped her arms around my neck. "You." Her lips still tasted like salt and tequila.

I tilted my head, diving in deeper to savor her.

She let out a soft whimper, pressing into my chest. "I tried not to tell them anything but I think Cassandra had them put double the alcohol in my drink."

"Don't be fooled by the 'mom act.' Becks is just as diabolical."

She giggled. "It was good, I think. I don't know. I don't really fit in with them."

"They knew each other before they came to the ranch. They worked together in New York. It'll just take some time."

Her crisp blue eyes turned to puddles of cerulean. "You think I have time?"

I tucked her hair behind her ear and cupped her cheek. "As much time as you want."

∼

DINNER WAS A LIVELY AFFAIR. I couldn't remember the last time I had laughed this much or felt this at ease around my family. Mom opted for burgers and fries, which was nice. It didn't require utensils or cutting, and I appreciated that.

Brooke sat to my left while Gracie sat on my right.

After our conversation this afternoon, I was hoping Bree and I would have started mending fences, but it seemed like she was keeping a safe distance for now. I knew I couldn't expect much. Still, despite our distance across the table, she talked to me and laughed at everyone's jokes.

I kept my arm around Brooke's shoulders throughout the meal. It was the best I could do to hold her close while we ate.

I had been distracted, spending time with Nate and CJ and the new horses while the girls went to lunch, but I had missed the fuck out of her.

I didn't want to let her go.

"Brooke?" Gracie asked, leaning around me to see Brooke while my mom put a giant platter of cookies in the middle of the table for dessert.

Brooke grabbed two, dropping one on my plate and one on hers. "Yes?"

"So, are you like... Uncle Ray's girlfriend? Or do you work for him? Because I just thought you worked for him."

Hushed laughter rose up from the table.

Brooke's cheeks turned bright pink. "Um—"

"Geez, you can't ask that," Bree whispered in the loudest whisper known to man. "Everyone knows it's both."

Gracie scoffed. "Well, I didn't know it was both and that's why I asked."

I rubbed my temples. Brooke held onto her cookie like it was the last life jacket on the Titanic.

"I—um—" Brooke stammered.

"Grace, that's none of your—our—business," Christian chided.

Honestly, I wanted to agree with Bree and put the debate to rest.

Brooke was both.

But that also didn't sit right with me. Part of me doubted if she would stay if she didn't have a fat paycheck dropping into her bank account every Friday.

I didn't want to believe she was with me for the money, but it had certainly started that way and I couldn't fault her for it. That was what had brought her to me to begin with.

But if I was being honest with myself, I didn't want to keep paying her to stay with me.

Brooke had said she wanted me. That she wanted to see where this spark between us would go. I didn't want to make her unemployed, but I needed to know she meant it.

I had to figure something out.

"She works for the company that we hired to send help," I said to Gracie as evenly as I could. It was as middle-of-the-road as I could make it. I didn't deny what was going on with Brooke, but I wasn't ready to officially throw our relationship into the court of public opinion.

Brooke took a sip of water and nodded slightly. "Yeah…"

The single syllable was crushed beneath the weight of her overwhelming disappointment.

Shit.

26

BROOKE

"I'm gonna change," Ray said as we caravanned into his house after dinner at Claire and Silas's house with the whole family.

It should have been a great night, and it was. For the most part, at least.

Until he confirmed the reality I was avoiding.

This was temporary.

I was just his employee.

It didn't mean anything, no matter what he said or how much I wanted my feelings to be real. No matter how much he made me believe they were real.

It was all smoke and mirrors. A convenient way for us to pass the time.

I couldn't imagine a world without Ray. Without his family. Without this place. I didn't want to.

For so long I had felt like I was drifting on the breeze, flitting and floating at the whim of the wind. Being here felt like I finally had a purpose. Like I was doing something that mattered, even if it was small.

I waited until Ray's bathroom door closed to let the first

tear slip down my cheek. I didn't want him to see me cry. It was stupid to cry over something that never was.

I scribbled out a note that I was going on a walk and left it on the kitchen counter. I was the one who was supposed to be ignoring him, but now I needed space.

Guilt chipped away at me like acid chewing through metal as my flip-flops snapped down the dirt path.

I was so stupid. I shouldn't have gotten involved with him in the first place. What did I think was going to happen? We were going to just fall into life together and live happily ever after?

Things like that didn't happen to me.

As much as I wanted to believe that good things happened to good people, it just wasn't true.

I found myself in the stables, trading my flip-flops for a pair of communal rubber boots to clean the empty stalls. I like the monotony of the tasks. It was nice to put my energy into something and see the payoff when I was done. The mostly mindless tasks gave my brain a rest.

But with that rest came the intrusive thoughts that picked away at my already fragile feelings.

Sweat beaded on my forehead as I propped the pitchfork against the wall and grabbed the broom to sweep out Anny's stall. She was grazing in a fenced area, which meant CJ would be down here sooner or later to ride her out to the herd or put her in her stall for the night.

With any luck, it would be the latter end of "sooner or later," and I could disappear after taking my frustrations out on some dirty hay and bedding.

Truck engines and ATVs rumbled in the distance. It wasn't uncommon to hear people out and about at all hours of the night.

The ranch hands worked odd hours. Because as much as the cows slept and rested, trouble didn't.

The dust and cobwebs were gone from Anarchy's stall, but the ones in my mind were thicker than ever.

I would need a good rain to get rid of those.

The coldness that chilled Ray's voice when he answered Gracie was the crack of thunder before the downpour.

Tears streamed down my cheeks in a torrent as I slid down the stall partition and sat hunched up on the swept floor.

I lost my family, but at least I slept knowing I had been wanted and loved. Life just had other plans. But this time, I couldn't work through grief by holding on to small fragments of gratitude.

He really was just tolerating me. Making the best of us being stuck together.

I shouldn't have slept with him. Every time one of his brothers or sisters-in-law teased us about hooking up, I wanted to crawl into a hole and die.

They would never respect me. Ray would never respect me. I was just a convenient piece of ass.

Heavy footsteps echoed through the barn. "Brooke?"

I didn't make a peep, but I was fairly certain my sniffles gave me away. CJ poked his head into Anny's stall and found me in a heap on the floor.

"What are you doing in my barn?" He crossed his arms and huffed. "You know, even the ranch hands don't sleep with the animals. We're somewhat civilized in the bunkhouse."

I wiped my cheeks, accidentally smearing dust and dirt across my skin. "I just needed a breather."

He looked around. "And manual labor was the answer? You know, you don't get paid to muck stalls."

"I know. I just wanted something to do. I'm sorry if I messed it up."

CJ grabbed a bale of straw from the stack and tossed it into the stall. It landed with a thud. Two more followed it. "Ray's looking for you."

I spread the straw out to make a suitable bed for Anny. "I'm off the clock."

CJ took to cleaning the water and feed bins. "I don't think that means much to him."

"He can deal with it. He's fine without me, and I need space."

CJ chuckled. "He's never been good at taking 'no' for an answer."

I paused and looked at him with pleading eyes. "I just want to hide for a little bit."

He shrugged. "Suit yourself, but Ray will figure out a way to find you."

We finished turning over Anny's stall in silence, and CJ brought her in for the night.

She immediately started nuzzling into my neck when she got close enough.

"Hey, gorgeous," I said as I loved on her. "You're not as mean as everyone says you are."

CJ laughed. "No, she is." He smoothed his hand down her glossy black coat. "But for some reason she likes you."

"I won't be out here too much longer," I promised.

He shrugged and headed out. "Can't say I didn't warn you. Good luck with your night."

I found companionship with the horses. They judged, but there was no unwanted commentary. If they liked me, they'd let me stay around. If not, they were gone. I appreciated the simplicity of that. Animals were good judges of character.

The sputter of a golf cart rattled me out of the silent chat I was having with myself.

"Brooke?" Ray roared through the quiet of the stables.

Anny glared at the barn doors, and I didn't blame her.

"Brooke—" he paused. "I don't know your fucking middle name or I'd use it."

The clatter of metal piqued my curiosity and drew me out from Anny's stall. I peered around the corner. Ray was sitting in the driver's seat of a golf cart, in the process of pulling his wheelchair out of the back and opening it up on the ground beside him.

Shit.

"Brooke," he shouted again when he heard me shuffling in the hay. Brown eyes landed on mine. His jaw was locked tight as he slid out of the golf cart and into his wheelchair.

I swallowed. At least we were alone. The horses wouldn't tell anyone about him yelling at me.

"Where the fuck have you been?" he snapped as he rolled into the barn.

I turned my back to him and smoothed my hand down Anny's nose. "I left a note. I said I was going on a walk."

Ray let out the most sarcastic laugh I had ever heard. "You left a note. Right. Because the last time you went on a walk you almost died of heatstroke. So unless you're going to let me put a goddamn tracking chip in the back of your neck, then no. A note is not fucking good enough."

"I don't understand why you're angry," I said calmly. "How'd you even get down here? Did CJ rat me out?"

"CJ didn't tell me shit," he snapped. "Don't ask me why, but I just knew you'd be in here."

"Well, if you knew I'd be here, then you know why I'm here and not at your house. So, if you'll excuse me, I'll be spending the rest of my time off the clock away from my *boss*."

"Brooke," Ray said as he shoved on the wheels and pushed himself into the entrance of Anny's stall.

Anarchy lunged at him, snapping at his head as a warning.

"Jesus—fuck—" Ray shoved backward. "What the hell is her problem?"

"She doesn't like people who don't respect her space. And neither do I. You don't get to be angry at me, Ray."

Heat blazed in his eyes. "I do get to be angry. Do you understand how fucking worried I was? You can't just walk away from me without an explanation. You don't get to do that. Not when I care about you."

I gritted my teeth. "I absolutely get to walk away. Especially because I'm just the girl who works for the company that you hired to send help."

He was visibly taken aback.

"Yeah." I grabbed the broom and pitchfork and stomped out of the stall to hide the fact that tears were filling my eyes. "That felt great after spending the weekend thinking that I meant something to you."

Ray caught me around the waist, and the tools clattered in my hands. "You do mean something to me. Do you understand that? Coming out of the bathroom and finding you gone scared the shit out of me."

I jerked out of his grasp and put the tools back on the hanging organizer. "Could have fooled me."

"I care about you!" His shout cracked like a whip.

I spun on him. "You don't get to say that and think it'll make everything better. Your family knows we've been fooling around. You saying that I'm just 'the help' hurt me, and you know it."

I felt stupid for the tears running down my face, but I stopped caring what he thought of me the minute I didn't mean anything to him.

"I've never been anything but honest," I said as I pulled off the rubber boots and slipped back into my flip-flops.

"It's the truth. I pay you," he said.

My vision blurred and burned. "Fuck. You," I spat.

"Brooke." His hand shackled my wrist. "I'm not denying anything."

"What happened to all those things you said to me in the truck? Huh? Where was that guy? I get that this isn't easy for you, but if I'm not mistaken, you're the one who figures it out. So stop being a fucking coward and figure it out."

"I'm trying!" he shouted. "But every fucking time I think I can do this, something reminds me that I can't. Someone broke into my house. What if we had been there? What if I couldn't protect you? You don't think that weighs on me?"

"That's your problem," I yelled back. "I'm sorry, but I've told you how I feel. I can tell you that I want you just like this until I'm blue in the face, but believing it is on you."

He froze.

I had a headache from crying, and I was over it. "I'm going back to my house," I said, utterly exasperated. "I'll see you on Monday."

I could hear the crunch of his wheelchair rolling over debris and hay as he came up behind me.

Warm hands slid up my hips. "Stay," he rasped as he leaned forward and rested his forehead on the small of my back. "I promise I'm working on it. I swear to you. I just need... I just need more time. I'm trying to figure it out."

I wanted to fall into him and trust that he wasn't playing games with my heart. "You don't get to say that. It's not a fix. You don't get to buy time with empty promises."

"I love you," he said softly and calmly from behind me. "I do. And that's why I'm trying really fucking hard not to hurt you. That's why you can't be with me."

"That's the dumbest thing I've ever heard."

"I love you and that's why I want better for you. I want someone good for you."

I turned to face him. "You are the greatest good."

His hands slid up my hips and pulled me closer. He pressed a kiss between the waist of my shorts and the hem of my tank top, taking advantage of the strip of skin that peeked out from between them.

"You matter to me. Please know that." His words were a whisper, caressing my body.

I slid my fingers through his hair, holding him closer. "I don't want you to beg. I want you to prove it to me."

Ray pushed the cuff of my shorts up my thigh and pressed his lips to my leg. "I will." He left a path of warm kisses up my inner thigh. "I'll prove it to you every fucking day."

A soft sigh escaped my lips as his stubble scraped my skin. "You know what happens when you get hurt, right?"

"Hmm?"

"You have to kiss it and make it better."

His chuckle was dark and comforting like a glass of whiskey by a rain-spattered window. "Drop your shorts, baby girl."

I wiggled them down without hesitation as he slid his middle finger through my soaked pussy.

"Take off your shirt and bend your back over the saddle stand. I want to see how flexible you are. I want to see your eyes while I make good on my promises."

I eyed the empty saddle stand. It was about three feet off the ground and had a smooth, curved wooden top. Two ornate knobs were fastened to the top on either end to keep the saddles from sliding off. I pulled off my tank top and bra and left them in a pile with my shorts and underwear.

"Like this?" I asked as I laid back against the side of the curved top. It forced my back into a tall arch. My hair hung off the other side in a waterfall of curls. A breeze tickled my breasts and I was suddenly all too aware of where and how naked I was.

Ray wheeled over and locked his chair in front of me. "That's my good girl. Just like that." His hands glided up my thighs, spreading them apart. "On your tiptoes now."

I pushed up onto my toes, a little further over the saddle stand, and his mouth latched onto my clit.

I let out a high-pitched whine, startling the horses in their stalls. Ray growled into my pussy as he sucked and bit until I was a wet, writhing mess.

"One foot up onto my chair. It's locked," he said as he reached forward and grabbed the knobs on the top of the stand. Ray dropped his gym shorts and boxers, and pulled himself up. The blunt head of his cock teased my entrance as he lined himself up. "Lean back as far as you can."

I peered over my chest through heavy eyes, watching as he held onto the ends of the saddle stand to support his bodyweight. "You good?" I asked quietly.

He let out a sharp breath as he nudged inside of me. "I'm steady. I've got it—got you." Ray's biceps rippled as he snapped forward, pushing inside of me.

I whimpered as I was filled and stretched. The second and third thrusts knocked the air out of my lungs.

"I'm gonna figure my shit out," he grunted as he fucked me hard over the saddle stand. "Might take a while. But I'll do it. I'm not letting you go."

"Keep me," I whispered in desperate pants as he stole

my breath. Heat boiled inside of me as he shifted all of his weight to the grip he held with his right hand and used his left to toy with my clit.

My toes curled and my back went rigid.

"Goddamn, baby girl. I feel you squeezing my dick. Come for me." He switched to slow, massaging strokes and shallow pumps. "I want you to shatter. You can break. I'll be here to pick you up. I'm not going anywhere."

His arm started to tremble as I reached my peak. Ray pulled out and slammed inside of me once more. The slide of his dick into me ignited my release. I cried out as I came, reaching for him. Ray grabbed the top of the saddle stand and held on, his body pressed to mine, as he came inside of me.

Our breath mingled as our heart rates slowed together.

"I need to sit down," he croaked as he pressed a reverent kiss to my sternum.

I nodded as he pulled out of me and dropped down into his chair.

His grin was Cheshire. "Goddamn, you're a sight to see. Bent back like that, tits in the air, my cum dripping down your leg." He licked his lips and inhaled deeply before leaning forward to kiss my knee. "I'm sorry I made you feel unwanted."

I pushed myself up and stopped when my head spun. "Keep proving to me that I am wanted. That's all I need."

Ray helped me clean up and dress quickly. As much of a turn on as the possibility of getting caught was, I didn't actually want to get caught.

When I had put on my shorts and shirt, he took my hand in his and kissed my knuckles. "Let's go."

I made sure everything was where it was supposed to be

and followed him outside. An old golf cart was parked just outside the door.

I stopped in my tracks. I knew he had somehow gotten down here, but I hadn't thought about the logistics. "You drove?"

"CJ got some parts at the hardware store to convert it to hand controls," he said as he maneuvered out of his chair and into the driver's seat. "He brought it over for a test drive after the horse delivery while you were out with the girls."

I helped fold the chair and placed it in the back before hopping in with him.

Ray started the engine and pushed a lever for the gas pedal, then turned the steering wheel to head back to his house.

"You know," I said as I rested my head on his shoulder and felt the night air swirling around us. "I think I like you driving me around."

Ray chuckled and leaned over to give my head a quick kiss. "That makes two of us."

27

RAY

Brooke snored.

I had to admit—it was cute. She was curled up on the couch like a cat with her head in my lap. The movie we had been watching was muted. I had turned the volume down as soon as her eyelids closed.

It had been a long day for both of us. We spent most of the morning and afternoon in town, bouncing between appointments.

Brooke went with me to my PT appointment. We stayed in town for lunch, then separated while I went to my first mental therapy appointment.

I hated it.

But I didn't want to crush Brooke's spirits. She seemed so hopeful that I was going. That it would fix me.

I was going to give it a shot, but I didn't have her optimism.

While I sat in an office that was far too air-conditioned for my liking, Brooke picked up groceries, prescriptions, and parked at a coffee shop to use their WiFi. She had been looking into class options at the community college.

I knew she was bored as hell with me. I felt bad that she was wasting her time hanging around my house, waiting for me to need something.

Sometimes I asked her to help me just because I knew she was bored.

Her snores snapped me back to the present. I combed my fingers through her hair, brushing it away from her face. Her features were soft and angelic. Freckles dotted her nose and cheeks from being out in the sun.

After we made it back to the ranch, we crashed on the couch with leftovers pilfered from the fridge and hadn't moved since.

Brooke stirred and nuzzled into my thigh. "Is the movie over?" she mumbled.

"It can be," I said as I rubbed her back. "Are you ready to go to bed?"

She nodded but didn't get up.

I wanted to scoop her up in my arms and carry her to bed. I wanted to lay her down and strip her bare. I wanted to pull her into me and hold her all night.

But I couldn't do that.

The psychiatrist had left me more raw and sore than my physical therapy appointment. Maybe it was the whole "break you down before you're built back up" thing, but I hated every second of it.

Christian texted me to ask how it went and promised it would get better, but I wasn't so sure.

It took eight seconds for me to win a championship, and one second to lose everything else.

Turning the tides would take more than the weak pull I was left with.

Brooke's soft snores resumed. Even the sun needed to set and rest.

She was the reason I had energy and drive to keep trying. Her hope and optimism fueled me.

"Come on," I said softly. "You'll sleep better in bed."

We moved like zombies through the dark house. I made sure the doors were locked while Brooke brushed her teeth and washed her face.

"Ray?" she asked quietly as she stood in front of the door to my room.

I frowned because she sounded worried. "What's the matter?"

"I was just gonna ask if I could sleep with you tonight."

We had slept in the same bed together at the motel, and we had fallen asleep together a handful of times—usually by accident—at the house. But we had never intentionally gone to bed together.

Brooke gave me space, probably because she was afraid to ask for intimacy. That was definitely my fault.

I wheeled over and slid my hand up and down her thigh. "Always, baby. I want you in my bed."

"You sure?" She dug a pink-painted toe into the floor and wobbled her ankle back and forth.

"I'm sure."

Her smile was soft and sleepy.

I finished brushing my teeth, then cut the lights and eased over into the bed beside her. Brooke had taken up the left side, leaving the right side for me.

"How'd you know what side I sleep on?" I asked as I kissed her head.

"Your phone charger is over there," she said with a yawn.

I chuckled. "Observant."

I didn't need to ask her to come closer. As soon as I was settled under the covers, Brooke curled into my side. She was asleep in seconds.

I was jealous of her peace. I couldn't remember the last time I slept that well. If I wasn't waking up from phantom pains or discomfort, I woke up with mental anguish.

But Brooke didn't. She was steady and stalwart like the sunrise.

My hands ached from physical therapy. Callie gave me a break from gross motor skills and made me hold a fucking pencil for what felt like ages.

Maybe it was the warmth and pressure of her body against my chest, but my mind calmed much more quickly than it usually did.

"Ray."

I stirred, rousing to Brooke's whisper. I had been in the best sleep I could remember.

"What's the matter, baby?" I mumbled into her hair.

"I think someone's in the house," she whispered.

My eyes blinked open and I froze. Brooke's body was rigid against mine.

The house was silent. Maybe one of the animals had gotten out and was making noise outside. That happened fairly frequently.

A thud echoed from the living room, making us both jolt.

Brooke's eyes widened in the moonlight.

Shit. What the hell was I going to do? The police response time this far out wasn't worth a crap. I couldn't do jack shit. Just getting in my wheelchair would make a fuck ton of noise.

Brooke ripped the covers back as I grabbed my phone to call CJ.

"What are you doing?" I hissed. "Get back here."

Brooke, in her panties and my t-shirt, slid out of bed and

grabbed one of my cuffed forearm crutches that was propped up against the wall.

"Get your ass in bed," I snapped in a whisper. "I'm calling CJ."

"And I'm going to see what the fuck is out there," Brooke whispered.

"No."

"Yes."

The call to CJ connected, but Brooke was at the door before I could stop her. I yanked the covers back and felt around in the dark for the arm of my wheelchair. "Brooke—"

She tiptoed into the kitchen then screamed. I heard the clunk and thud of the crutch connecting with a body. My blood ran cold.

"Brooke!" I roared as I dropped into my wheelchair and peeled out of the bedroom.

Brooke grunted as she pulled back and swung again like a slugger.

Headlights flashed across the front of the house. A shadowed figure grunted and let out a shout before bolting out the back door and off the deck. Brooke lunged towards the back yard, and I grabbed her arm.

"Stop," I roared.

"But he's getting—"

"I don't give a shit!" I snapped. "Get in the bedroom and lock the fucking door."

Brooke scoffed. "Fat chance of that!"

The front door cracked as CJ kicked it open and barrelled in. He flicked the lights on and paused.

Brooke was wielding a forearm crutch like a sword, I had her arm in my grasp, and we were both in our underwear.

"Get. In. The. Bedroom," I said through gritted teeth.

Brooke pointed to the open sliding door. "Call. The. Cops."

I let her go and pinched the bridge of my nose. "You're gonna give me an aneurysm."

"Hey now," CJ said as he eased into the situation. "What the hell happened? You called me at three in the morning and didn't say anything."

All at once, the adrenaline seemed to drain away from Brooke and reality set in. "Someone broke in," she whispered.

CJ raised an eyebrow. "And you chased him out with a crutch?"

"I hit him twice and then he ran," Brooke said. Her breath quickened as she looked at the crutch in her hand.

Anger burned inside me like a pool of fire.

I glanced at CJ, and he glared at me. Because of course he did. He and Brooke got along great.

Just one more fucking reminder that she should have been with someone else.

Someone who could wake up in the middle of the night and make sure the house was empty. Someone who could hold her when she was frightened. Someone who could protect her.

"I'll call the police," CJ said as he fished his phone from his pocket. He glanced at me and nodded his head towards the bedroom.

"Come on, Brooke," I said as I took the crutch away from her and rolled back into the bedroom.

She followed, as quiet as a mouse.

"Get in bed," I said as I hastily opened my dresser drawer and grabbed a pair of shorts and a t-shirt.

"But what about—"

"I'll handle it," I said as I turned and rolled to the door. "Go to sleep."

∼

THE LIGHT of day made everything worse.

I hadn't slept a wink since that fucker had broken into the house in the middle of the night.

The cops showed up an hour later and did the perfunctory rounds of taking statements, making notes of the sliding door that had been lifted off its tracks, fingerprints on the glass, and the tossed kitchen. Tire tracks were found on the service road that edged the south side of the ranch. They came and went out the back.

Nothing had been taken, but it was clear that they knew what they were going for. The cops promised to track down Brooke's roommates, but they were probably already getting out of dodge.

Which left me with one giant loose end: Brooke.

More accurately, how I had snapped at her in the heat of the burglary. In a turn of events that I hated more than anything, she was ignoring me.

Christian had dragged my ass out of the house and into town for an impromptu therapy session after CJ snitched.

I both loved and hated how protective my brothers were of Brooke.

After being calmly and professionally bitched out by that therapist, I had been delivered back to my house like a goddamn pizza. But Brooke was nowhere to be found.

Regret left a sickening taste in my mouth. For once, I wasn't bothered by my disability. I was disgusted with how I had acted.

I sat at the kitchen table, trying again and again to get my apology right, but it all seemed so trivial. Empty, frivolous words were a paltry offering when I knew I had inflicted deep wounds.

The pencil felt foreign in my hand, but the discomfort of trying again and again to form letters was the penance I had to pay.

When Brooke didn't show back up by the afternoon, I went after her.

The barn was empty, except for a handful of horses and their judgmental glares. I steered the golf cart up the lane toward the ranch's office.

Brooke's car was still in my driveway, so she had to be on the property, right?

But what if Cass or Becks had driven her into town?

I pulled up to the office and got my wheelchair out. Voices carried through the corrugated metal frame. They silenced as I wheeled myself inside.

Christian, Cassandra, Nate, Becks, CJ, and my father stared at me in silence. Mickey was asleep on the dog bed in the corner.

"Family meeting I wasn't told about?" I said as I wheeled in.

No one said a peep.

"Where's Brooke?" I snapped.

Cassandra lifted an eyebrow. "Try that tone with me one more time. I dare you."

"Do it," Becks said. "I'd like to see what happens."

I strangled the armrests of my wheelchair. "Will someone please tell me where Brooke is," I gritted out.

"You've got the words, but you don't have the music," Christian said as he leaned back in his chair and stroked his beard. "Try that one more time."

I growled. "This family drives me fucking crazy, you know that?"

Nate grinned. "Right back at you."

I ran my hands down my face. "I need to apologize to her."

They exchanged glances with one another.

Finally, my dad spoke up. "She's up at the house with momma. They're doing some baking."

I huffed and turned to leave, but CJ quickly blocked the door. "Sit."

"I am," I countered.

He crossed his arms. "You know what I mean."

"Fine. Let's get this over with."

"That's the spirit," Cassandra said. "Who wants to start?" She looked around. "No one? Good. I will. What the hell is your problem?"

My fingers clenched the armrests. "I don't have time for this."

"Yeah, you do, son," Dad said. "Sit still and listen before you fuck it up."

It wasn't often that my father swore, but when he did, I knew it was serious.

"This is not your problem. It's mine," I said. "Let me handle it. Y'all have enough going on."

"Which is why you left the ranch in the first place," Christian said.

That made me pause.

"Because we had a lot going on. So you packed up and decided to ride bulls." Christian lifted his cowboy hat and ran his hand over his long hair. "Nate got hurt. The ranch expanded, then we started struggling. So you left."

I knew what he was getting at. It was something I had shared with him in confidence over a decade ago.

I never wanted to burden anyone, but I did. Packing up and heading to Colorado was the solution. Bull riding was my ticket out. I didn't want to be another mouth to feed or put more strain on the family.

I returned when I was needed.

Christian needed help with his girls and the ranch after Gretchen died. So, I came back, did what needed to be done, and then left.

Being thrown off a bull and paralyzed reset the clock. It undid everything I had been working toward. Brought me back to the place I'd been hell-bent on leaving.

I came back without any say in the matter, and now I was an even bigger burden.

"Family isn't a burden," Dad said. "Assholes are. Stop acting like one. You've got a sweet girl who loves you to pieces and you're acting foolish. Cut it out."

"Someone broke into my house last night, and I couldn't do a damn thing about it," I shouted. "None of you know what that feels like."

"Maybe not, but I know what it feels like to need help. We all do," Christian said. Cassandra opened her mouth to object, but Christian pointed at her. "Even Cass."

She bit her lip and glared at him.

"Why do you think Becks and I chose to live on the ranch in the middle of nowhere when she has to fly to New York or around the world every month for work?" Nate asked. "If you don't understand how family works, then you need to figure that out before you involve Brooke. Because this family isn't going anywhere."

"You have to decide if you want to be a part of it or not," CJ said. "Because if you're in, that means we get to help you. If someone breaks into your house, you call us because you know we'll be there."

My jaw throbbed from clenching my teeth together.

Becks's eyes fell on mine. "We don't think you're being a dick because of your injury. You're being a dick because you're a prideful son of a bitch. You were that way before you needed to use a wheelchair."

"Brooke doesn't care about what you can and can't do," Christian said. "I see it in her. But she should care about you losing your shit on her."

I rolled my eyes. I didn't sign up for this little intervention today. "Easy for you to say."

Nate hunched forward. "Downpours happen. You either drown in it or grow after it."

"You owe her an apology," Dad said. "Your momma and I raised you better than how you're acting."

I already had that part ready. I just needed to get her to talk to me.

"A good one," Cassandra said. "Or I'll kill you myself."

"Please," I grumbled. "You just talk a big game."

Cass rocketed out of her chair. "Wanna try me? You mess with my little sunflower, and I'll—"

Christian caught her around the waist and pulled her against his chest. "Settle down, princess. I think he's had his fair share of crow for the day."

Becks snickered behind the balled fist she pressed to her mouth. "What's your plan, Ray? If you need a woman's point of view, you know where to find us."

I tipped my head at Cass. "I don't think I want hers."

The group snickered.

Sighing, I said, "I'm working on it. I'm... I'm gonna make it right. I just have to find her a job, then find her so I can fire her."

That seemed to appease the mob. They shared brief nods.

"Start with the apology," Cass said. "I'll handle the job."

The door to the office creaked, and a shadow dashed away outside.

I looked at Christian. "Where are your girls?"

"At a friend's house."

Shit.

28

BROOKE

My stomach felt like an anvil as I walked from Claire's house back to Ray's.

I couldn't sleep after the break-in. I was scared and shaken. What if the person returned?

But Ray had banished me to his room.

When dawn broke, I slipped out and went up to his mom's house. I clung to threads of hope that her open-ended invitation to bake together was genuine. I wanted to be anywhere but Ray's house. And as much as I wanted to be near him, I needed space.

The anger that flashed in his eyes during the break-in haunted me. I understood being scared. I was scared. But he wasn't angry at the burglar. He was furious with me.

Claire met me at the door, as if she was already expecting me. She didn't pester or prod, just led me to the kitchen and handed me an apron.

When making a batch of banana bread didn't fix anything, we moved on to cookies. Then brownies. And pie.

Claire swore up and down that baking that much was a regular occurrence for her, although I didn't quite believe she had planned it for today. Still, we pulled out giant Tupperware containers from her cabinets, sliced and boxed assortments of desserts, and made front porch deliveries.

While Claire took a boatload to the ranch hands' bunkhouse, I stopped at Becks and Nate's and Christian and Cassandra's houses. Surprisingly, no one was home.

The long walk back down the dirt path gave me time to clear my head and settle my nerves.

When I passed the ranch office, I froze.

Ray's golf cart was parked outside, and I could hear a cluster of voices talking over one another.

I clutched the plastic container like a life preserver and peeked through the crack.

Laughter bubbled up at something someone had said, then Ray's voice cut in. "I just have to find her a job, then find her so I can fire her."

I went numb.

Just when I thought we were figuring things out... Just when I thought Ray was working on himself so we could be together...

I was so stupid.

Tears burned like acid rain as I turned and ran back to Ray's house. I wanted to pack and be gone by the time he came back. But the moment I stepped inside, I couldn't handle it.

Everything smelled like him. It looked like us. Our lives were blended so seamlessly within these four walls.

I dropped the container on the kitchen counter and ran out the sliding door to the backyard.

The grass was soft on my toes as I slid my feet out of my flip-flops and sank them into the neatly clipped blades. The distant din of ranch life carried on the breeze.

I would miss it here. It had been a long time since I felt something like home. Like belonging. Like safety.

Even in the terror of a burglary, I knew there would be people to keep me safe. To watch out for us. I loved Ray with my whole body—so much that it hurt. But it wasn't just him. It was the whole Griffith family that I loved.

I wanted to be a part of it.

The rhythmic thumps of a wheelchair rolling down the ramp startled me, but I didn't flinch. Why would the condemned jump at the sound of the executioner? They knew what was coming.

I stared at the glassy pond and refused to turn around to look at him.

The soft swish of his wheelchair rolling through the grass grew closer. "Hey."

I found a pebble and pitched it at the surface, skipping it twice before it sank.

"Okay," Ray said as he locked his chair and eased out to sit behind me. "I deserve the silent treatment."

I flinched when he sat behind me because apparently, the damned do jump. Tears rolled down my face, and I didn't care enough about my pride to wipe them away.

Ray sat me between his legs. I could feel the heat radiating from his chest. Usually, I would have immediately curled into him, but not this time.

I was tired of being played the fool.

"I'm sorry," he said as he rested his chin on top of my head.

"Just get it over with already," I rasped as I snapped a blade of grass out of the ground. "I'll get my stuff and be gone by the end of the day."

Ray stiffened. "What are you—" His arms tightened around me. "You heard me say I was going to fire you."

The corner of my mouth trembled. "Just let me go," I whispered.

Ray's inhale was slow and steady. Why was he so calm while I was borderline hysterical? It was infuriating.

"I don't need your help," he said.

I let out a caustic laugh at the sky. "Yes. You've made that perfectly clear."

"I need *you*." Ray pressed his mouth to the back of my head. "I *want* you."

"Then why do I have to go?" I choked out. "You know how much I need this job."

It was only half true, though. I needed a job, but I could have found something. I just didn't want to leave him.

"Baby, I don't want you going anywhere. That's why I don't want you working for me. I want you to be here because you want to be. I don't want to keep you trapped. Cass is going to help us find something for you that you love." He gently cupped my cheek and forced me to look at him. "I'll get to the rest of my apology in a minute. But you're going stir-crazy. I want more for you than occasionally giving me a hand and getting my groceries."

"I like helping you."

"I know you do." He pressed a kiss to my temple. "And I know I don't deserve you. I don't deserve to be loved the way you love me."

I hunched forward and hugged my knees. "What are we doing, Ray? This is... this is never going to work."

"You're right."

Wait. He wasn't supposed to agree with me.

He gently rubbed my back. "It's not going to work if I don't get my shit together. So, I'm working on it. Because I want this to work. It's not going to work if you're my employee. I want a partner. Someone who's here willingly.

So, I'm working on that too. And as you may have guessed, I just had my ass chewed out by my family because they like you better than me and want you to stick around." His thumb grazed my cheek. "And, you know what? I like you better than me too."

My eyes dropped to the ground. "You've made all of those promises before."

"I know, baby. I know I let you down. I know I hurt you. I know I have to let go of what I thought my life was gonna look like whenever I got around to hanging up my chaps for good. I've got to work on that, and I think it's going to be harder than physical therapy."

He said everything I wanted, but did it make me a pushover if I accepted it? Could I believe him after he had said it all before? Was I just a naïve girl getting back in line to have her heart broken again?

"I want to believe you," I said.

"That's good enough for me. Because I want you. So, if that's where you're at, then I know where I stand with you and where I need to put in the work." Ray cupped my cheeks, his eyes soft and kind. "I'm a proud man, Brooke. I don't like asking for help, so I'm only going to ask for one thing."

"What's that?"

"One more chance to love you right." He reached into the pocket of his gym shorts and pulled out a folded piece of paper. "I, um... I went to therapy again this morning. Christian called in a favor after what happened last night and got me in before the office opened. When I got home, you were gone, so I sat and tried to figure out how to apologize while I waited for you to come back."

"I went to your mom's house," I muttered.

He slid the paper into my hand. "I've given you too many

empty words before. So, this time, I... I wrote them down. I know my handwriting sucks. It looks like a kindergartener wrote it out. But I'm trying, Brooke. I swear to you. I just..." His voice broke as he tightened his arms around me. "I just needed you to know that I'm gonna put in the work because I love you."

Carefully, I unfolded the note. The letters were large and misshapen. Eraser marks were evident on the page where he had tried and tried again to get it right. Some words had been scratched out and changed. The effort and intention he had put into every word was overwhelming.

If I had to choose between you and the sun, it's you.

In every lifetime, you are the most brilliant thing in existence.

Your love is blinding and sustaining. I crave your warmth.

The incandescence of you is what gives me light when my nature is to seek darkness.

In every form that you exist, you are my sun. And I'll be your moon.

I'll be the light that drives the nightmares away. The glow that soothes. And the calm you seek refuge in.

Because you can burn eternally without me.

But not me without you.

A tear splashed onto the page. I quickly folded it to keep his words from washing away. I turned in his arms. "Ray..."

He pulled me against his chest and cradled the back of my head. "I know it's not much—"

"It's everything," I whispered into his neck. "Because it's you."

"You told me that good and bad exist in tandem. That sunshine and sorrow are two sides of the same coin. And I believe it. I don't care if the clouds ever go away, because you're the silver lining inside them."

My lip quivered, and I bit down on it. But the trembling never stopped.

"I love you, Brooke," he said as he cupped my jaw and guided me to his lips.

The kiss was warm and laced with the salt of tears. But so was life.

"I love you too."

"You wanna know something?"

"Hm?"

"The day we met, I remember getting out of Christian's truck and seeing you for the first time. It was the middle of the day, and the sun was high. It looked like you were glowing." He dragged his thumb across my cheek to wipe the tears away. "And that was the first day I remember feeling how warm the sun was. How good it felt. You eclipsed my darkness that day. And you've done it every day since."

I tucked into his chest as the exhaustion from the last twenty-four hours washed over me.

"One more thing," he said.

I opened my eyes and watched as he reached into the cupholder on his chair and pulled out a plant with a small red bloom.

"What's that?"

Ray chuckled and set the small pot in my lap. "Your plant. The one that only blooms when you meet the love of your life."

I blinked. "But... I dropped it. And it was mostly dead anyway."

"But it wasn't all dead. I found a cutting on the pavement and—for some reason—took it inside and put it in a glass with some water in my room." He skimmed his fingers up and down my arm. "And each day the roots got a little longer. I found a pot and put it in some dirt and kept watering it."

I fingered the soft red petals.

Ray's cheek pressed against my temple. "And the day we got back from our night away, it bloomed." His lips found mine again. "I don't believe plants lie. They just seek the sun and keep growing. And so will I."

"I have to find another job," I whispered against his lips.

Ray grinned. "So do I."

That surprised me. I knew Ray was well-off, but he had always shrugged off any thoughts of what was next.

"What are you thinking?"

His nose bumped against mine. "Life's a bull. Sometimes you can hang on. Sometimes it throws you off. Sometimes you get completely fucked. You gotta get up, dust yourself off, and keep riding."

29

RAY

"She looks good up there, doesn't she?" I said, watching from the edge of the outdoor riding arena.

Brooke had tacked up Indy for the inaugural ride in the new arena. CJ's boys had finished the fencing two days prior, and a truckload of sand had been brought in first thing this morning. Brooke had insisted we come down to watch it get graded out.

CJ sided up to me and rested his elbows on top of the fence. "Real natural. I haven't seen someone take to a horse like that since Bree."

Brooke's long hair whipped in the wind as she and Indy kicked up to a canter. Her smile was infectious.

"Yeah, I always thought Bree would get competitive with it. I was kinda surprised when she didn't want to."

"Chris put the girls in activities outside of the ranch so they wouldn't feel like this was a foregone conclusion for them," he said. "Besides, now she's got that boy she's been asking about."

I let out a low growl at the thought of some prick with

raging teenage hormones getting anywhere near Bree. "Let him come around. It's less suspicious if he brings the body to us."

CJ laughed. "How's the job hunt going for her?" he asked as he tipped his head toward Brooke.

"Nothing yet. Not many places are hiring. I was hoping she'd get the receptionist spot at my PT office, but they gave it to someone else."

"Cass come through with any leads?"

"Not yet. I know it's driving Brooke crazy. She asked if I thought you wanted help working cattle this morning."

CJ chuckled. "Respectfully, no. As much as I like her, I don't let outsiders near my cattle. Cass knows it. Becks knows it, too."

Hooves pounded the ground, growing closer and closer until we were engulfed in the shadow of a horse that stood sixteen hands high.

"How's it feel?" CJ asked Brooke as he shaded his eyes from the sun.

She brushed her hair out of her face and propped her hands up on her hips. "Good. Still not as fun as a full gallop through the pastures, but if my opinion means anything, I think it's a good setup for the equine program. Big enough to get a good speed if you want to or stay slow and have a few horses in at once." She smoothed her hand down my horse's mane. "Indy seems to like it."

Indy dropped her head over the edge of the fence, sniffing around in my direction.

I leaned out the side of the golf cart and gave her a treat. "You gotta take care of my girl. Alright, In?"

Brooke laid forward and rested her arms and chest on the back of Indy's neck. "I think we get along just fine."

I chuckled. "I know. But she can get a little sassy and

headstrong sometimes. You gotta remind her that you're in control."

Brooke grinned. "So can you, and I handle you just fine."

CJ snickered. "You gonna take one of the new horses out when you're done busting Ray's balls?"

Brooke's eyebrows lifted. "Can I?"

"They need to get used to being ridden by different people if they're gonna be used for the equine program. I gotta head out, but Christian might be around to help."

"I'll stick around," I said.

CJ looked surprised. "Are you sure?"

I shrugged. "She knows how to tack them up and down. I'll guide her through any hang ups."

"Alright." CJ pushed off the fence. "See y'all at Momma's for dinner."

"Do you need some water or anything?" I asked Brooke when CJ disappeared.

"I'm fine," she said as she removed the elastic band from her wrist and tied her hair back. "I'll probably call it a day soon. I'll need to shower if we're going to your parents' house for dinner."

I leaned back in the golf cart seat and took a moment to admire her beautiful legs. Goddamn. Brooke had the most attractive legs I'd ever seen.

I adjusted my cock. "My shower is plenty big for both of us. We can save time and shower together."

Brooke laughed. "I meant that I actually need to get clean and wash my hair."

"I can help with that."

She snorted. Or was that the horse? Actually, it was both. I hated that my girls were ganging up on me.

Brooke took hold of the reins. "A little longer, then I'll be done."

"Or you could be done now, and we'd have plenty of time for that extra-long shower."

She smiled. "You're not my boss anymore. I'll be done when I'm done."

Brooke looked radiant as she rode away. Indy broke into a quick gallop that made my heart skip a beat.

What if Brooke fell? What if Indy got spooked and bucked? What if they got too confident on the sand and took a tumble on a turn? Brooke could break a bone. She could get a concussion. Or worse, she could—

"Ready?"

I blinked. Brooke was on her feet, walking alongside Indy and leading her out of the area.

"What?"

"You looked like you drifted off on my second lap." She laughed. "Was I that boring?"

I swallowed my pride and shook my head. "No, you just startled me. That's all."

Her expression softened. "How about I get Indy untacked and meet you at the house for that shower?"

But instead of going our separate ways, I followed her to the barn in the golf cart. I didn't think she'd want to walk back to my house after being out in the sun for most of the afternoon.

Brooke was calm and focused as she went through the motions of removing Indy's tack. She didn't miss a beat in getting my horse comfortable before brushing her down and examining her.

Once everything was finished, Brooke sank into the golf cart seat beside me.

"I'm going to need a pre-dinner dinner," she said, resting her head on my shoulder.

"Go take your shower, and I'll make you a snack."

She beamed. "My hero."

"So, um...I spoke to Marty today," I confessed when I felt like we were far enough away from the barns and warehouses that no one could overhear us.

Brooke looked up at me. "Really? About what?"

"Sorting through some of the requests that Cass has been fielding. He said he'd negotiate the deals if I wanted to jump on them."

"That's great!"

I shrugged. "It might not be steady work, but it'll be a few things here and there."

She snickered. "Not all of us can be millionaires, I suppose."

I parked in front of the house and kissed her temple. "Come on."

While Brooke rinsed off and changed her clothes for dinner, I sat at the kitchen table and scrolled through a few of the emails Marty and Cass had shoved into my inbox.

If I was being honest, I didn't have a single desire to rehash my accident in some memoir that would end up on Dollar Store shelves in five years. I didn't want to go on some speaking tour. That sounded miserable. I didn't want to be "inspiration porn" for bored corporate types looking to motivate their teams.

A few minutes later, we were back in the golf cart, heading to Momma's house.

Driving with my hands instead of my feet was a learning curve, but it wasn't too bad. I liked being able to get around and see what everyone was up to—especially since Brooke had become something of a permanent fixture in everyone's lives.

She baked with my mom. She babysat my littlest niece and hung out with Bree and Gracie so their parents could go out on dates. But she had made herself most at home with the animals.

I was half-convinced she was one of those movie princesses who could make birds and mice sew dresses for her. The horses and cows seemed to like her. Even that asshole barn cat had come around and would weave between her ankles when she came and went.

I loved how easily she assimilated into ranch life. Into my life.

The smell of shellfish and spices wafted out of the main house as we parked. Most of the family was already seated at the long table. It had been covered with newspaper instead of a tablecloth.

The mountain of potatoes, corn, sausage, and crawdads made my mouth water.

"Alright, y'all. Lowcountry boil tonight," Momma said as she wiped her hands on a towel. "Pull up a chair and get to eating. I didn't make all this food for y'all to look at it all night."

Brooke went to move one of the kitchen chairs out of the way for me, but I caught her hand.

"That's alright, baby. I'll just sit there tonight."

Her lips parted in surprise, but she kept her tone quiet. "You sure?"

Christian and his brood spilled through the door, fashionably late.

I cupped my hands behind my left knee and lifted it off the footrest and onto the ground.

Everyone seemed to stop what they were doing as I repeated the process with my right leg. Brooke slid her hand into mine as I slowly rose to my feet and held onto her for balance.

A pin dropping would have sounded like a gunshot as I shuffled toward the table.

I lost my balance the moment I was within arm's reach of the table. I grabbed the edge and refused to let go. Brooke lifted our clasped hands a little higher to give me leverage to slowly lower into the chair rather than dropping like a sack of potatoes.

"And there's my workout for the day," I said when I was seated. I pulled the chair out beside me for Brooke. "Let's eat."

She pushed my wheelchair aside and sat down next to me.

Nate looked at me as if I'd just walked on water. "So, are we just going to ignore what just happened?"

"I'm hungry." I glanced at Brooke, who was fighting back a smile. "Are you hungry?"

"Starving."

"Fine. Stuff your faces. But get ready to talk with your mouth full," CJ said as he reached into the pile of food on the table. "Because what the hell was that? How long have you been able to fucking walk, dude?"

"Watch your language, Carson James," mom scolded, tears welling up in her eyes. She pointed her spatula at me. "You have some explaining to do, young man."

"I've been working on it in physical therapy."

"*For how long?!*" Christian shouted.

Everyone fell silent.

Cassandra's jaw dropped. "Did you just raise your voice? I think that's more shocking than Ray walking."

I filled up my paper plate with potatoes, crawdads, and corn. Brooke grabbed some crawdads, corn, and sausage.

"Don't get your panties in a twist," I said. "I can shuffle a few feet and that's it."

Bree settled into the chair next to Brooke. "So that means you still need to use your wheelchair?"

Brooke chimed in since my mouth was full. "It's called being an ambulatory wheelchair user. But Ray is still considered paraplegic."

I gave her thigh a grateful squeeze.

Gracie reached for an ear of corn. "So, it's not all or nothing?"

I shook my head. "It's not all or nothing. Very few things in life are."

The conversation quickly shifted to the progress of the lodge and restaurant. Cassandra had been caught in the middle between the investors of the development, the local authorities who believed they had a say in the property's easement, and the construction crews.

It was a logistical nightmare.

"How close are we to launching the equine program?" I asked.

Cassandra wiped her lips. "The website and social media platforms are ready, but I'm waiting until I finalize the program schedule."

Becks frowned. "Why haven't you finalized the schedule yet?"

Cassandra pointed at Christian and CJ. "Until I can get those two to set aside time in their schedules to run the program, progress will be slow."

"I can help if you need an extra hand," Brooke offered as she refilled her plate from the pile in the middle. "I don't have much else going on at the moment."

CJ glanced at Cassandra. "She's the one I would hire for it."

"High praise from Mr. Nobody Sets Foot on My Ranch," I teased.

"I'm just saying," CJ replied. "If someone has to do it, it should be her."

"It's not just hanging out in the barn all day," Cassandra countered.

Brooke's eyes ping-ponged between them.

Cassandra looked from CJ to Brooke. "I need someone who can schedule boarding and grooming appointments, coordinate with the farrier and veterinarian, set up and run beginner programs, and be the ranch's liaison for school field trips—"

"We're having field trips?" Brooke gasped.

I loved the "we" that came out of her mouth.

Christian looked at Cass. "I think we found our hire."

Brooke crossed her fingers under the table.

I sat back and draped my arm over her shoulders. "As her former employer, I'm happy to provide a letter of reference."

Cassandra rolled her eyes. "Of course you are." She turned her terrifying gaze to Brooke. "My office. Tomorrow. Nine in the morning. Don't be late. Be prepared to sit still and learn the scheduling software. And I do not tolerate small talk."

Brooke smirked. "I think you'll come around."

Cassandra glared. "I guarantee you, I will not."

Christian lifted his beer to Brooke. "Welcome to the ranch."

Brooke glowed as everyone raised their glasses and toasted her. I tapped my glass against hers. "I wouldn't want you anywhere else."

30

BROOKE

"You know, I didn't expect the annoying part of training Brooke to be you lingering in my office," Cassandra said as she glared at Ray.

Ray had parked his wheelchair on the other side of Cassandra's desk and had resorted to asking her if I was done for the day every five minutes.

I snickered under my breath and tried to stay focused on the calendar Cassandra and I were setting up.

She let out a low growl and turned back to the schedule. "Anyway. Red blocks are for exclusive arena rental. You'll need to time them far enough apart to clean the arena between riders and set up the obstacles that are requested. They'll show up with their own coaches and trailers if we're not boarding the animal for them. You just need to be present and check in occasionally, during the rental period. Green blocks are—"

She snapped her head to Ray when he hunched over to peer at the screen. "Dear god, *what?*"

"Seriously, how much longer? It's already a quarter till seven."

Cassandra pinched the bridge of her nose. "You of all people should know that the ranch isn't a nine-to-five. Didn't you grow up here?"

He leaned back and laced his hands behind his head.

"Anyway," she said with a huff. "The green blocks are for ranch-led individual lessons. For the time being, you need Christian or CJ with you until they're ready to kick you out of the nest. So, make sure you ask them before you schedule lessons. Yellow blocks are for—"

"Field trips," I said, recalling what we had talked about earlier in the day. "No more than two a month, with a max capacity of thirty kids per field trip. And I need another ranch hand or Griffith present for crowd control."

Cassandra blinked for a moment. She seemed a little surprised I had gotten that right. "That's correct. You could even get Nate or Becks or Claire and Silas if they're willing. Just an extra body."

"What about—"

"Silence," Cassandra snapped at Ray.

He snickered and went back to playing on his phone.

"Phase one is handling reservations individually. Once the program is up and running and we have enough cash flow to warrant it, we'll find some kind of online scheduling software so people can reserve time on their own."

Cassandra clicked around and showed me how to add and edit reservations to the calendar and where to find them in the grand scheme of the ranch's master calendar.

Seeing all those time blocks made my head spin, but I liked the challenge.

I let out a slow breath. "I hope I don't mess it up."

Cassandra was stern. "You will not fail."

"But what if I accidentally—"

She grabbed my shoulders and turned my rolling desk chair to face her. "You will not fail. Do you understand?"

Okay. My new boss was officially scarier than my old one.

"Yes, ma'am," I squeaked.

Christian laughed as he strolled into the office. "She hates that. Just so you know."

Cassandra nodded. "Don't call me ma'am and I won't fire you... Today."

Ray chuckled, and I rolled my eyes. "You two are peas in a pod," I muttered as I hunched forward to play around with the calendar.

"What are y'all still doing in here?" Christian said as he came up behind Cassandra. "It's quarter till' seven."

"Anyone without boobs has to leave!" she shouted. "Out!"

"Oh cool. I can stay," Bree said from the doorway. "When's dinner? It's almost seven."

"That's it," Cassandra said as she slammed her hands on the desk. "You're off the clock. Go home."

Ray, Bree, and Christian shared conspiratorial grins. He wiggled his phone at me and winked.

That man...

"I'll be here bright and early," I promised Cassandra.

"What are y'all still doing here?" CJ said from the doorway. He was drenched in sweat and out of breath. "It's seven."

"You're late," Ray said. "But I appreciate the effort."

Cassandra rolled her eyes. "I should've known you orchestrated that. I usually have to drag Christian back to the house."

Gracie poked her head in. "Why are you still working? It's—"

"Seven! I know!" Cassandra shouted. "I swear, this family is going to drive me batshit crazy."

"Should've clocked out at five," Ray said.

"Y'all should come up to the bunkhouse after supper," CJ said. "We're having a bonfire."

Christian frowned. "A bonfire in the middle of summer when it hasn't rained in months is the stupidest thing I've ever heard. How about *don't*."

CJ rolled his eyes. "It's a little one. We'll keep it contained. Bring the girls."

"Please, Daddy?" Gracie said as she grabbed a red permanent marker from the cup on the desk and started coloring on Ray's arm, filling in a flower that was part of his sleeve of tattoos.

"It's already pretty late," Christian said.

Bree found a blue permanent marker and took Ray's other arm, coloring in a pocket watch and chain that wrapped around his elbow and forearm. "I cleaned my room and did all my chores."

Christian glanced at Cassandra. She returned the look to him, passing back whatever silent communication they had going between them.

"Well then," Christian said. "Since I know you did all those things because you know it's your responsibility, bonfire it is. But you still have to be in bed by ten."

Bree's marker stilled on Ray's arm. "And because I've been so responsible, you'll think about letting me go out with Mason on Saturday?"

The room froze.

The eighteen-plus crowd looked at Christian. Gracie looked at Bree, then Cassandra.

Ray frowned. "Who's Mason?"

"Mason Cruz," Bree blurted out. "He's a grade ahead of

me, and I've done everything Dad said I had to do to be able to go on dates. I get A's and B's. I keep up with my chores. And he *still* won't let me go out with him."

Christian crossed his arms. "Because you don't have your driver's license yet. Do you want me or Cass going on dates with you?"

Bree slammed the marker back onto the desk. "No!"

"You need your driver's license so that you can leave the date whenever you want to. It's for your own safety and agency," Cassandra said.

Bree looked up at Ray. "Will you talk to them? Please? If I have to tell him that my dad won't let me go one more time, he'll stop asking me out and move on."

Ray shrugged. "Let him move on."

Her features curled up in anger. "But... no."

Ray pointed to the tattoo she had been coloring in. "You missed a spot. If that kid wants to move on, let him move on. If he likes you, he'll wait. Simple as that."

Bree rolled her eyes. "You're not supposed to take their side."

"Sorry, kid. I'm full of disappointments these days. If you want a popsicle, you know where to find 'em. Your dad and Cass are just looking out for you." Ray glanced at Christian. "But maybe you could compromise and let the kid come to family dinner. After Cass runs a background check."

"Already done," she clipped.

Something warm inside me bloomed as I watched Ray diffuse Bree's frustration. He would be such a great dad...

"Brooke."

I snapped out of the haze. "Huh?"

Ray was pushing away from Cassandra's desk. "You ready to go back to the house?"

Hearing him call it that—like it was mine too—was everything I ever wanted.

We made our way out of the office and back to the house for a quick dinner before heading out to the bunkhouse.

Trucks, ATVs, and horses carried everyone to the bonfire that glowed in the middle of an open field. Ray needed both hands to drive the golf cart down the dirt path, so I simply rested my head on his shoulder and took in the view.

The sun lit up the pastures in seas of gold. The dark silhouette of the construction site jutted out of the earth. The exterior to what would eventually be a luxury lodge and restaurant was almost done, but they still had a long way to go before it would function.

The lodge was a mix of stonework, cedar beams, and massive glass panes. The architecture was breathtaking. I couldn't wait to see it completed.

"You're late," CJ hollered from the circle of camping chairs, hay bales, and tailgates.

One of the ranch hands had a guitar out and was playing an old country tune.

Ray grinned. "Had to eat dinner."

It was me. I was dinner.

"Where do you want to sit?" I asked him.

Ray glanced around. "I, uh... I'll just hang out in the golf cart."

My heart sank a little. I wanted to sit close to the fire, but Ray and I were a team. I wasn't going to abandon him. There were a lot of people around; a lot of people he didn't usually interact with.

"Sounds good," I said as I settled in.

Ray laced our hands together and looked down at me with a weight to his gaze.

"I don't think I've told you how fucking thankful I am that you're here," he said, just between us. He brushed his thumb over the top of my hand. "I know I don't deserve you. But I'm grateful for every day I get to wake up with you beside me."

I chewed on my lip. "Do you think we'll make it?"

The lines around his eyes relaxed, but deepened over his nose. "Why do you ask that?"

"We don't have a lot in common. You're a lot older than me. I fell for you the moment I saw you for the first time, and I never stopped to think. I have a bad habit of not thinking before I speak or act, and I just—"

Ray chuckled. "Look at Chris and Cass. Do you think they're alike? Or Nate and Becks? She was a lot more like Cass when she first moved to the ranch. I know one thing for certain. I want this, so I'm gonna work for it."

He reached into the caddy behind us and pulled out a plastic bag of blue and pink Sweet Tarts.

"My hero." I laughed as I opened the bag and picked out a blue one. "What do you do with the other ones?"

He chuckled. "I eat the purple and yellow ones, and throw away the green ones. They suck."

I tucked my feet under my butt and curled up beside him on the bench seat. "I love you."

He kissed the top of my head, then my forehead, then my lips. We sat in silence, watching the flames lick up into the sky. Ray had a small length of rope he was working on. The monotony was soothing.

"Y'all just gonna hide over there all night?" Christian hollered from the tailgate of his truck.

"Yep," Ray shouted back. "You're lucky we graced you with our presence in the first place."

Light flashed in my peripheral vision. I looked over

toward the lodge and smiled as the sun dipped below the horizon, casting a royal blue hue across the sky.

Ray pressed his lips to my temple. "What's the matter?"

"Nothing. I just thought I saw lights on at the lodge. It was probably just the sun on the windows."

He grabbed a piece of candy from the bag. "I don't think they've got the electricity up and running yet."

Anarchy was grazing from a patch of grass behind where CJ was seated. She stopped and glared in the direction of the lodge. Her ears twitched, and she let out a displeased grunt.

Laughter and music bubbled up from the bonfire. I closed my eyes, soaking it all in.

"This feels like home," I said softly, so it stayed just between Ray and me. "I haven't felt this in a long time."

He wrapped his arm around me and held me close. "Sometimes I worry you like my family more than me."

I laughed softly. "They have less groveling to do."

"Are the construction crews still here?" Cassandra asked as she checked the time on her phone.

Heads turned toward the lodge, where flashlights danced through the second floor.

"The crew left two hours ago," a ranch hand said as bodies began to rise.

"We'll go check it out," Ray said as he put the golf cart into drive.

CJ called Anny over and mounted her. "I'm coming." A handful of his boys joined in.

The golf cart jostled and bumped along the divots in the road. As we got closer, the flashlights dancing inside the lodge grew more frantic.

My heart jumped in my throat, and I squeezed Ray's arm. "There's people in there. More than one."

"Maybe one of the workers forgot to put the tools up or something," he said.

The ominous pounding of Anny's hooves echoed like a sinister roll of thunder. CJ rounded the front of the lodge and hopped off her back.

"Who's up there?" he shouted into the framework.

Profanities were mixed in a scuffle as the lights danced over the site.

"Hey!" Ray shouted at CJ as he stormed into the lodge. His knuckles went white against the steering wheel.

I knew where his head and heart were. Ray wanted to be the one going up there to see who was messing around inside.

Boots thundered on plywood sheets. Shouts rose up, drawing the attention of the rest of the ranch hands and Griffiths.

A shadow darted out of the lodge.

"Oh my god!" I clapped my hands over my mouth. "That's—"

CJ tackled the man, and he yelped. I recognized that voice instantly. I used to dread hearing it through my bedroom door.

CJ and my former roommate, Nick, grunted as they rolled across the dirt.

Something slick and black glinted in the moonlight.

"Carson!" Ray roared.

BANG!

I screamed and ducked into Ray as a gunshot cracked through the air, not sure where it had been pointed.

Another shot went off as CJ's boot connected with Nick's jaw. He went limp. The bullet slammed into something metallic.

CJ crawled off Nick, then froze. We all heard it at the same time.

A slow, unsettling hiss.

"Get out!" CJ shouted.

The ranch hands that had gone into the lodge bolted out into the pasture as glass exploded from the windows in a hailstorm.

Ray grabbed me, pulled me across his lap, and tucked me under his stomach, hunching down as orange flames billowed out of the lodge.

The whoosh and crackle of flames bigger than the bonfire lit up the night sky. The ranch came alive as everyone jumped into action.

"Here," Ray shouted to CJ as he tossed him the rope he had been working with. "Tie him up and get back."

CJ caught the rope and had Nick trussed like a turkey in seconds.

"The lodge is on fire," I whispered as reality set in.

My roommates had done this.

They did it—for whatever reason—because of me.

Christian's truck growled as he came to a screeching halt next to a picturesque pond and started unloading a pump and hoses. I could hear someone talking on the phone to a 911 operator as the fire ate up the future of the ranch.

Everything went numb. "This is all my fault."

31

RAY

Smoke hissed from the charred corner of the lodge as firefighters and ranch hands worked to get water on the structure. My brother had hauled down the pump they used for wildfires to keep the blaze at bay until emergency services could arrive.

The worst of it was contained to a section that connected the lodge to the restaurant.

The bullet had slammed into an acetylene welding tank and made it explode. The blast traveled along the path of least resistance, blowing out the windows and licking up the lumber.

Brooke was stiff in my arms, staring blankly at the flurry of activity.

"Baby, it's not your fault," I murmured into her hair as I gently rubbed my hand up and down her back.

Blue lights flashed across the sky as Nick and Chandler, her former roommates, were shoved into separate police cars.

"Everyone's okay," I said softly. "It's gonna be fine."

At least I hoped it would be fine. Cassandra was pacing

close to the bunkhouse to get enough bars on her cell to make emergency calls to the investors forking out the money for the lodge and restaurant.

I cupped Brooke's cheek. "You didn't do anything wrong."

"I brought them here," she whispered. "If I hadn't taken this job they wouldn't have come. They wouldn't have stolen equipment from the construction site. They wouldn't have broken into your house. They wouldn't have been here tonight." She cupped her hand over her mouth. "CJ... He—he almost got shot."

"But he didn't. He didn't, okay? He's just fine."

"Nick had a gun," she whispered. "I've never seen him with a gun."

A body approached, striding through the grass with purpose. A badge glinted on his chest. "Sir. Ma'am," he said.

Brooke wiped her cheeks and looked up at the cop who had taken our initial statements.

"What can I do for you, officer?" I asked.

"We're about to head back to town," he said. "As much as I told those two to save it for the judge, they just kept talking." He looked at Brooke. "You're the roommate with the rich grandma?"

"Former roommate," Brooke said. "Am I in trouble?"

He shook his head. "No, ma'am. I'm just curious. Have they been harassing you for money?"

I stiffened and looked down at her.

Brooke's tight lips told me everything.

"Baby—"

"I just... paid for a lot of things at the house we lived in," she hedged.

The cop nodded. "Seems like they panicked when the easy money stopped flowing and started trying to get it elsewhere. I'll tell you the same thing I told that lady who's yelling at her phone." He pointed over his shoulder to Cassandra. "You can lawyer up and try to get it back, but these kids don't have two pennies to rub together. I don't know how much you'll be able to get back."

Brooke nodded. "Thank you, sir."

It made a lot more sense in hindsight. Trying to shake her down on the sidewalk for quick cash. They probably pawned the tools they stole from the construction site. Breaking into my house for drugs to sell.

"Come on," I said as I cranked up the golf cart. "Let's get home."

Brooke was silent on the drive back, not saying a word as we entered and changed out of our smoke-filled clothes. I reeked from the bonfire. Ash coated my arms and hair.

"Shower with me," I said as I led her into our bathroom.

The light had vanished from her eyes, leaving them empty like a day without sun or a night without stars.

I settled onto the shower seat. "Come here, baby girl."

Brooke stood before me, completely naked, while I adjusted the water temperature and let the rain shower pour over us.

Sliding my hands around her hips, I pulled her closer, kissing a soft line from her navel to the swell of her breast.

"Sit," I said, opening my legs and gesturing to the space on the bench between them.

Brooke sat between my legs without hesitation or protest. Still, there was a vacant look in her eyes, something I had never seen before.

Her warm skin pressed against mine, removing any barrier between us. Water droplets danced down our bodies, forming rivulets.

I grabbed her shampoo and poured some into my palm, gently working it into her heavy ringlets.

"Talk to me," I urged, pressing a kiss to her shoulder.

She sniffled and wiped her eyes as I ran my fingers through her hair. "It's all my fault."

"Brooke, I already—"

"It is." She shook her head. "I love you," she whimpered. "But I ... I love your family too. And I just wanted to be a part of it. I thought things were finally working out for me. That I had a place to belong. A really cool job. And a boyfriend. And a—"

I grabbed her jaw and kissed her hard, stealing all her doubts away.

"You have all of it. Every single thing. You want me? You have me. You want my family? They adore you. You want to be part of this ranch? You're the best thing about it. You want my last name? It's yours. I didn't want to come back here, but now I can't imagine leaving. So, before those doubts consume you, let me fill your mind with something else. I love you. I fucking love you, Brooke. Nothing—absolutely nothing—will change the fact that you belong here."

Tears filled her eyes and cascaded down her cheeks, only to be washed away by the shower.

"You're wanted here." I pressed my lips to her forehead as our hearts raced together.

"I hope so," she whispered.

Every morning I woke up, that old saying about ashes to ashes and dust to dust floated in my mind. We were little more than skin and bones; just temporary vessels on a finite timeline.

Every morning, I'd open my eyes and inhale for eight seconds, then exhale for another eight seconds. Every breath reminded me that my life had changed in the blink of an eye. But in the finite time between ashes and dust, I was determined to find a greater purpose for the next breath than I had with the last.

Falling in love felt like the most profound breath I would ever take.

Brooke sat under the downpour as I washed away the smoke and ash from her body, and then my own.

It had been my experience that trials brought clarity. Brooke's words reminded me of how true that was.

It broke my heart that she was hurting. I wanted to take away her pain. But her confessions of wanting my family, wanting to be a part of the Griffith legacy, and wanting to be with me was everything I had ever wanted.

Together, we finished rinsing off, dried ourselves, and slowly made our way to bed.

My sparse bedroom had begun to show signs of life. That damn love plant with its one pitiful bloom still sat in the window. A bag of candy I had started to sort was on my bedside table. Brooke's pillows were wedged against mine. On her nightstand, there was a book she had started.

Thunder rumbled in the distance as we crawled under the sheets and wrapped our arms around each other.

"I didn't know it was supposed to rain," she said, yawning.

"I like the rain," I said, kissing her goodnight and pulling her closer to my side.

Brooke rested her head on my chest. "Why is that?"

"It's a reset. Tomorrow, we can go outside. The grass will be greener, the air clearer, and the pond higher. Sometimes, life needs to pause. And sometimes, it takes something beyond our control to make that happen."

"You're poetic," she said, resting her head on my chest. "I

would have never guessed that about you when we first met months ago."

I chuckled. "I had plenty of months to think." I kissed the top of her head. "Not all of those thoughts were positive. You should be glad you weren't here during those months. They were dark."

Her fingers danced across my chest, tracing abstract patterns. "Your darkness doesn't scare me."

I pulled her on top of me so that we were chest to chest. Brooke's knees straddled my hips and she rested her head on my shoulder.

"How could it scare you? Light is never afraid of darkness." I pressed my lips to her head. "But you know what?"

"What?"

I interlaced my fingers with hers and brought her hand to my lips. "The moon reflects the sun and stores its energy until the moment comes when the sun cannot be seen. During the moments when you can't find your light, I'll be here to give it back to you."

～

I woke up the next morning with Brooke still straddling my torso. Her gentle breaths were soft and steady.

"I know you're staring at me," she said.

"Can't help it." I kissed her head. "But you gotta get off me. You have to get to work, and I have to get to PT."

"I still feel bad about not taking you. I'm—"

"Not on my payroll anymore," I reminded her. "Besides, I told Bree she could take me into town. She's gotta get thirty hours of driving time before she can get her license."

"Do I have to face Cassandra today? Or is there a chance she'll have something else to do all day?"

I chuckled. "I don't think you'll get that lucky. But I'll go with you to the office before Bree picks me up."

She pecked my lips. "Deal."

Brooke wiggled into a pair of navy shorts while I got the coffee started. By the time we were dressed and caffeinated, it was a quarter till eight, and someone was knocking on the door.

"I'll get it," I hollered to Brooke as she finished braiding her hair. I unlocked the front door and pulled it open.

I wasn't quite sure who I was expecting on my porch this morning, but it wasn't Cassandra holding a bag. Christian was with her, so I assumed it wasn't someone's decapitated head.

"Morning," I said.

Christian lifted his chin. "Figured we'd catch you and Brooke before the day started."

I glanced at the oven clock again. "Your day started three hours ago."

He shrugged. "Brooke here?"

"Who's at the—" Brooke froze in her tracks when she spotted Cassandra and Christian.

I backed my wheelchair away from the door so they could enter. Brooke was still frozen in place.

"Y'all want coffee?" I asked, trying to break the silence.

"No. This won't take long," Cassandra said.

Brooke twisted her fingers together. "Am I fired?"

Cassandra cocked her head. "Why would you be fired? You've barely started."

"I just thought that after last night—"

Christian put his hand on her shoulder. "Brooke, none of that is on you. Don't even give it a second thought."

"So what brings you to my house?" I asked.

Cassandra sneered. "What are you? A swamp ogre who thinks he owns the pond? We live on the same fucking property. It's not a different continent." She reached into the bag. "Your jackets came in."

Brooke edged closer, cautious but curious. "Jackets?"

Cassandra pulled them out and handed the smaller one to Brooke. "You're part of the ranch now. You get a jacket." She tossed the other one to me. "You too, Grumpy."

The smile on Brooke's face said it all as she tried on the tan corduroy jacket. But my last name stamped on her in the embroidered ranch logo was my favorite part.

She was here. She was ours.

She was mine.

Brooke threw her arms around Cassandra and squeezed. "Thank you!"

Cassandra stiffened. "Alright. That's completely unnecessary. I'm leaving."

I laughed.

Christian pulled Brooke into a gentler hug as Cassandra peeled herself away and dashed out the door. "Welcome to the ranch." His eyes lifted to me. "Welcome back."

32

BROOKE

The new colt was a handful. I don't know why I was surprised. His name was Riot.

"Keep your head on your shoulders," CJ called from outside the arena. "He's acting like a kid—testing your boundaries. You're in charge."

I let out a slow breath and focused on control.

CJ had been putting me through my paces for the better part of the afternoon, making me jump from horse to horse to get used to riding all of them. Some of the old faithfuls—like Bree's horse, Dottie—were easy as pie.

The new ones? Not so much. They were in unfamiliar territory with unfamiliar people. It would take time and peppermints. Luckily, I had plenty of both.

Riot whipped his head back and forth when I tugged on the reins, but he trotted back to CJ without much more fuss.

"I gotta head out," he said. "You good getting back to the barn?"

"Yeah," I said as I grabbed a canteen off the top of the fence post and took a long drink. "I'll get him untacked and turned out."

Riot's attitude seemed to calm down when we strolled into the shade. The barn was blissfully quiet. Dusty, the barn cat, snoozed away in the corner of Indy's stall.

"Are you gonna give me trouble?" I asked Riot as I started to remove the riding equipment. He didn't seem bothered by me talking away as I brushed him down.

I officially had a week at my new job under my belt and it was ... going.

Working for Cassandra was like working for a porcupine. Frankly, she seemed like the kind of animal who would eat her young. But Christian stopped by the office a few times a day to make sure I was still alive.

Ray stopped by too, but he had more or less settled into the routine of letting me go every morning. But as soon as the clock hit five, if I wasn't home, he would be in the office pestering Cassandra to let me clock out.

Frankly, I was a little surprised he hadn't shown up at the arena when I was out with Riot and CJ.

I finished up in the barn and headed to the office to clock out. Some days it still felt strange to leave Ray during the day. I had grown so accustomed to being with him nearly every waking moment, that watching him leave the ranch with Bree, Claire, or one of his brothers was an out-of-body experience.

I felt like I was missing out. For the longest time, it was him and me hiding out together and sneaking off to his appointments in town. The transition back to working a real job where I wasn't paid to ignore my boss was brutal.

I liked the routine of caring for the horses, doing chores, and tackling scheduling and a budding business launch. The physical labor helped me sit still and focus on the office work. I would have never thought that living and working on a cattle ranch was the right fit for me. But with each passing day, I realized how perfect it was.

Even more so since I got to go home to Ray at the end of each day.

Mickey wandered into the office as I was punching my timecard in the archaic machine. I gave him a scratch under the chin and readjusted the pool noodles on his horns that kept him from breaking everything in sight.

The walk home was my favorite part of the day—that, and the fact that I called it home.

Part of me, an incessant part of me, was waiting for the other shoe to drop. For Ray to realize he wanted someone older, someone settled, someone who could bring more to the table.

But every day I walked through the door, I couldn't imagine being anywhere else.

Ray made me feel wanted like I had never been before.

"I'm home," I called out into the house as I hung my bag on the hook by the door. "Ray?"

No answer.

Maybe he was out with Christian or something. I shrugged it off and dipped into the shower to rinse off.

I swear, I took more showers now than I ever had. Between the heat, animals, and dust, I was filthy in seconds. I had no idea how Cassandra managed to waltz around the ranch in crisp white pantsuits. Either her dry cleaning bills were outrageous, or the dirt was simply afraid of her.

The calming aroma of eucalyptus and lavender floated in from the bedroom as I slipped out of the shower with a towel wrapped around my chest.

Candles had been lit, and the lights were dimmed. Ray was sitting on the bed, waiting for me.

"There you are," I said as I tiptoed to the stack of clothes sitting by my side of the bed. I really needed to ask him if I could move the dresser from the guest room into the room we shared. "Were you outside?"

Ray leaned back on his elbows. His eyes raked over me as I dropped the towel. "I was up at Momma's house waiting for a package I ordered."

"How was your day?" I asked as I pawed around for a pair of underwear.

"Better now," he said, reaching over and curling his hand around my hip. "You don't need those."

I laughed. "I don't need underwear? What? You just want me to walk around naked?"

He chuckled. "I'm not gonna argue with that."

"I like the candles."

"Yeah?"

"It's relaxing."

"Good," he said. "Lay down."

"But it's barely six o'clock."

Ray lifted an eyebrow. "Are you arguing with me?"

I clammed up and stretched out on the bed. Ray leaned down and lightly brushed his lips against mine. The touch of his kiss was gentle and warm, like a familiar hello. As he deepened the kiss, his hand caressed my stomach and his tongue slid against mine. A whimper escaped my lips as he moved his hand up and over my breasts.

"Roll over," he whispered.

My eyebrows furrowed. "But..."

Ray chuckled as he leaned back. "Roll over, Sunnyside."

I grumbled and turned onto my stomach. The breeze from the ceiling fan caused goosebumps to cover my back and legs.

Ray sat up on the bed and positioned himself next to

me. Something clicked in his hands, then he rubbed them together.

I moaned as soon as he slid oiled-up palms down my back. "Oh my god, I love you."

Ray laughed. "Good. Because I love you too."

"My back is jacked up," I muttered into the covers. "That feels so good."

He pressed his thumbs into the small of my back. "It's from riding. Eventually, you'll get used to it."

I whimpered when he exerted a little more pressure. "Not there yet."

He chuckled and moved up to massage my shoulder blades. "I watched you on Riot for a little while. You looked good."

I took a deep breath and closed my eyes. "It feels good to be up there."

He poured more oil into his hand and smoothed it all the way down my back to my ass. "Open your legs."

I parted my thighs and bit down on my lip as he circled one leg, kneading and working out the knots in my hamstrings. The side of his hand grazed my pussy, but I tried to focus on the massage.

I felt as though I was floating as he relieved the tension in my legs. I bit my lip when his hands circled my thigh, just under my ass, to work on my sciatic nerve. His fingers grazed my cunt and danced over my clit. It was enough to tease, but not nearly enough to satisfy.

"On your back," he instructed, moving to sit at my head.

I groaned. "You're teasing me."

"I'm not teasing you, baby girl," he said in a low rasp as he moved my head to rest in his lap.

I closed my eyes as he massaged the oil into my collarbone and chest. "You only call me baby girl when you're horny. Otherwise, it's Sunnyside or Brooke."

"Am I that obvious?"

I grinned. "I like it."

He squeezed my arms, working the stress out of my biceps before cupping my breasts.

"Best massage ever," I mumbled.

Ray interlaced his fingers in my hair, massaging my scalp and temples. I had almost drifted off to sleep when I felt his hand cupping my breast again. A sudden pinch on my nipple startled me.

My eyes flew open, and I gasped as he attached a second clamp to my other nipple.

"Just relax," he soothed, returning to massage my shoulders. "You look so beautiful like that."

He flicked one of the hanging gems that hung from the left clamp.

I squeezed my thighs together. An odd haze of lust and leisure washed over me. I was a puddle of relaxation and arousal.

"Touch me," I pleaded.

Ray scraped his fingers across my scalp, sending pinpricks of delight down my spine. "I am," he replied.

"You know what I mean," I whimpered, shifting my body closer to his so that my chest pressed against his hands. The jolt made my tits bounce, and I felt the tug of the clamps on my nipples.

"Maybe I enjoy watching you squirm," he said, licking his thumb and then grazing it over my nipple in small, steady circles.

A high-pitched whine slipped from my throat, and I spread my legs apart.

"That's it—open your legs for me. You know exactly what I want," he whispered, leaning over me.

Something cool and smooth teased my exposed folds. Ray pressed a button, and vibrations coursed through me as he used the toy to circle my clit.

I gasped, arching off the bed. My hips pushed into his hand. He placed the toy against my clit and held it there with his palm until I became a desperate, writhing mess.

Flashes of light and heat radiated from my nipples as the gentle weight of the clamps pulled on the sensitive nerves.

He inserted two fingers inside of my pussy and parted them wide, stretching me open before sliding the egg vibrator deep inside.

His hand shackled my throat. "That should tide you over until I'm ready to fuck you."

Nowhere near close.

It was a sick tease, bringing me right to the edge of ecstasy, but not quite giving me release.

His chuckle sent chills down my spine as he grazed my lips with his thumb. "I probably don't need to say this, but don't you dare orgasm. I expect you to wait until I give you permission."

"No promises," I gasped as pleasure washed over me in waves.

Ray slipped two fingers between my parted lips, pressing down on my tongue. I moaned around them and sucked as my body was hit with pulses of electricity, dancing from my breasts to my core.

"Be a good girl for me. Wait to come and I'll make it worth your while," he whispered, stroking my cheek with his knuckles. "Or I can just keep you like this all night." He tugged on one of the clamps, eliciting a moan from me. "Will you be good for me?"

I nodded.

"Up on your knees. Face the headboard."

I struggled to move as the sensation from the massage left me in a daze.

"Hold on tight and arch your back," he instructed, running his hand down my ass and then slipping his hand between my cheeks.

Something cool and slick pressed against my tight opening, and I gasped. "Ray—"

"Relax and breathe for me. It's just a small plug."

I whimpered as he applied pressure and massaged, allowing my body to gradually accommodate the bulb before it closed around the tapered neck.

"Just a little one. There you go," he murmured, tugging on the flared base. "Doesn't that feel nice and snug?"

The movement made the vibrations from the toy in my pussy transfer through the thin skin separating it from the plug in my ass.

"Oh my god," I gasped.

"Go ahead. Pray," he said, sinking his teeth into the side of my neck. "You're going to need it."

Ray held both of my hands and drew them over my head and behind my neck. Smooth rope meant for bondage bound my wrists, keeping my arms up in a V shape. Ray tested the tension to make sure it wasn't too tight or too loose.

I pleaded as the toys inside me brought me closer and closer to release. I desperately wanted to come.

"I love how much you trust me," he murmured as he criss-crossed the rope around my chest.

The harness lifted my breasts, making me acutely aware of the clamps still dangling from my nipples. My whole body was a live wire, sparking and dancing with unshed energy.

"I love that you're in this with me."

Ray had undressed somewhere between the forming the loops and knots. He pressed his chest against my back.

I begged as he placed his hand low on my stomach, providing pressure where I wanted his touch.

He cupped my breast and squeezed. My muscles clenched around the toy he had put in my ass.

I licked my lips. "I think I would have loved you in any form, at any point in life. It would always have been you. Your soul and mine. Then, now, and whatever is still to come."

My head spun as he wrapped the rope between my thighs, around my hips, and pulled until my legs were forced apart. I cried out when he slid his forearm behind the knots running down my spine. The harness was tight, but not uncomfortable.

I felt supported, safe, held.

He pressed the head of his cock against the entrance of my pussy. "So wet for me, baby girl."

He slid a finger into my pussy, circling my walls as he removed the egg vibrator from inside me. My legs trembled as he pressed it against my clit.

"Ray!" I cried out. "Please—please—"

"Beg for it," he growled.

He nudged the head of his cock into my pussy, holding onto the headboard. His other arm was secured through the ropes, keeping me close against his chest.

"It's going to feel tight when I fuck you with the plug in your ass, but you can handle it. You're going to take me, and you'll look so pretty doing it."

Tight didn't begin to describe it. His girth filled me

snugly, almost painfully. I gasped and begged as he slowly sank inside of me.

"It's too much," I choked. "Too thick—"

"It'll fit," he promised with darkness dripping from his words. "Now take it."

When he was fully inside me, he released the headboard and caressed my nipples with his thumb.

"So damn beautiful, baby. All dolled up for me with jewels hanging from your tits, and your body bound so I can make you come until you beg for mercy."

I was a desperate, writhing mess. "Please let me come. I can't—I can't hold it—"

He thrust hard into me. "Come around my cock. You feel so fucking good."

He let go of the headboard, grabbed the buzzing vibrator, and pressed it against my clit, then my swollen, throbbing nipples.

I thrashed, fighting against the ropes as he pushed himself deep inside me.

Ray nipped at my ear. "Doesn't that feel good, baby?" He moved the vibrator back to my clit. "You are so beautiful. I want to spend every last breath making you feel your highest, your most powerful. You're everything. *Everything.* Now come for me."

The orgasm hit me out of nowhere. My pussy squeezed and clenched around his cock. My body seized, but he held me close.

Ray slid the vibrator down and teased his balls until he jerked and came inside me. "Breathe. I'm gonna lay you on your side to untie you."

I nodded, gasping for air. The calm came as quickly as the rush did.

Our mingled release slid down my thigh as Ray laid behind me and began to undo the knots.

He rubbed my hands and wrists, checking them over until he was sure I was okay. I hissed when he opened the clamps and pulled them off my nipples.

"Bring your knee to your chest," he soothed as he tugged on the plug. "Did you like using this?" he asked as he slowly slid it from my body and set it on the nightstand.

Heat and embarrassment flooded my cheeks. "I liked it... a lot." I whimpered when his arm brushed against my swollen nipples.

Ray eased me onto my side, facing him. He lavished my breasts with sloppy kisses. His touch soothed the lingering aches until I felt warm and at ease. Ray covered me in fervent kisses, making it clear that I was positively, wholly, and incandescently *his*.

33

RAY

"Everyone's gonna have to squeeze in tonight," Momma said as she opened the door for Brooke and me. "We've got some extra folks joining us."

She gave Brooke a tight hug. "Hey, sweetie. How was work?"

Brooke was still wearing her official Griffith Brothers Ranch polo shirt, having managed the first field trip full of excited school kids who wanted to learn all about horses.

I had watched from a distance as she guided them through the barns and delivered the speech she had rehearsed a thousand times in our bedroom.

Brooke beamed from ear to ear. "It was great. I think the kids had a really good time."

Momma squeezed her hands. "Cassandra told me you did a great job."

Brooke gasped. "Really?"

"Well, she said it went smoothly. That's basically the same thing to her."

Brooke laughed. "I'll take it."

"And how was your day?" Mom asked as she leaned down and wrapped an arm around my shoulders.

"I see how it is. I bring a pretty girl around and suddenly I'm an afterthought," I said, teasing her simply because I could.

Mom scoffed. "Well, I talked to Brooke first because I know I'll get more words out of her. But if you want to have a chat, then I'll ask how you are first next time."

I chuckled. "My day was fine. I was on a video call with Marty for most of it, dealing with contract negotiations."

Mom pressed her palm to my cheek like I was still the six-year-old boy who ran amok all over the ranch. "I'm glad you're getting back at it. I know it's not the same."

It wasn't. The rodeo was my first love, but *she* was my forever.

I would have been perfectly content following Brooke around like a lost puppy for the rest of my life, but I was fairly certain she would get tired of that. I needed to find a new dream, whatever that was.

I didn't think appearing in ad campaigns was my life's calling but, for now, it was a start.

"We'll see if they're willing to shell out what Marty's asking. He drives a hard bargain."

"Who else is coming tonight?" Brooke asked as she looked around.

It seemed like we were the last to show up. CJ was already here, talking to Nate and Becks. My dad had their daughter, Charlie, on his knee as he read her a story. Christian and Gracie were on the couch. Bree was pacing in the corner, looking at her phone.

It looked like Cassandra was the only one missing.

"One of the bigwig investors in the restaurant was here today to look at the damage from the fire," Mom said.

"Cass called a little while ago and said their meeting was running long, so I offered to have everyone up here for dinner."

A car pulled down the drive, and Bree bolted past us and onto the porch.

Christian jumped off the couch.

Mom looked at me and Bree. "And your brother compromised with his daughter. Bree can't go on dates with the boy just yet, but he's allowed to join us for dinner."

"This is going to be entertaining," I said to Brooke as I wheeled into the house.

She laughed. "Have a little faith. I think it's sweet that Christian came around."

"This kid doesn't know what he's in for."

The door opened, and the living and dining rooms went silent as Bree walked in, holding the hand of some floppy-haired, good-for-nothing punk.

"Be nice," Brooke whispered.

"Well, hey there," Mom said to the future corpse. "You must be Mason. It's nice to meet you. I'm Bree's grandma."

"Hi, Mrs. Griffith," Mason stammered out. He spotted Gracie and offered a wave. "Hey."

Gracie gave him a chin tip. "'Sup."

"This is my Uncle Ray and Brooke," Bree said, braving the gauntlet as she led the kid I wanted to barbecue into the house.

"Nice to meet you, Mason," Brooke said with a sweet-as-pie smile as she jabbed her elbow into my shoulder.

"Hi. Uh..." Mason looked down at me and cleared his throat. "Bree's told me a lot about you. She said you're her favorite uncle."

"Hey!" CJ and Nate shouted from the living room.

Brooke snickered.

Mason squeezed Bree's hand. "But, uh... I'm a big fan, actually."

"Flattery will get you nowhere," I said. "There's plenty of space out here to hide a body, and you're not that big."

Brooke dropped her head into her hands. "Please excuse Bree's uncles. They're still being house-trained."

Bree giggled.

I looked at Bree and tipped my head toward Christian, who had come up behind me. "Better get it over with, squirt."

Bree looked up at her father with doe eyes. "Daddy, this is Mason. Mason, this is my dad."

Mason's Adam's apple bobbed like a cartoon. "Hello, sir."

Christian silently crossed his arms over his chest, and worry filled Bree's eyes. I pulled against the wheels and backed my wheelchair up and over his foot.

"Hey!" he shouted, jumping back. "What the hell? That hurt."

"My bad," I said innocently as I tossed a wink to Bree.

Christian sighed. "Nice to meet you."

"You know," I teased. "I think you can do better than that. Wanna try again? You've got another foot."

Bree dragged Mason into the living room to meet the rest of the motley crew.

Brooke crossed her arms and glared at me. "Really?"

"What?" I said innocently.

She huffed. "Don't pull the tough-guy act. You know damn well you would do anything for her."

I loved when Brooke looked angry. It was adorable.

I hitched my thumb over my shoulder at Christian. "I ran over his foot, didn't I?"

"I fucking hate this," Christian grumbled.

I peered into the living room and saw that Bree and

Mason had taken up residence on the loveseat. They were sitting an appropriate twelve inches apart and both looked like they were about to throw up. Still, that punk-ass kid looked at Bree like she hung the moon and stars.

I couldn't really be mad at that.

I went ahead and got settled at the long line of tables that had been pushed together so there were enough seats. I didn't want to be struggling to get in and out when there were people I wasn't familiar with joining us for dinner.

"What crawled up your ass and died?" I asked CJ when he stormed into the kitchen.

He grabbed a beer from the fridge and sat down across from Brooke and me.

"More fuckin' people," he grumbled.

I raised an eyebrow. "What? On the ranch?" I rested my hands on the table. "You knew this was coming. All these deals were signed before my accident."

He took a long drink. "Doesn't mean I have to like it. You saw what happened at the build site. Putting all these things on the ranch is just asking for trouble. Mark my words, there's gonna be more of it."

CJ would live and die for the ranch. More than my father. More than Christian. He was a purist, loving the land more than the ability to keep it afloat. He didn't take kindly to change, and I had a feeling he would hold on to that anger as long as possible.

We were alike in our ability to hold grudges.

The door swung open and Cassandra strolled in with some fancy-pants man on her heels. He was in a tailored suit, squeaky clean loafers, and had a watch that I knew sold for at least five figures.

"Oh my god," Brooke whispered.

I glared at her. "Eyes on your own man."

She snickered.

Cassandra's face was stern and all business as she strode to the center of the living and dining room. "Everyone, this is Luca DeRossi."

He tipped his perfectly coiffed black hair. "Pleasure to meet you all."

"He's the head of the DeRossi Hospitality Group and will be the co-owner and executive chef of the steakhouse," Cassandra said.

Mom wiped her hands on a dish towel. "We're glad to have you for dinner, Mr. DeRossi. We're not fancy, so I hope you like sloppy Joes."

He flashed a toothpaste-commercial smile. "I love them. Thank you for having me. It'll be great to get to know everyone. I'm excited to partner with a family for this venture."

And with that, CJ finished his beer, slammed it down, and pushed away from the table. "I'll eat in the bunkhouse," he grumbled as he stormed out.

Worry flashed in Brooke's eyes.

No one said a word until Bree broke the silence. "Cass, this is Mason."

Cassandra's intimidating gaze turned on the teenager. "Right. No red flags on your background check, but just know that I have eyes and ears everywhere."

He nodded nervously. "Yes, ma'am."

"Don't say that!" Bree whispered to him.

"Uh—Um—Yes, Ms. Parker," Mason recited.

"Well," Mom said as she glanced at the door. "I suppose we should start eating before it gets cold."

The tension from CJ's sudden departure faded as we dug into our meal. Luca shared his vision for the restaurant and, I had to admit, it didn't sound half-bad. Laughter filled the table as he talked about a woman he was going to propose to

—a pastry chef from a restaurant his group recently acquired—and how they met.

An hour later, Luca said his goodbyes and headed out to catch a flight to North Carolina.

Bree and Mason had slipped out for a walk around the front of the property that was supervised by Gracie, leaving Christian to commiserate with Becks and Nate. I stole Brooke away from her conversation with my dad and led her out to the porch to watch the sun set.

Cicadas sang as Brooke helped me transfer to one of the rocking chairs.

"Thanks, baby," I said as I adjusted my legs and leaned back.

Brooke made a move for the other rocking chair, but I caught her around the waist and pulled her onto my lap.

"This is nice," she said as she rested her temple in the crook of my neck and closed her eyes.

I pressed a kiss to her forehead. "Can I ask you something?"

"What's that?"

"Are you happy here?"

Brooke laughed. "What kind of question is that? Of course I'm happy here."

I tucked her hair behind her ear. "I mean it. If all your days looked like this one, would you be happy?"

She tapped her chin. "Let me think... Waking up to you? Yes. Walking to work? Yes. My job? Yes. Coming home to you? Yes. Not having to cook dinner? Absolutely. Falling asleep with you? Yes." She kissed my cheek. "I couldn't have dreamed up anything better. You've given me everything I never knew I wanted."

She felt so good in my arms. And, for the first time in a long time, I was at peace with where I was.

"What about in there?"

"In the house?"

I nodded. "What if your life looked like that? A big family. A front porch to sit on when the day is done. A whole bunch of kids running around, causing chaos."

Her fingers glided over the tattoos on my forearms. "I think that sounds like a dream."

I kissed her lips. "What about all of that here? With me?"

Her hands pressed against my cheeks as she tipped her head to the side and kissed me long and slow. "I'm in for the ride."

EPILOGUE
BROOKE

Seven Months Later

I smoothed my hands over Ray's shoulders, working the baby oil over his muscles. "Are you excited?"

He gave me a sheepish smile in the reflection of the dressing room mirror. "A little nervous." His eyes were soft. "You sure you're okay with this?"

I slid onto his lap and laughed as I poured a little more oil into my hand to coat his chest. "Of course I'm okay with it."

"Brooke—"

I rolled my eyes. "Remember that time we went out to Maren and I took my top off and rode that mechanical bull? You're still clothed." I glanced down at the snug pair of men's briefs he had just put on. "Well, mostly clothed."

His eyes dropped to my cleavage. "Trust me. I remember everything."

The last six months had been filled with falling into a routine and figuring out our new lives together, but I wouldn't have had it any other way.

"How're you feeling?" he whispered as he slid his hand up my shirt and rested it on my stomach.

I let out a shaky breath. "A little nervous about tonight."

Two pink lines had caught us both by surprise a few weeks ago. After the initial shock had worn off, excitement and anticipation set in.

Ray was going to be the best dad.

"Don't be," he said softly. "They're gonna be fucking ecstatic for us. Have you eaten?"

I rolled my eyes. "Yes. I've eaten today and thrown it up."

"You better watch your attitude, Sunnyside," he teased. Ray tucked a curl behind my ear. "Want me to send Marty to get you something to snack on?"

"I'm good. I threw a granola bar in my bag before we left the house."

Ray reached for his phone. "I'm gonna have him go get—"

"Babe, I'm fine. Today's about you." I eyed the stuffed thing on the dressing room vanity. "Are you really supposed to shove that thing in your underwear?"

He laughed. "Yeah. It's no big deal. I've done it before."

My baby daddy—the underwear model.

Ray stole one more kiss before wheeling away from the mirrored vanity with me on his lap. "But I don't think I'll need it today."

I laughed and slid off of him. "You better think some cold shower thoughts, or you'll be flashing everyone when your dick gets hard and pops out of those underwear."

"I can keep it under control," he promised.

"Really? Because you did this." I pointed at my stomach.

Ray backed me up against the vanity with his wheelchair and slowly lifted the hem of my shirt. "Yeah I did."

Pride and satisfaction filled his voice as he dotted butterfly kisses across my stomach.

A knock sounded at the door, startling us both.

"Mr. Griffith, Andre is ready for you on set," an underpaid yet chipper lackey said from the other side of the door.

I grabbed the robe that was hanging on the coat hook.

"Thank you," Ray called out as he put the robe on backward so he didn't have to lift out of his wheelchair.

Like everyone, Ray had good days and bad days. He still went to physical therapy a few times a month, but had started doing most of his exercises at home. He had outfitted his truck with hand controls and drove himself around most of the time. Therapy, both physical and mental, had helped.

There were still days filled with storms of anger, but sunshine always followed.

I followed Ray onto the photoshoot set and politely elbowed the assistant out of the way when she reached for his robe.

I held the fluffy fabric to my body to keep my heart from thumping out of my chest as lights flashed for test shots.

He was sinfully sexy with wet, tousled hair, neatly trimmed stubble, and a lazy smirk on his face.

Bree and Gracie had come down to the house that morning to color in his tattoos for luck. They had only colored a few, but it meant the world to all three of them to have their Uncle Ray back.

I chewed on my fingernail and clenched my thighs as Ray slumped casually in his wheelchair and draped his arm over the back of it, opening his body to be photographed for the ad campaign.

He flicked his eyes at me and licked his lips. I could read the devilish thoughts racing through his mind. I could still feel the ropes twisting and twining around my body.

The photographer called out for him to change poses. Everyone was patient as Ray readjusted his legs, lifting one off of the footrest to stretch out on the floor. He cupped the back of the opposite knee and drew it up so his foot was resting on the edge of the wheelchair seat.

Oh... That wasn't a bad view.

My heart raced as he looked off into the distance and tangled his hand in his hair.

The camera shutter raced as the photoshoot flew by. I was fascinated by the computer screen off to the side that showed each black and white shot lining up in real-time.

It was incredible how the shift of Ray's mouth or the flick of his gaze could change the mood of the photo. Some were casual and relaxed. Some were playful, with the corners of his eyes crinkling as he laughed.

Others were devilishly provocative.

When the shoot ended, I handed the robe to Ray and crossed my arms protectively over my stomach. I watched as the father of my child interacted with people with joy in his eyes.

He had never looked sexier.

"You know, we should probably think about getting you a bigger vehicle," Ray said as we made our way to his truck. He opened the passenger door for me, then wheeled around to the driver's side.

I put his wheelchair in the back while he got behind the wheel. "Why's that?"

Ray shrugged as he cranked up and waited for me to get buckled. "Your car's small. A carseat in my truck will be a pain in the ass. We should get a minivan."

A bark of laughter escaped me. "A minivan?"

"Yeah. Why not?" He pulled out onto the highway. "We're gonna have a baby. It just makes sense."

"We're just having one baby, unless you know something I don't know."

He snickered. "I'm serious, Brooke. We should go ahead and do it. We've talked about wanting a lot of kids."

Those conversations had always been hypothetical until I missed my period.

"In the future. Not today or tomorrow or in nine months," I pointed out.

"In the future," he conceded.

I couldn't help but stare at him as he drove us back to the ranch. "You're excited about this aren't you?"

His grin was infectious. "It's the best thing that could have happened."

Vehicles and animals were clustered around the front of Claire and Silas's house when we pulled down the drive. We were a little early for dinner, but that had never stopped us before.

Besides, I was starving and I was certain Ray's mom would have something sweet tucked away in a Tupperware container.

My stomach lurched as soon as my flip-flops hit the grass.

"Baby—" Ray looked at me from the driver's seat with concern. "What's the matter?"

I grabbed his wheelchair out of the back. "Just nerves."

"I told you," he said as he got down into his chair and shut the door. "They're gonna be excited."

"Easy for you to say. You're one of them."

As much as the Griffith family made me feel like one of their own, Ray and I were still dating. I wanted to believe that they would be excited, but the pregnancy hormones were making me insecure.

Especially when Ray didn't say another word.

I was surprised to see everyone already piled into the kitchen when we went inside. Dinner wasn't supposed to start for another half hour.

My stomach roiled as everyone said their hellos and asked how the photoshoot went. Ray kept me close with an arm around my hips or his hand holding mine.

Finally, when the food had been doled out and everyone was seated, he cleared his throat.

"Before we eat this delicious dinner Momma cooked, Brooke and I have something to tell y'all."

He found my hand under the table and gave it a squeeze, just like I had done to him during the first family dinner we came to. A smile worked across his face as he looked at me.

"We're having a baby. Brooke's pregnant. I'm—" He choked up as tears welled in his eyes. "—I'm gonna be a dad."

The simultaneous gasp must have sucked all the oxygen out of the room.

Then, a crash of cheers and congratulations spilled over like a dam breaking.

Ray's mom bolted around the table and threw her arms around me. "Oh, honey. I'm so excited. You're gonna be the best momma."

I couldn't stop the tears from falling. "Thank you," I whispered into her shoulder.

Silas was next, squeezing me tight. "You're gonna be great, little momma."

I sobbed.

Nate, Christian, and CJ came around with gentle hugs, then rearranged all the seats around the table so they could pepper Ray with questions. Becks and Cassandra did the same to my side.

"I have tons of Charlotte's baby stuff packed away in the

attic," Becks said. "We won't be using it again, so it's yours if you want it."

Cassandra's excitement was less effusive, but not lacking in sincerity. "I'll organize all of Becks's hand-me-downs and compile a spreadsheet of what's available so we can reconcile the inventory with what you still need. Do you have a registry yet?"

I laughed and wiped my eyes. "No. We just found out. I'm not that far along." It dawned on me that the table wasn't full. "Where are the girls?"

"Mason took Bree and Gracie out to a movie," Cassandra whispered, trying not to spook Christian. "They should be back soon."

"That's sweet that he took Gracie too," I said.

And, speak of the devil, Bree and Gracie made their grand entrance, along with the boy Christian had begrudgingly come to accept.

Bree dipped behind my chair and slipped something into Ray's hand.

A hush fell over the table like summer showers filled with sunshine. Ray turned and took my hand.

"I know we surprised them, but now I've got one more surprise. And before you ask, I had this planned well before we found out about the baby."

Oh no. The tears were back.

"Brooke, you saved me. You brought me back to life in ways I will never be able to repay you for. You sat beside me at this table and you held my hand when I needed your strength. And I promise you, if you'll let me, I will spend every last breath I have trying to give that back to you. You are gracious and good. You're hardworking and optimistic. You're kind and loving. And goddamn, you're beautiful. And I can't think of a better person to be the mother of my children. But more than that, I can't think of a better person to be my wife."

Nate pulled back Ray's wheelchair while Christian and CJ helped brace his arms until he was down on one knee.

He had asked them to do this. To be a part of it.

The diamond ring was blurry through my tears, but I felt its weight as Ray slid it on my finger.

"Will you marry me?"

I was a blubbering mess as I nodded and wrapped my arms around his neck. "Yes, yes!" I kissed him again, though I couldn't stop laughing or crying. "All of my yeses are yours."

BONUS EPILOGUE
RAY

17 Years Later

Returning to the arena after seventeen years felt like stepping into a dream. The dirt under my boots stirred up a torrent of memories. This was the place where everything had changed. I'd seen a few events over the years, but today marked my return to the heart of it all.

I scanned the list on my clipboard and lifted the microphone. "Up next—number eighteen—six-year-old Loretta Thompson from Maren, Texas."

From the stage, I watched a little girl in boots and flannel climb onto the back of a sheep named Blizzard, holding on for dear life. She did a damn good job too, smoking the rest of the kids who had tried their hand at mutton busting.

I scanned the crowd, trying to spot my motley crew, but there were too many faces to pick them out. The place seemed overrun with Griffiths.

"Hey, handsome." Brooke appeared on stage, offering me a water bottle.

Goddamn, she was as pretty as a picture.

She had aged like fine wine. Her curls were streaked with silver and piled atop her head in a bun. I worshiped the body that had given me our children every moment I could.

She was an exceptional mother to our brood. It felt like just yesterday we were nervously waiting for our firstborn. Now, he was about to go off to college. He'd be the first of us to get a degree after high school, and I was so fucking proud.

"Where are the kids?" I asked, sipping from the bottle.

"Oh, they're around somewhere." She pulled up a stool and sat down, sharing my wheelchair's armrest. "I think Claire is with Seth, and Olivia and Summer are together."

That was predictable. Claire, at six years old, was nearly inseparable from seventeen-year-old Seth. Our middle two, Olivia and Summer, were practically twins despite being two years apart.

Brooke stayed on stage with me while I announced the last two kids competing for the mutton busting championship.

When the final scores were in, I handed out ribbons and the championship buckle.

It still amused me that kids wanted photos with an old bull rider, but I obliged each of them before the next announcer took over for team roping.

A pair of hands clapped down on my shoulders. "Okay. How long do you think I could actually last on a bull?"

I chuckled at Seth's question. He was a mirror image of me in my teenage years. "You wouldn't get out of the gate. He'd throw you in the chute."

"Be for real. I'd do alright."

"Keep thinking that. Where are your sisters?"

Claire appeared from behind Seth's leg. "Hi, daddy." She

crawled into my lap and hung her feet over the armrest of my wheelchair. "Can we get a snack?"

"In a minute, baby. I'm almost done." I kissed her head.

Our youngest had Brooke's curls and a pair of blue eyes that spelled t-r-o-u-b-l-e.

Brooke slid her arms around me from behind and rested her chin on top of my head. Her breasts pressed against the back of my neck.

"I'm proud of you," she said. Her voice was soft, meant only for me. "You did great."

Olivia joined us on the wings of the stage. "Can we get food?"

"Oh my god, yes. I'm starving," Summer chimed in.

I looked up at Brooke. "Should we feed them?"

She hummed thoughtfully. "We fed them once and they just kept following us home like stray cats."

"*Mom*," three of them whined.

We snickered.

"Alright. Let's go get some food," I said as I backed up and pivoted to avoid the extension cords taped down across the stage.

Claire was perfectly happy letting me cart her around like a princess. I didn't mind it in the slightest. Before I could blink, she'd be grown and out of the house along with the rest of them. I just wanted to hold onto these moments for as long as possible.

Brooke had given me the greatest title of my life. *Dad*.

It was better than any championship buckle, trophy, or accolade. My wife and kids were the highlight of my life.

The six of us had road-tripped across the country together, watched the ranch grow and change over nearly two decades, spent countless birthdays with hoards of friends over for horseback rides and movie nights by the pond. We had managed cramped living quarters and dealt with the mess of construction for an addition to the house when we needed more bedrooms.

We had survived the passing of my dad—their grandfather—and all the mourning that followed.

Through the mess and mayhem, the beauty and elation, the grief and gratitude—we held onto each other.

I paused to admire Brooke as she ushered everyone out of the arena and into the minivan with practiced efficiency.

Yeah, we got the minivan.

Early evening sun danced through her hair, illuminating the regal grays that had been earned over seventeen years of parenting. She was my silver lining.

"You too," she said as the sliding doors closed and she made her way around to the passenger's side. "I might be hungrier than all of them combined."

I caught her arm and tugged her down. Brooke stumbled into the kiss but gave way just as quickly.

"I love you."

She laughed like it was a forgone conclusion because—for us—it was. "I love you too."

Still, I held onto her. "I know you weren't here when it happened or in the months after. But you were here for the days and months and years that really mattered."

Her brows lifted, and her eyes softened. "As much as I wish I had been there, I'm glad I wasn't. Because it brought me to you."

I pulled her in for another kiss, just because I could.

The window rolled down, and the kids groaned. "Bruh, stop making out with mom. It's weird. And we're hungry."

"I'm not your *bruh*," I said before stealing another kiss.

Parenting was half daily grace and half pissing them off on purpose. Especially the teenagers.

Bonus Epilogue

"Dad," the girls groaned.

Brooke laughed. "We better go before we have a mutiny on our hands."

That was true. Two of them could drive. We finished loading up and pulled away from the arena. As the debate about where we were going to stop to eat on the trip home raged in the back, I looked over at Brooke.

She had a lazy smile on her face. Her fingers traced the somewhat faded tattoos on my forearms. It seemed like just yesterday the kids would crowd around to color them in. Claire still did, but she was quickly growing out of it.

Maybe I'd get them permanently filled in.

"What are you thinking about, Sunnyside?"

She rolled her head across the back of the seat and looked at me. "Are you happy?"

I laughed. "Of course."

"I mean it," she pressed. "You had it all before."

"I didn't," I said. "I had things. I had people. I had a life. But I didn't have you. I didn't have a home. I'd give it all up. My money. My body. My breath. All of it, over and over again, if it meant that I got you for just one day."

WANT MORE GRIFFITH BROTHERS?

Cow boss CJ Griffith likes three things: land, cows, and people with the last name **Griffith**.

Anything and anyone else is a threat to his way of life.

Especially **her**.

Fire Line: An Enemies to Lovers Romance is available now!

AUTHOR'S NOTE TO THE READER

Dear Reader,

If you've read *Pretty Things On Shelves* (the second chance romance that I co-wrote with my husband), you may have guessed that we got married quite young.

As hard as it was, there was such beauty in figuring out what our lives were going to look like together.

We didn't have to blend two separate lifestyles—we created one together.

I loved looking at Ray and Brooke's love story through that lens: two people starting and re-starting in life. Figuring out what they wanted *together*.

Ray and Brooke have such a hold on my heart. I loved watching him work through his anger and hurt. I loved seeing her find her peace and calm in an unlikely place.

With just one more book to go in the Griffith Brothers series, I'm already sad that we're closing in on the finale. I love this family so much, and hope you do too.

Time to saddle up for one last ride.

With Love and Happily Ever Afters,
  Mags

PS. Because you're super cool, let's be friends!

ACKNOWLEDGMENTS

Landon: For listening to me. For telling me my book doesn't suck. For being my partner in this crazy life that we have together. For being the best dad. For pushing me and supporting me. I love you! Go bobcats!

Mikayla and Mandy: For your kindness, support, and badassery. Cheers to smashing porcelain figurines to death with bowling pins to keep us from doing it in real life. Here's to a friendship that survived the group chats.

Kayla: For your social media prowess, reliability, and quiet sass that always makes me laugh. I'm SO thankful for you!

Mel: For being the most BADASS cover designer!

To Jen, Megan, and the Grey's Promotions Team: Thank you SO much for all your hard work and for hyping up this book!

Kyle and Michael (Badass Attorneys): For being my email filter and anger translator. I could never do what you two do. Your patience is unmatched. Thank you for everything!

Kayla, Sierra, Catherine, and Jen (Promo Badasses): Thank you for your hype and social media prowess!

The HEA Babes: For laughs, inexplicable microtropes, and a cool place to overshare.

My 2024 Street Team: Emily J, Kayla N, Paula S, Melina F, Megan B, Courtney P, Amber B, Morgan H, Emily K, Hayley K, Jann R, Betsy C, Lauren C, Ashley M, Randa D, Allison C, Carissa L, Alex M, Sandie C, and Sam Y, and Sam W. Thank you for your enthusiasm and encouragement! You all are an imperative part of my book team and I'm so grateful for every recommendation, video, and post!

My ARC Team: You guys are the greatest! Your excitement and support astound me daily. You make me feel like the coolest human being alive. I'm so grateful for each one of you. Thank you for volunteering your time and platforms to boost my books!

Starbucks Baristas: You don't talk to me and never question why I'm sitting in the corner 40+ hours a week. Thank you. Also, please bring back the almond croissant. I'm begging you.

My Readers: Because naming all of you one by one would double the length of this book: You all are the reason I keep writing books. I'm thoroughly convinced that there's no greater group of people in the world. Y'all are amazing human beings! Thank you for loving these characters and getting as excited as I do about their stories! Thank you for your hype, encouragement, and excitement!

Taylor Swift: For giving us Female Rage: The Musical!

Also, to Santa: Because I can.

ALSO BY MAGGIE GATES

Standalone Novels

The Stars Above Us: A Steamy Military Romance

Nothing Less Than Everything: A Sports Romance

Cry About It: An Enemies to Lovers Romance

100 Lifetimes of Us: A Hot Bodyguard Romance

Pretty Things on Shelves: A Second Chance Romance

The Beaufort Poker Club Series

Poker Face: A Small Town Romance

Wild Card: A Second Chance Romance

Square Deal: A Playboy Romance

In Spades: A Small Town Billionaire Romance

Not in the Cards: A Best Friend's Brother Romance

Betting Man: A Friends to Lovers Romance

The Falls Creek Series

What Hurts Us: A Small Town Fake Engagement Romance

What Heals Us: An Age Gap Romance

What Saves Us: A Small Town Single Mom Romance

The Griffith Brothers Series

Dust Storm: A Single Dad Romance

Downpour: A Grumpy Sunshine Romance

Fire Line: An Enemies to Lovers Romance

ABOUT THE AUTHOR
MAGGIE GATES

Maggie Gates writes raw, relatable romance novels full of heat and humor. She calls North Carolina home. In her spare time, she enjoys daydreaming about her characters, jamming to country music, and eating all the BBQ and tacos she can find! Her Kindle is always within reach due to a love of small-town romances that borders on obsession.

For future book updates, follow Maggie on social media.

facebook.com/AuthorMaggieGates
instagram.com/authormaggiegates
tiktok.com/@authormaggiegates

Printed in Great Britain
by Amazon